"Let him go."

"He can't get away with this."

"He won't." Derek hoped his promise wouldn't become a lie. "Let's take a look at you." He leaned back so he could look her over, but she turned abruptly into his embrace, her body quaking with shock as Uniform's boots continued to pound against the stairs.

"We should call security." He held her close, needing the assurance that she was alive and well. He kept breathing in the soft clove scent of her shampoo, imagining they were back at their last campsite, under the stars. Anything to block that moment when he was sure she was going over the rail.

"We should." Grace Ann didn't move, her hands fisted in the fabric of his shirt as the sound of a door clanging open and closed echoed up the stairwell.

Would she be in a heap at the bottom of the stairwell if he hadn't come along?

* * *

If you're on Twitter, tell us what you think of Harlequin Romantic Suspense! #harlequinromsuspense

Dear Reader,

Army nurses have fascinated me since *M*A*S*H* was first on television, so I'm thrilled to introduce Grace Ann Riley. Following in her mother's footsteps as a nurse with the US Army Nursing Corps, Major Riley knows all about service and sacrifice and she's learned to handle life on her own terms.

She's tough and resilient and the type of nurse we all hope for during challenging circumstances: competent, kind and dedicated. She's also a woman you'd want to call a friend: someone who will be in your corner, ready to crack a joke or leap into action as necessary.

In Derek Sayer she's found an easygoing friend who gives her space from the demands of military service. But when her life and career come under fire, Grace Ann must decide if she has the courage to open her heart and receive Derek's help—and love: an offer that could make what she thought was a full life truly complete.

Live the adventure!

Regan

HIS SOLDIER UNDER SIEGE

Regan Black

HARLEQUIN
ROMANTIC
SUSPENSE

HARLEQUIN®
ROMANTIC SUSPENSE™

Recycling programs
for this product may
not exist in your area.

ISBN-13: 978-1-335-62643-1

His Soldier Under Siege

Copyright © 2020 by Regan Black

This edition published by arrangement with Harlequin Books S.A.

For questions and comments about the quality of this book,
please contact us at CustomerService@Harlequin.com.

Harlequin Enterprises ULC
22 Adelaide St. West, 40th Floor
Toronto, Ontario M5H 4E3, Canada
www.Harlequin.com

Printed in U.S.A.

Regan Black, a *USA TODAY* bestselling author, writes award-winning, action-packed novels featuring kick-butt heroines and the sexy heroes who fall in love with them. Raised in the Midwest and California, she and her family, along with their adopted greyhound, two arrogant cats and a quirky finch, reside in the South Carolina Lowcountry, where the rich blend of legend, romance and history fuels her imagination.

For all of our military heroes who give so much of themselves, at home and abroad, to protect our beliefs, freedoms and way of life.

Chapter 1

At the nurses' station of the orthopedic post-op ward, US Army Major Grace Ann Riley peeked at the monitor showing the status of various ongoing procedures in the surgery suites. So far this morning there'd been no update on Kevin Sayer, the patient everyone in her unit was watching for. Coping with a seriously injured friend was proving to be one of the biggest challenges in her career.

It was too soon for updates, even without factoring in the notorious unpredictability of spinal surgeries. Deliberately, professionally, she shifted her focus to the busy day ahead. Brooding wouldn't be any help to her or the patients under her care. She could indulge that need— and burn off any other stressors—after her shift.

Most days Grace Ann relished the demands of her current rotation here at Walter Reed. Each day posed new hurdles and new successes. She put her heart and mind into every shift, leaving pleasantly exhausted, but rewarded as well. Today couldn't be different, couldn't be less, not even with the distraction of a teammate in the operating room. The post-op patients under her care needed her full attention. What she did made a difference, in the lives of her patients and for the families waiting for them to come home whole. Or as whole as possible, in some cases.

Her father always said a good nurse could change a soldier's world. Of course her father, the highly decorated and equally beloved General Benjamin Riley, had met an army nurse early in his career and been smart enough to marry her. Thinking of her parents eased some of the ache weighing on her heart today and put a little spring in her step. The rubber soles of her shoes squeaked against the flooring as she aimed her stride toward the room at the end of the hallway.

She checked the name on the chart: Trisha Jenkins. Pushing open the door, she smiled and introduced herself. "Good morning. I'm Grace Ann and I'll be your nurse today."

The woman lying in the bed gave a weak smile in return, squirming to sit up a bit more. "Trisha," she rasped. "Your patient."

"My mother is a Patricia. Occasionally a few people have shortened it to Tricia," Grace Ann said, establishing common ground. "But it never caught on. I heard my dad call her Patty once and I thought she'd deck him."

Trisha coughed out a little laugh. "My parents didn't give anyone the option."

"Smart." Grace checked Trisha's pulse first and then used her stethoscope to check heart and lung sounds. "My advice? Get as much mileage out of that sexy voice as possible," Grace Ann teased while she noted the vital signs in the chart. "How is your knee feeling?"

"Like an overstuffed sausage," Trisha replied.

"That sounds about right for the first day after an ACL repair." She assessed the dressing and anti-inflammation protocol. Satisfied, she gave her patient a rundown of what to expect through the day. "The surgeon, or one of his associates, will probably come by in another hour or so. Physical therapy should be here by ten," she explained. "Getting up will be an adventure, but worth it."

"Adventure as in a water park vacation or adventure as in training to become a paratrooper at airborne school?" Trisha asked.

"Well, I suppose that depends on whether you're more afraid of water or heights." Hearing the raspy chuckle, she knew this soldier would be back on duty sooner rather than later. "Keep in mind, Rome wasn't *re*built in a day."

"Got it."

Grace Ann double-checked Trisha's pain levels and medications. She listed the names of the care team for the day and encouraged Trisha to press the call button if she needed anything. At the sound of the cafeteria cart rattling down the hallway, Grace Ann stepped out to collect Trisha's breakfast tray.

On a normal shift, concerns ran the gamut from pain management to mind-set and soothing anxious family members. Some patients pushed the envelope of recovery, getting up and out of bed too soon. She preferred that kind of trouble over the challenges of those emotionally crippled by their injuries. She put a little tag on Trisha's chart so the team would watch out for the too-much-too-soon sort of problems there.

Continuing with her rounds, Grace Ann kept one

eye on the clock, along with everyone else on duty. The orthopedic ward wasn't the easiest of assignments and burnout was real. The wounded warriors they cared for put specific faces on the concepts of sacrifice and risks of a military career. But her sense of drive and commitment to helping others helped her, too. Whenever she saw hope or courage chase despair from the faces of recovering patients, it gave her positive ammunition against the ugly memories haunting her after her last deployment overseas.

Having one of their own in surgery for injuries sustained during a training exercise made each minute feel like an hour. There were risks in training, of course, but precautions as well. Drills and exercises weren't supposed to be career-ending. Sure, accidents happened, but rarely enough in the current environment that most of them took fitness and wellness for granted.

Not anymore.

Like her, Kevin was a registered nurse; he was also currently a captain within their unit and a good friend. By some miracle, he'd survived a crash when the helicopter went down a few days ago in a crisis rescue training exercise staged in a remote part of Texas. His back broken, he'd somehow also managed to survive the transport to a local hospital for stabilization and another transport for reconstructive surgery here at the Walter Reed National Military Medical Center in Maryland.

Grace Ann believed—*had to* believe—he'd come through the operation with flying colors and eventually be cleared to get back on duty. Any other outcome was unthinkable.

Kevin wasn't just a friend or an extended part of her army family. He was the younger brother of Derek Sayer, the man she'd been sleeping with for the past couple of years whenever their crazy schedules allowed. They'd kept their friends-with-benefits relationship a secret, but if Keven didn't pull through, if this surgery ended his career, how would she ever look Derek in the eye again?

Guilt prickled at the back of her neck and she blinked away tears she couldn't let fall. She'd been on the roster for that training exercise. At the last minute, her orders had been changed. She'd remained at the hospital and Kevin had been sent her place. Although she had zero evidence, she couldn't shake the feeling that the crash had been an attempt on her own life rather than an unfortunate accident.

She passed the nurses' station again for another glimpse at the screen that showed statuses for all orthopedic surgery patients. Kevin had not yet been moved to recovery.

"What do you think it means?" an aide asked, worrying her ID between her fingertips.

Grace Ann thought of Kevin's irreverent sense of humor and managed a smile. "He probably asked for a little liposuction or a tummy tuck while they were in there."

The aide chuckled in agreement as a patient call signal sounded at the desk, and they parted ways to return to their respective duties.

Grace Ann was grateful for the full roster of patients and demands today. Whenever she stopped moving, the stinging regret threatened to paralyze her. Kevin had only been on that helicopter because she'd been passed over due to security concerns. Someone from her father's past had decided to target the Riley children in what investigators believed was a revenge effort designed to cause the general the most pain.

A few months ago, her oldest brother Matt, an army

major currently stationed at the Pentagon, had barely escaped the elusive madman's efforts. What had started with a vague "you will pay" threat had escalated as the man set out to expose and embarrass the family. His plans had nearly killed Matt. At the same time, her car had even been vandalized with the now-familiar "you will pay" message the jerk favored. Investigators had dubbed him the Riley Hunter and were scrambling to unravel more about his real identity, why he'd gone on the attack and how he hired the mercenaries who carried out his orders.

In light of the ongoing investigation and the aggressive nature of the man calling the shots, the military was keeping a close eye on the locations and assignments of Matt, Grace Ann and their three younger siblings who also served.

No matter how the five of them protested, the decision had been made by those higher up the chain of command. Training exercises and deployments had been frozen. Communications were monitored for any mention of the general, Grace Ann or her siblings. Extra eyes, electronic and human, were tasked with keeping tabs on all of them.

Wallowing in the frustration after the fact wouldn't change a thing. It would ease her mind and the fraying edges of her soul if she knew that those higher-ups were looking for clues that would prove the helo accident had more sinister origins, but it wasn't her place to ask.

"Woolgathering, Major Riley?"

Grace Ann flinched at the nasal voice of Hanson Bartles, their current executive officer and assistant to the commander. Everyone called him H.B. when they could get away with it. Basically a decent guy, his talents ran to administration rather than hands-on nursing care. She supposed someone needed to have admin skills. Although they would never be friends and frequently butted heads on the priorities and how-to of running a field hospital, they got the job done.

She pulled herself together before facing him. "Good morning, Major Bartles." He preferred proper titles to friendliness. A slender man, edging toward skinny, he had stiff posture, which always reminded her of the rigors of basic training. Never a comforting thought. The discomfort was only compounded by his precise military haircut, deep-set mud-brown eyes and razor-thin nose.

"If you don't have enough to do, I could use help with the filing." It was an old, humorless joke that never earned a laugh. Still, he kept at it, apparently believing one day the result would change.

"If you don't mind getting your hands dirty, we could use your help down here," she countered as he fell into step beside her.

His narrow eyebrows lifted toward his hairline and then settled back into place. He might not be happy with her occasional sass, but she never gave him enough grief to take any action against her. "Any word on Captain Sayer?" he asked, pitching his voice too low to be overheard.

She shook her head. More guilt nipped at her heels. Of course H.B. had come down to check on Kevin. Everyone in their unit was on edge, and petty personality differences had to be pushed aside.

"I haven't heard anything since the commander went down to the surgery waiting room to sit with his brother," H.B. said. "David, right?"

"Derek," she corrected automatically. Grace Ann had to work to keep her expression neutral as the warm, laughing eyes of Kevin's older brother flashed through her mind. He would be too worried to laugh now. He hadn't so much as sent her a text message since the accident. "That's nice of her to wait with him," she said of their commander, Lieutenant Colonel Molly Bingham.

Grace Ann had briefly considered going downstairs to check on Derek and managed to find every viable excuse to avoid that scene. Dodging him made her feel like a lousy person, a terrible friend with or without benefits, and added another layer to the guilt weighing her down. Eventually Derek would know she'd been on shift this morning. If she wasn't careful, he'd learn she should have been on that helicopter instead of Kevin.

Probably a good thing he hadn't reached out yet. What could she have said to ease his worry? Her more immediate concern was how she'd face Derek when his brother reached the post-op ward. Professionally, it was her job to be available to answer his questions, but she didn't want to be professional with Derek. She wanted to lean on him, bare her soul and never stop apologizing. Another part, equally needy, craved distance from what was sure to be anger and resentment that his brother had taken her place and was now staring down a long tunnel of recovery.

She knew reality would fall somewhere in the middle.

The signal at the door between the surgical suite and her ward sounded and the wide doors parted. "You'll excuse me, duty calls," she said to H.B. without waiting for a response. Though she wished it was Kevin on that gurney—safely out of surgery—she was grateful to have a clear, valid reason to ditch H.B. and get back to work.

Once the recovery team had her newest patient settled in the bed, she took over. She was just charting the vitals on her initial assessment as the man's mother and wife arrived. Both women were sniffling and dabbing at

red-rimmed eyes. Having been through this scene frequently, Grace Ann asked and confirmed that this was
the first time they'd seen their soldier in months. She offered upbeat reassurances and reviewed what they should
expect in the next few hours. Recognizing the situation
had the potential to get sticky, she smiled confidently
and explained where they could find the family lounge
before making a swift exit.

Never in her life had she felt like more of a coward,
but getting snared in all that raw grief and angst would
make the rest of her shift unbearable. She could go 24/7
for a patient, but her tolerance for family drama had
changed. Today, she had to put Kevin's situation first.

She was making another pass by the monitor to check
his surgical status when a code alert sounded for a patient
at the opposite end of the hallway. In a well-orchestrated
flurry, every visible member of the staff leaped into motion. Grace Ann was a half step behind the crash cart as
the emergency response team poured into the room, and
she began carrying out orders as fast as they were given.

Together they moved through each life-saving protocol with competent precision, the only goal to save
the patient. And they lost both battle and war as the soldier's body gave out in fits and starts. When the doctor
pronounced time of death, there was a tangible sense
of defeat choking the air as Grace Ann and the others
cleared the room.

In a field hospital on the other side of the world, there
might have been hugs or even a fair bit of cursing over
the circumstances and failure. None of the people she
worked with knew how to give up gracefully in the fight
for life. Here, in this beautiful, state-of-the-art facility,
with families present and watching, they were expected

to maintain a standard of professionalism that bordered on superhuman.

Grace Ann lifted her chin, rolled her shoulders back and strode down the hallway away from the shadow of defeat and frustration. The patient hadn't been under her care, but that didn't lessen the sense of loss. They were a team, the concept drilled into them from day one of their basic training, all the way through nursing school and beyond. Although the human body was astounding and resilient and mysterious, sometimes the wounds were too severe or the will to survive too fragile. And yet they had to keep going, keep pressing on to save those they could.

Smothering reactions and distress were part of the job. This was merely the first time in the current *hour* she'd had to hide the emotions roiling inside. At home she could break down and have a glass—or a bottle—of wine with a frozen pizza and let the tears flow. She couldn't wait.

In the process of locking down her grief, she smiled absently at the man who turned into the corridor without really seeing him.

"Grace Ann?" He shifted toward her, not quite blocking her path. He reached out before he caught himself and tucked his hand into his pocket. "I'm glad to see you."

The voice cut through her haze of grief first. Derek. She looked up into his gentle blue eyes and saw a friend. The urge to lean on him grew like a giant bubble at a children's party. He'd understand. He might even take comfort as he offered it.

Feeling weak and sad, she felt this was the worst time to bump into him. She held herself back, shoulders straight, hands shoved into her pockets. "Hello, Derek." She squeezed out the greeting through the vise grip of emotions clamped on her throat. "How are you holding up?"

The tension churning deep inside her belly eased just being near him. The man was so easy on the eyes with his sandy-brown hair and vivid blue eyes. He hadn't shaved and the burnished gold stubble emphasized his strong, square jawline.

She found him as attractive now, rumpled and exhausted, as she had when they'd first met at a family picnic for the unit. Today, his suit jacket was folded over his arm and his shirt unbuttoned at the collar, his tie nowhere in sight. She imagined he'd driven straight to the hospital from the office when he'd gotten the call about Kevin's injury and impending surgery. Under the sunkissed skin of a man who loved the outdoors, his face was a little gray and his lips bracketed with worry lines.

When had he last eaten?

And just like that the day's trouble and her lingering guilt faded to the background. Her mind soared well away from the hospital, back to the tent they'd shared on a kayaking trip six weeks ago. She opened her arms and pulled him into a hug. Clearly startled by her demonstration—no one knew they saw each other regularly—he hesitated before reciprocating the embrace. She couldn't say which of them held on to the other as people and activity flowed around them.

Giving was simply the way Derek was built, as intrinsic as his lean muscles and bone structure. She knew they both benefited from the nurturing contact, though she tried not to take too much.

Reluctantly she stepped back. "Is Kevin out of surgery?" she queried as her guilt surged to the fore again. She hoped he was too distracted to notice.

"Yes," Derek replied. "I just got word." He pushed a

hand through his hair, wrecking it more. "The surgeon told me he came through the procedure in great shape."

The urge to pull him into another hug, to celebrate and let herself ride a wave of happiness for him and his brother, nearly overwhelmed her. She clutched her stethoscope with both hands until the feeling passed. Remorse and culpability were strange emotional burdens.

"That's fantastic." How long had they been working on the patient they'd lost? "Everyone in the unit will be so happy. Have you seen him yet?"

He nodded. "For maybe all of a minute in recovery."

"That's good. I know it doesn't seem like much." She wanted to reach up and soothe as the lingering distress rippled across his shoulders. "Have you eaten lately?"

"I'm fine." He shifted his feet. "Just not a big fan of hospitals."

"Who is?" she asked brightly. "We're used to that completely natural bias around here." She was fully aware he wasn't a big fan of the army, either. To be in a place that combined both must be excruciating. As family went, Kevin and Derek only had each other. For a fleeting moment, she wanted to confess that it should've been her in that helicopter. But what good would it do to give him more what-ifs to think about right now?

"Do you know Kevin's room number?" she asked.

"Not yet…" His voice trailed off as his gaze drifted over her face. "Are you okay?"

"Absolutely," she lied. "Would you like me to look up the room number or show you around the floor?"

"Lieutenant Colonel Bingham just gave me the full tour. I know they have Kevin assigned to that wing." Derek tilted his head toward the opposite end of the hallway.

She glanced in that direction. "He'll have an excellent team."

"Not you?"

Was that disappointment in his voice or only her wishful thinking? "Not me." Medical crises could instigate all sorts of reactions, but she didn't want this situation to alter the foundation of their friendship. At the core of it, they were good together *because* they didn't have any expectations or pressures from external sources. "Don't worry, everyone from the unit will make time to pop in and pester him until he's on his feet again."

One corner of Derek's mouth curled into a hint of the smile she missed more and more between each of their meetups. "Kevin will appreciate that."

"Probably not for long," she teased. "I'll check in on you both in a bit, okay?" She had to get back to her patients. Even with the lingering guilt, she'd have an easier time maintaining her positive, calm professionalism after these few minutes with Derek.

"Grace, one more second." Derek smoothed the fabric of the suit coat draped over his forearm. "Can I buy you a coffee? After your shift, of course."

An answer evaded her. Was the invitation an attempt to move their covert, casual relationship into something more public? Coffee was an activity friends or colleagues shared when they didn't care who might see them together. A lonely butterfly flew a tight spiral in her belly before she grounded it. She was reading too much into it. Her arrangement with Derek was *private*. Sharing a conversation over coffee wouldn't expose their secrets, even if someone from the unit happened to see them.

"We'll see," she hedged, needing time to sort out if her hesitation stemmed from guilt or something less easily defined. "I'll stop by once Kevin's settled in his room.

We can decide then." He might be too tired or too worried to leave his brother's side.

A pucker appeared between his golden-brown eyebrows as he studied her. "Okay."

She hurried away, the soles of her shoes squeaking rapidly in her wake. Her mind flickered back to Derek as she moved between patients and responsibilities. Did she *want* to have coffee with Derek? *Oh, yeah.* Especially if coffee was a euphemism for something far more physical, distracting and life affirming.

She had to get a grip. Biologically, she was well aware that sex was one of the most common coping mechanisms after a loss or in a crisis. And though hooking up with Derek had proved mutually beneficial, she didn't feel fair connecting with him physically just to take her mind off her ever-expanding abyss of guilt over what happened to Kevin.

Of course, fairness wasn't something life tossed out very often. Both she and Derek knew that firsthand. A cajoling, suggestive voice in her head reminded her that this affair had been his idea. And hadn't she happily continued their casual hookups every three or four months for the better part of the past two years?

She'd felt more than a passing interest spark when she'd been introduced to him at a gathering for families prior to Kevin's first deployment with the unit. Those sparks had fired a bit stronger at the homecoming picnic that wrapped up that particular tour.

Her lips tingled, as they did every time she recalled their first kiss. A rushed moment, stolen in the shadows as the sun set on a full and happy day, it had been a kiss full of tantalizing promises. Promises they'd kept to each other through various camping trips and outdoor excursions no one else knew about.

His friendship was priceless. He was so different from the men and women who made up the rest of her world. Though they didn't see each other on a regular basis, he'd become her haven in a world that could turn from beauty to frightful on a whim. On rough days, her stolen time with Derek buoyed her spirits and gave her something positive to look forward to.

She didn't want to lose that or hurt him with might-have-beens. She had to tell him it should've been her on that helicopter, even if it meant the end of their friendship.

Derek craved a breath of fresh air. The odor of hospital and antiseptic was embedded in his clothes. He could feel it seeping into his skin. And he was doing what he always did in hospitals—overreacting. He closed his eyes and focused on that sweet feeling of Grace Ann's hug. The one she'd given him in public, at her workplace. Marveling over the gesture calmed him enough to take another deep breath. To stay put. He hoped that hug would be enough to carry him through the challenging moments to come.

By the time they had his brother settled in the hospital room, Derek found his second wind, or maybe it was the third or fourth. He'd lost count of how many times he'd fought back from the undertow of exhaustion and panic since the unit had notified him about the crash.

Unfortunately, he was pretty sure one more adrenaline spike was the last thing he needed. Steady as he'd been through all the waiting, the familiar mixture of worry for his brother and aggravation with essentially feeling helpless was creeping in. It put an edgy buzz in his ears, under his skin, that he couldn't shake off.

From the moment Kevin had announced his intent

to join the army, a piece of Derek had been waiting, braced for "the call." The call that would make him the last Sayer on his family tree.

He dropped into the bedside chair. He should be used to this weight on his shoulders, having become Kevin's emergency contact at the age of eighteen when their parents had been killed in a car crash. Grief and the sudden onset of responsibility had changed everything about him. He'd willingly stepped into the breach—would do so again now—but the carefree teenager he'd been occasionally wanted to act out at the unfairness of it all.

Anger swelled at the sight of his brother in the hospital bed, tethered to several machines monitoring who knew what. Derek reeled in his temper. Negativity wouldn't help. Kevin wasn't on life support and he *would* make a full recovery, eventually.

After he'd waited out the surgery with Kevin's commanding officer, seeing Grace Ann had steadied him. Their brief conversation had been a spark of hope. And that hug… He'd nearly buried his head in the sweet-scented softness where her neck curved into her shoulder. Hardly fair and nowhere close to appropriate, considering their personal relationship was top secret. No one even knew they were more than acquaintances.

He liked it that way. The setup worked for both of them. No pressure, no questions, no conversations about what might come next. She must still approve, as well, or she would've stopped meeting up with him on the random weekends when their schedules meshed. On occasion, he'd debated the wisdom of the casual, no-responsibility thing they had going and couldn't manage any shame. They had mutual interests and were definitely compatible and so far, neither of them had met anyone worth making a change to an arrangement they both enjoyed.

"Knock, knock." Grace Ann's quiet voice preceded the sight of her face peering around the door. "Can I come in?"

"Please," he managed, practically jumping to his feet. He should keep his distance, especially here. This was her place of business, the unit her second family, yet he couldn't resist the appeal and comfort of having her near.

Her relaxed, easy smile as she walked into the room was reminiscent of early mornings on their many camping trips. Under a clear sunrise, her cap of short dark hair gleamed and her soft fair skin and deep brown eyes radiated warmth. He never tired of seeing her in those remote, solitary settings, knowing the moments they shared were only for the two of them.

Selfish? Maybe. He cataloged it as self-preservation. Other women eventually expected more than he could give. Grace Ann, raised in a boisterous and busy military family, was too independent to make demands on him.

Today, with the whir and beeps of machines and the cold, clinical smells surrounding them, their backdrop was a far cry from the pace and peace of nature. Here, dressed in her scrubs, her stethoscope in her pocket and a bulky watch on her wrist, she was a professional, though he desperately wanted to lean on her as a friend without fear of being caught in the act.

"How's he doing?" She stopped at the foot of the bed, adjusting the blanket tucked around Kevin's feet.

"You probably know better than I do." Derek winced at the hard edge in his voice. He hated hospitals almost as much as he hated standing by, helplessly waiting. He held up his hands, surrendering. "Sorry. Apparently I'm too tired to be civil."

"That's to be expected," she murmured.

In the privacy of the room, with Kevin unconscious, her lips curved into one of those smiles he enjoyed only when they were alone. Her eyes warmed with compassion, chasing away the persistent chill he'd been fighting since walking into this building.

"Has he been awake at all?" she asked, turning her focus to one of the monitors.

Derek shuffled his feet and stuffed his hands into his pockets, uncomfortable with the needs at war inside him. He could handle this, had handled worse in the past. "A minute or two," he replied. "Long enough to tell me to lighten up."

"That's his special skill around here," she said, patting Kevin's shoulder. "He keeps all of us from taking ourselves too seriously." Sadness drifted over her like a fog, first shadowing her eyes, then flowing down over the rest of her in those shapeless scrubs. Was she afraid for Kevin? Were they keeping some dreadful detail from him? Curious and concerned, he studied her while she watched his brother's monitors.

"Well?" he asked.

She swiveled around as if she'd forgotten he was there. "Pardon me?"

He nodded to the various machines emitting periodic beeps. "What's your assessment?" Waiting for the answer, he watched her reclaim her composure, though the signs of a rough day lingered in her rigid shoulders and the way she gripped her stethoscope.

"He appears comfortable," she said. "You, not so much."

They stared at each other over the bed. The silence stretched between them, a wire ready to snap. He couldn't decide if he wanted to yell at her or kiss her or beg her to get him out of here. "I'm not myself," he muttered, turning toward the safer view outside the window.

"Did you get something to eat?"

"No." The idea of food made his stomach turn over.

"You should grab something," she suggested. "I'll wait here if you don't want him to be alone."

Her calm, professional demeanor was taking over. Was it too much to ask to keep Grace Ann, friend and lover, in this room instead of the experienced RN?

He stalked back and dropped into the chair by the bed. "I need to stay." Being there for Kevin had become his role the moment their parents died. It didn't matter where "here" was. He wasn't perfect, but whatever support Kevin needed—emotional, financial or physical— Derek did his best to provide.

"All right. Tell me what sounds good and I'll go get that for you."

Her completely rational tone grated on his nerves. "You're not a waitress." He had to get control of this nasty attitude. No one deserved this surliness, but especially not her. Not when he claimed to be her friend.

She angled her head, a grin teasing the corner of her mouth. "Well, I have been. It's just like riding a bike," she said. "What'll it be? Downstairs, they had burgers and pasta marinara on the line today."

He scrubbed a hand through his hair. "I'm being an idiot."

"No, Derek." She stepped closer, her gaze earnest. "You're being a concerned brother. I have a few, so I know firsthand what it looks like."

Her gracious understanding did nothing to settle this prickling under his skin. Surely she saw plenty of people at their worst every day. He didn't care to be lumped into that group.

"You and I are so different," he said. Not the first time he'd thought it, though it was the first time he'd dared to say it aloud. The cornerstone of their weekend getaways had been the avoidance of deeper topics and connections. Better, they'd decided early on, to keep the focus on their common interests. Love of the outdoors, new adventures and sex. Excellent sex.

She waited for him to gather his thoughts without saying a word.

He couldn't remember the last time a woman had been so patient. He couldn't recall the last time he'd argued with a girlfriend. Because he didn't. And she wasn't. He was a short-term kind of guy who knew when to make a quick or graceful exit. The randomness of their hookups had to be why things still worked with Grace Ann.

"Kevin's more like you," he continued. "Those days after the accident, when Dad didn't pull through, I never wanted to see a hospital, nurse or doctor again. Kevin set his mind on a medical career. Took me a long time to accept that."

He wasn't sure he'd accepted it yet.

"Kevin's going to make a full recovery," she said. Her quiet confidence was a cool balm to his ragged emotional wounds. "There will be hard days. He's going to need your legendary support in the weeks to come."

"Legendary?"

Her lips parted but her cell phone chimed, distracting her before she could explain. Frowning at the device, she excused herself and stepped into the hallway.

Legendary support? That had to be sarcasm. Derek had stumbled many a time, trying to raise a heartbroken little brother. They'd fought bitterly along the way and he'd been particularly unenthused about his little brother's career decisions. He reached for Kevin's hand, careful to avoid the bruising that mottled his skin from the helicopter crash.

Grace Ann came back in. "That was my boss," she explained, holding up her cell phone. "I can't pick up anything for you, but I asked the cafeteria to send something up."

"That was…" Just about the nicest thing anyone had done for him in years. "Thoughtful," he finished. "Thank you."

"Anytime. I'll see you tomorrow. If you need anything, don't hesitate to ask. Everyone wants to pitch in and help both of you through this."

He nodded. His voice wasn't trustworthy.

"Promise me," she pressed.

She'd never demanded a promise or anything else from him before. He found himself giving it easily. "I promise."

As she darted away, he felt the change. Lighter, hopeful again. It seemed a few minutes in her company had cut his burden in half. Should he chalk that up to her professional skill or their unique friendship?

It bothered him more than a little that he couldn't be sure.

Chapter 2

Being called to the commander's office wasn't completely out of the ordinary, but it wasn't an event Grace Ann categorized as fun. Hugging Derek in the hallway couldn't have raised any eyebrows. As Kevin's brother, he was unit family and offering him support or comfort was completely normal under the circumstances.

Maybe the Lieutenant Colonel wanted to put her on a new assignment or a special project. She was always up for a change of professional scenery and she'd happily dive into a task that would fill the hours between shifts and keep her mind off those relentless ghosts haunting her and the madman hunting her siblings. Only one way to find out. In the elevator, she took a deep breath and gathered her thoughts, prepared to give an update on her patients, as well as Kevin.

H.B. was shutting down his computer for the day when she walked into the suite of administration offices. "Go on in," he said. "She's ready for you."

"Thanks." She tried to pick up a clue about this meeting from his expression, but he might as well have been playing poker. Rapping on the door, she announced herself.

"Come on in." Lieutenant Colonel Bingham waved her forward. "Have a seat," she said. "It's been a long day for all of us."

"It has," Grace Ann agreed. The pleasantries did nothing to settle her nerves. There was a hard gleam in the commander's usually kind brown eyes. "I just came from Kevin's room. He's resting comfortably."

"That's good news." Bingham's gaze raked over a paper on her desktop before she looked up. "There is no easy way to say this," she began. "I just received notice you're under investigation for misappropriation of Department of Defense medical supplies."

The absurdity of the statement left denials and protests tangled up between Grace Ann's brain and her mouth, making her momentarily mute. There had to be some awkward, horrible mistake. She'd been stateside for two years, serving with her unit here at Walter Reed day in and day out. The only exceptions had been temporary assignments for training exercises elsewhere. Until the Riley Hunter's actions prevented her participation.

"I beg your pardon?" she managed. "I would never—"

"Of course, I don't believe it for a minute," Bingham said. "I do, however, have to take appropriate action. The report claims you broke the rules during outreach efforts on your last deployment."

Who would start pointing fingers now over a deployment two years done and gone? "The school," she murmured as the devastating memories burst free of the boxes where she tried to keep them.

The ghosts took shape, flowing around her, the happy

faces of children she'd come to know and love a little. She wasn't in the office. Not even in the States. She was back in that dusty village where boys and girls, eyes sparkling with life and energy, would dance and sing and giggle during the team's visits. One by one those faces withered, the eyes staring into nothing, all that life snuffed out.

"Major?"

Grief was an open, festering wound. Her mouth went dry, recalling the dust that coated everything and everyone. Her heart seemed to stall in her chest, aching more with every beat, her ears ringing as they had in the aftermath. Wouldn't it be nice to curl up and turn her back on the world with all its horrors?

She yanked herself back to the present before the past dragged her under permanently. "Yes, pardon me." Slowly she opened her hands, stretching her fingers, which had balled up in defense.

Bingham hadn't been their commander on that tour and Grace Ann wasn't sure what she might or might not know about the incident. When she had control of her voice, she explained, "We regularly conducted wellness visits at the village school. It was a high point in the tour for all of us. Until it was bombed."

Legally, DOD supplies could be used to treat locals in cases of blindness, loss of limbs, or life-threatening trauma. On the day of the bombing, she and the team had gone out to conduct routine checkups with the school-children. There hadn't been any trauma supplies on hand to be used, appropriately or not.

Someone must have misinterpreted the team's actions in that crisis. Why pin it all on her? Needing information, she forced herself to ask questions. "Is that the incident being investigated? Who accused me?"

"The whistleblower's name is redacted in my report," Bingham said. "As well as specifics."

The name wasn't important. Grace Ann was confident she'd guessed right. "That has to be it," Grace Ann murmured to herself. "The school was the biggest, most publicized community outreach effort in our area," she explained. "I suppose our time there, the improvements we were making, turned the village into an irresistible target for terrorists."

"You know better than that," Bingham said. "It had nothing to do with us. Terrorists habitually go for the jugular in a community. Positive growth isn't tolerated."

Bingham was right, but Grace Ann couldn't shrug off the weight of blame. She'd come home, debriefed and reestablished a healthy work-life routine. And still when she closed her eyes to sleep, the children who would never grow up were with her.

"I don't like this, Major Riley." The commander glared down at the paper again, closed the folder with a snap. "However, my responsibility is to cooperate for the integrity of the investigation, regardless of how ridiculous it is. To that end, your security clearance has been suspended—"

"Pardon me?"

"—and your access to medications and controlled substances is revoked. Due to those status changes, you've been removed from the schedule until the investigation runs its course and you're cleared."

"Ma'am?" Grace Ann stared at her commander, dumfounded. The words wouldn't fall into any sensible order. How would she fill the hours without her work? "I didn't do anything wrong over there." Who had she offended so badly that they'd file a false report?

"I know this comes as a shock," Bingham continued

gently. "Your first call should be to the JAG office. After that, I recommend you take a real vacation. According to your personnel record, you haven't taken much more than a long weekend since your return from Afghanistan."

"There was a week in Key West," she said absently. She could hardly mention her secret trips with Derek every few months. "We all met down there to celebrate when my parents picked up their boat."

Most of the time she filled her days off between short jaunts to the Rileys' new beach house in North Carolina or rambling through nearby state and national parks with Derek. Surrounding herself with activity was the only way she'd found to mute the agony of that day and keep those vicious memories locked down.

"Your scattered days here and there aren't nearly enough downtime to balance how much you give us here, Major Riley," Bingham said. "Consider the extended time off a silver lining to this frustrating and inconvenient situation."

"How long?" She blurted out the question before she had control of herself. "I mean, yes ma'am."

Bingham narrowed her gaze. "If you want my opinion, no one who knows you is putting any stock in this. Still, the investigators are obligated to follow through."

"Of course." Transparency and accountability were the catchphrases these days. That logic was no comfort to her while her career deflated like a popped balloon and her heart cowered in her chest.

"I did try to keep you on the rotation," Bingham said. "They wouldn't have it. I anticipate you'll be cleared and back with us just as soon as the initial interviews are over."

Her head pounded. They were conducting interviews already. On a violent incident that had taken place on the other side of the world. She couldn't think of a single person who would set her up this way or a single witness who might verify this outrageous claim.

"I'm free to go?" She should feel lucky she wasn't in handcuffs.

Bingham nodded in the affirmative. "Major Riley. Grace Ann. You are a trusted, valued member of the Army Nurse Corps. I do *not* believe there is anything credible in this accusation. Take some time to yourself and let the system sort it out."

"Thank you, ma'am." It meant a great deal to be trusted, to hear that she was valued.

Unfortunately, the confidence and compliments wouldn't change the sudden abundance of free time looming in front of her. Hours and hours with no distractions, no work to exhaust her physically or mentally, posed a terrifying and untenable prospect.

She couldn't even invite Derek for a quick weekend away. He needed to be here with his brother.

Guilt and grief tied knots in her belly. She should be the one recuperating from spinal surgery—would have been if the Riley Hunter's antics hadn't kept her off that exercise. Now another storm cloud was throwing random lightning bolts into her life, threatening her career. She had no idea who she was without the army, without nursing.

Derek rubbed his palms together briskly, determined to stay awake. Overtired, now that he had a decent meal in his belly it was hard to keep his eyes open. He could sleep later. With so many things that could, and often did, go wrong in a hospital he was driven to keep watch over Kevin.

He and his brother held vastly different memories of

the days their dad lingered in ICU after the car crash. Kevin had been old enough to understand the concept of serious complications but still young enough that Derek sheltered him as much as possible from the increasingly grim updates.

Yes, Kevin's situation was different. Medicine had made huge advancements since they were kids. And unlike their father, Kevin had squeezed his hand once during Derek's brief visit to the recovery area and periodically roused enough to remind Derek he'd be fine. Now, while Kevin slept, Derek had only his thoughts and the incessant beeping of various monitors for company.

The television had been more annoyance than diversion. He'd called his office in Baltimore and updated his assistant that Kevin would recover fully, explaining it would be a few weeks yet before he could manage day-to-day tasks on his own. She'd promised to pass the information along as needed and keep him up-to-date on issues at the office. He was in-house counsel for a medical supply company, so there weren't any pressing cases to juggle.

Though it was selfish, he wished Grace Ann would come back. Her confidence in Kevin's recovery made it easier to believe life would return to normal again someday. Just knowing she was in the building gave him something positive to think about when the clinical sounds and smells overwhelmed him.

Eighteen years ago Derek had changed up his life and adjusted his personal plans to stay home and get Kevin through high school. The few weeks or months ahead of them were simply another drop in the bucket. Derek would telecommute or…

His thoughts evaporated when he caught a glimpse of Grace Ann hurrying by the open doorway. He'd expected her to pop in again after she dealt with whatever had called her away, had been counting on her return. He started to stand up and follow her and forced himself to stay put. Though Kevin didn't need him right now, he didn't have to trail after her like a lost puppy.

He pushed to his feet again. He should apologize for being rude when she'd been trying to help. An apology was a valid, mature reason to interrupt her and it had nothing to do with wanting to spend another few minutes in her company to store up that soft scent of her skin. She was intelligent, witty and kind and she'd managed to make this never-ending day almost tolerable.

Although, as he hustled down the hallway, he had to concede everyone here had been nicer than expected. The weight on his shoulders lifted with the silent admission. Kevin frequently joked about Derek's colossal bias against the military. His prejudice wasn't even based on his own experiences or an inherent philosophy. No, Derek's problem boiled down to a pervasive unease about Kevin's inevitable deployments to dangerous and remote locations.

His little brother had no idea how much Derek didn't want to be the *last* Sayer on their family tree.

At the intersection of two hallways, he looked around, having momentarily lost sight of Grace Ann. She was a little taller than average, a fact he appreciated whenever they kissed and when he spotted her dark head moving against the sea of scrubs. He almost called out her name before he remembered where he was and that shouting wasn't a smart idea.

He rushed forward, determined to catch her before she reached the employees-only doorway. He skidded to a stop as someone wearing a combat uniform—he

couldn't be sure if it was a man or a woman—rounded
the corner, grabbed her and shoved her into the stairwell.

What the hell?

Catching a glimpse of the shock on her face, he moved
on instinct and bolted after them. Through the narrow
window in the heavy door, he saw the uniform held
Grace Ann in a chokehold, pressing her back over the
railing. She fought back, twisting and straining to break
the grip, while keeping one foot hooked around the back
of the attacker's knee for leverage. Or balance.

Derek's heart slammed into his rib cage. He couldn't
lose her. Soldier or not, she wouldn't deal with this
alone—he wouldn't let her. Shouting for help, Derek
surged forward and grabbed Uniform's collar and hauled
him back.

The person under that boxy uniform put up quite a
fight. Closer now, Derek could see it was a man by the
big hands dusted with hair wrapped around Grace Ann's
neck. The edge of a tattoo on his inner right wrist peeked
from under a sleeve. Derek struggled, pushing and shov-
ing, determined to get the man off her.

She continued to scrape and grapple, using the distraction and shifting momentum to break the chokehold
at last. In a lightning-quick maneuver, she pinned Uniform's hands helplessly to his side and struck the man
hard on the jaw with her elbow.

Uniform's head snapped back, but he didn't give up.
Backpedaling, he thumped Derek into the wall with his
body and lunged for Grace Ann again. The element of
surprise gone now, she smoothly ducked under the attempt to corral her at the railing and raised her leg, trip-
ping Uniform. He pitched forward, tumbling down the
slope of concrete steps.

Uniform hit the first landing with a thud and a low

groan before he scrambled to his feet and kept running, pinballing between the wall and the rail in his haste to escape. When Grace Ann moved to follow, Derek caught her, holding her back. "Let him go."

"He can't get away with this."

"He won't." Derek hoped his promise wouldn't become a lie. "Let's take a look at you." He leaned back so he could look her over but she turned abruptly into his embrace, her body quaking with shock as Uniform's boots continued to pound against the stairs.

"We should call security." He held her close, needing the assurance that she was alive and well. He kept breathing in the soft clove scent of her shampoo, imagining they were back at their last campsite, under the stars. Anything to block that moment when he was sure she was going over the rail.

"We should." She didn't move, her hands fisted in the fabric of his shirt as the sound of a door clanging open and closed echoed up the stairwell.

Would she now be in a heap at the bottom of the stairwell if he hadn't come along? Jerking his gaze away from the unforgiving concrete at the bottom of the stairwell, he shifted them closer to the door and safety as the tremors rolling through both of them subsided.

"Thanks," she said, stepping out of his embrace. "I'm better now."

He wanted to believe her. His gaze fixed on the red marks circling her throat above the neckline of her scrub top and his heart lodged in his throat. "You sure?"

She suddenly bent over, her hands braced on her knees, and sucked in slow, measured breaths. "Just need a minute."

"Take your time." He stroked her back with his palm,

soothing, willing her to be okay. "Did you recognize him?"

Still doubled over, she shook her head. "The name on the uniform was Smith. The rank was PFC—private first class. That's all I got." She coughed, the rough sound making him wince.

"He had a tattoo on one wrist." Straightening, she arched an eyebrow. "I only caught the ink," he explained. "Not enough to identify an image."

"So he might as well be invisible," she said, then fell into another spate of coughing.

"We need to call security," he repeated. He patted his pockets, couldn't find his cell phone. "They can pull more information from video feed." He'd spotted surveillance cameras above the stairwell door and high in the corner. "And you need a doctor."

"I'm fine." She handed him her cell phone and rasped out the code for security. "I should have known this kind of thing was coming," she muttered.

"What are you talking about?" he asked while he waited for someone at the security desk to pick up. If someone was harassing her, the hospital, with all of the protective measures, identity checks and people coming and going, seemed like an audacious place to launch an attack.

She reached for the door, held it for him. "It's a long story."

"Good thing I have plenty of time on my hands," he said. "Which way to the base security office?" he asked as the phone kept ringing.

Her reply was interrupted by the person who'd finally answered his call. In low tones, he gave an explanation of the incident and promised they would both head straight over to give a full report.

"You need to stay with Kevin," she said when he returned her phone. "I'll go over and handle the report. If they have questions for you, I can share your cell number with them. Assuming that's all right."

Let her out of his sight after that? Not a chance. "You're not going anywhere alone," he told her. His heart hadn't yet returned to a normal rhythm.

"But—"

He cut her off with a look. "Wait here. *Please*," he added as he ducked into the room. Returning after grabbing his cell phone and jacket, he was glad to see she hadn't left without him.

"This is silly. You know I can handle myself." Her chin lifted in defiance, making the red marks on the delicate skin of her throat stand out in stark relief.

"You can," he admitted. She probably would have hog-tied the assailant with her stethoscope and dragged him down to security by his bootlaces if Derek hadn't interfered. Instead, he'd jumped in and the guy escaped. "You can," he repeated. "But you don't need to."

"Derek." Clearly exasperated, she made his name sound like an oath.

"You've said it yourself," he pressed. "Kevin just needs time to recover. No one's attacking him." He leaned close. "From where I'm standing, it looks like you need me more than he does right now."

"Fine."

Relieved it hadn't required more of an argument, he followed her to the employee area for her floor, waiting outside the door. She returned within a minute or two, a tote over her shoulder and a jacket zipped up to cover the marks on her neck. It only sent more questions rolling through his mind, but he held them all back for a later time. She was clearly irritable and he didn't want to stress her voice any more than necessary.

"I wish you'd let a doctor look you over."

She glared at him and shook her head. Her phone chimed with an alert and she checked the smartwatch on her wrist. The glare turned into a fierce scowl.

Whatever the message was didn't improve her mood. "Problem?"

"My brother," she replied with a dismissive shrug. "He's mad I refused a formal protective detail."

"More of that long story?"

"Yes," she replied with a grimace.

At the security desk, a base police officer took their detailed statements of the incident in the stairwell. Though she refused medical evaluation, they swabbed her throat for any possible DNA from her attacker and took several pictures of the marks left behind. Before they left, the officer assisting them pulled up the video from the nearest cameras and promised to try to track down the soldier who had attacked her.

On the surface Grace Ann appeared satisfied, but Derek's gut instinct told him there was something more going on. On their private trips, he'd learned to read her pretty well. The tension was there in the way she kept nipping at her lip and working her thumb over her index finger. Those little habits would fade during their time together, only to resurface when she had to head home.

Maybe the two of them should have been sharing more than superficial, steamy outdoor getaways these last couple of years. He'd kept secrets for both of them. Didn't she know she could trust him with anything?

"What next?" he asked.

"I'm going home," she said. "Hot tea and an ice pack."

Whether he blamed it on the traumas past or present,

he couldn't bear the idea of her heading home alone. What happened if the anonymous soldier returned? "Let me help. At least until you're settled." He intended to stick close until he got the whole story out of her.

She shook her head. "That's overkill."

"Maybe I could use a friend," he suggested. He'd been running on fumes before witnessing her attack. Time outside the hospital with her would be a welcome change of scenery.

"Uh-huh." She rolled those big brown eyes and he could tell she was close to giving in. "You'd do better with a friend who isn't in trouble."

What kind of trouble? He'd been around the unit long enough to know that time and again she put others ahead of herself. It had been obvious from their first introduction when she'd left her meal unfinished to take over in the serving line so another soldier could eat with his parents. "Probably," he said. "But you're right here."

"Convenient." Her lips twitched into a shadow of a smile. "For both of us."

Pouncing on the opportunity, he convinced her to let him drive her home. They took the base shuttle to his car and she programmed her address into his navigation app. During the short drive to her house, she sipped on a water bottle she'd pulled from her tote, staring at the neighborhood passing by.

He appreciated the silence as his thoughts were swirling with doubts and nerves about this move. Since agreeing to explore the potential of their first kiss, they'd deliberately avoided crossing the line between neutral-territory casual hookups and personal space.

Living in separate cities, about an hour away from each other, helped. Although they'd agreed dating other people was okay and that either one of them could bow out gracefully if a date took a serious turn, here they were. He hadn't dated anyone else in over a year. So he kept circling back to her, and her to him, every few months for a long weekend of hiking or rafting or some other outdoor adventure. It was the perfect solution.

No one else captivated him the way Grace Ann did and few had shared his interests with the same intensity. Unique, confident and strong, she was practical with an unexpected side of whimsy that cropped up at the oddest times. Despite the inherent risks of her career choice, she lived life large. He admired that, though he couldn't cope with it day-to-day over the long-term. On the rare occasions when he pictured his future wife, she didn't wear camouflage or follow orders to assist in a crisis overseas.

Pulling into the last driveway on her block, he studied the clean lines of the redbrick house on the corner lot with a one-car garage and a cherry tree in the front yard. He wondered if she had help with the well-kept lawn. As long as they had been together, he should know if she enjoyed yard work.

"Nice place," he said.

"Thanks. I'll get the garage door so you can pull in." She opened the door and slid out of the passenger seat, tote slung over her shoulder.

She punched a code into a keypad beside the door and a moment later the garage door rolled up. He put the car in Drive, but she didn't move. He couldn't pull in without hitting her and the garage interior was too dim for him to see beyond her. Turning off the engine, he climbed out of the car and walked up to stand beside her.

Shards of glass were scattered across the cement floor. His gaze followed the glinting trail to a broken window in the back corner. He reached for his cell phone, but he'd left it in the car. "Call the police," he said quietly.

"No." She swallowed. "It was just wind." She dropped her tote bag to the floor. "I didn't get the tree branches trimmed back when I should have."

He hadn't heard anything about damaging winds, having been indoors for the majority of the past two days. "You sure?"

"What else?" Moving forward with stilted motions that bore no resemblance to what he remembered as the fluid, energetic woman he'd gone kayaking with a few weeks ago, she walked over to the wall-mounted pegboard and pulled down a broom.

"Hold up." Derek stepped into her path, noticed her eyes had glazed over and her knuckles were white where she gripped the broom handle. With a gentle shake of her shoulders, he broke through the strange haze. "Grace Ann, you need to call the police. Now, honey."

A shiver rippled through her and her big brown eyes brimmed with tears. She blinked rapidly before they could spill over. "Why? I can't tell them anything."

Derek had never before felt this drive, this *need* to rescue a woman. Being there for Kevin had been his primary focus and he studiously avoided drama and troubling entanglements. Whatever Grace Ann was facing, he was determined to help.

"I'll make the call," he said. "We'll report this as a possible break-in." Thank goodness he'd insisted on bringing her home. "Take a look around," he said, using her phone to look up the nonemergency number for the local police department. "Is anything missing?"

She was so obviously overwhelmed he wanted to cuddle her close and assure her it was just another lousy moment in a bad day. His mind on the attacker who'd escaped, he couldn't help wondering if both instances were related. Briefly, he considered closing the garage door and taking her to a hotel. Preferably a hotel on the other side of the country.

Instead, he called the police department, gave her address and explained what they'd found. While she looked around, Derek took stock as well. There were a few items of value, but nothing other than the window seemed to be disturbed or vandalized. He glanced to the steps leading to the house, wondering if someone might be hiding inside. Although the hole in the window wasn't big enough for a person to fit though, he wasn't taking any more chances.

"Come on, we'll wait in the car."

She aimed a watery smile at him. "You should go. To your hotel or back to the hospital. I'll be fine."

Like hell he'd leave her to handle this alone. "Sure, I'll go. Is there a neighbor you'd like to come over to wait with you?" he asked innocently.

"Just *go*." Temper flared in her eyes. "I'm a big girl, Derek." She paused to clear her throat. "This isn't the first bad day I've had."

He'd bet good money it was among the worst she'd had in a long time. At least he hoped days like this weren't the norm. He moved her tote aside and tugged her down to sit on the steps with him.

"You might not have heard, but I'm coming off a pretty bad day myself," he said, keeping his voice light. "The experts promised that my worst nightmare isn't going to strike this time. Which gives me time to help you out."

"What's your worst nightmare?" she asked, pressing her hands together between her knees.

"Being alone." It wasn't a fear he'd ever confessed or tackled head-on. When had he come to trust Grace Ann so much? "I don't dwell on it," he added. He lived his life, managed his career and kept himself distracted with hobbies.

"Ah."

"Ah?" he echoed. "Meaning?"

She exhaled, her breath fluffing her bangs away from her forehead. "You know I'm second of five kids," she reminded him. "An army brat. My family seems to grow a little more every year through military connections alone. I'm not sure I have a grasp of the kind of loneliness you're afraid of."

Her answer painted a clear picture of how little he knew about her and filled him with a strange urgency to learn more. "Do you have a roommate?"

"No. I enjoy living by myself." A wry smile curved her lips. "Of course there's always a sibling or friend I can call, to vent or lean on when needed."

He supposed that's where he fit into her life. Someone she called when she needed a break from solitude or work. "Why don't you call your family now?"

"I should." Elbows propped on her knees, she rested her head on her hands. "I will once the police are done. No sense worrying everyone until we have more facts."

"You'll tell them about the attack in the stairwell, too?"

She rubbed her temples. "I hate to worry the family but I will tell them all of it," she muttered.

"What else are you dealing with?" He smoothed a hand across the bunched muscles of her shoulders.

"Stupidity." She picked up her cell phone, turning it around in her hands, lips pursed. "I got suspended today," she said. "Someone reported me for misuse of Defense Department supplies and my security clearance is suspended while they investigate."

Whoa. Work was everything for Grace Ann. "Why didn't you say anything?"

She picked at the knees of her scrubs. "Some guy was strangling me."

"Your family can help with this, right?" She was the daughter of a highly decorated general. Surely he still had connections.

"They shouldn't."

He draped an arm over her shoulders and pulled her close. "You have to tell them."

"I will." She leaned into him. "Again, better to have all the facts," she said.

"Do you need an attorney?" He didn't have the right legal expertise, but he had friends in all areas of law practice.

She frowned. "I didn't think you took private clients."

"I can help you find someone," he replied. He didn't even have to think about it, though it meant calling in a favor with a friend or two with more experience in military law.

She pushed up from the stairs, arms folded over her middle as she paced the width of the garage. "You're too generous," she said.

It didn't sound like a compliment. "You'd change your mind if I sent you a bill."

In the glare of the overhead light, he saw that her rusty laugh didn't quite reach her eyes. He really should have a ready solution—other than sex—to help ease her distress.

What began on a whim at his first family picnic with Kevin's unit could have been a sturdy foundation. In that soft evening light, away from the noise of so many happy, reunited families, he'd found contentment. Her wide, accepting smile and her doe eyes framed by long dark eyelashes drew things out of him too easily. With her, on that secluded path, all of his wishes and dreams were possible.

That one kiss had led to…nothing. Not right away. They'd exchanged numbers and after some careful planning, they'd spent a weekend hiking the gorgeous trails in the Shenandoah National Park. There, they'd developed a no-strings, friends-with-benefits arrangement that was the best of both worlds.

Now he felt as if they'd shortchanged all that early potential.

"I appreciate the offer," she was saying. "The accusation is bogus and the investigation will bear that out soon enough. I won't be out of work long."

He heard the faintly hopeful note in her statement and kept his opinion to himself. Waiting out bogus accusations was one thing, but adding in the attack at work and now the vandalism to her home, his uneasiness cranked up. "You think these are all just unrelated, unfortunate incidents?"

"Yes."

Her fierce, whispered reply wasn't convincing. He couldn't challenge her or ask for more details because the police cruiser pulled up, parking on the street.

"You can leave," she said as the officers approached. "I'll be fine."

"In a minute." He stood with her, not close enough to touch, unless she reached out. As much as he wanted to console her, it would be better if it was her idea.

The two officers introduced themselves as Willet and Radcliff. Willet, hair going gray at the temples, carried a bit more weight than the wiry, youthful Radcliff. Together they patiently listened to Grace Ann's account of finding the broken window, Willet taking notes. They asked about her security system and nodded in resigned acceptance as she explained there was only a motion-detecting floodlight at the back corner of the garage.

"Not much help in daylight," Officer Willet remarked.

"Any signs of trouble inside?" Radcliff queried.

"We haven't gone in yet." Grace Ann tugged at the high collar of her jacket. "It seemed prudent to wait for you."

"The door doesn't show any sign of damage," Derek said.

"I never lock this one," she admitted glumly.

"Understandable," Willet said. "It's the same at my house. Radcliff will take a look around outside to check for any evidence or concerns." With a nod, the younger man strolled off. "Once I clear the house, the three of us can walk through."

"I appreciate your time," Grace Ann said.

Officer Willet examined the doorjamb closely before entering the house, one hand on his holstered gun. "Just give me a few minutes," he said.

They stepped back to wait in the center of the garage. Officer Radcliff returned before Willet. He reported that other than a small, narrow footprint, there wasn't any other evidence to be found.

"Do you think the tree limb broke the window?" she asked.

"Not to my eye," Radcliff said. "I called for a crime scene tech to come out and gather whatever they can find."

She pressed her fingertips to her lips and nodded, accepting the assessment. Derek had never seen her so rattled. Of course he'd only really spent time with her on weekends, far from any real pressure. "Have there been any similar crimes in the area?"

"We always see a bump in burglary complaints when school starts up," Radcliff answered. "Pure vandalism comes and goes." He shrugged. "We'll run it through the system for any similar incidents when we get back."

Derek couldn't be sure what Grace Ann thought, but in his mind that added up to more trouble aimed directly at her. "You don't sound hopeful about catching the vandal."

"It's unlikely," Radcliff admitted. "No sign in here or out there of the object used to break the window." He shrugged again. "Probably a kid on a dare."

Derek hoped the officer was right. Because of the different jurisdictions, no one was likely to connect the attack at the hospital, on federal property, with this incident in her civilian neighborhood, unless Grace Ann suggested it specifically. Something he knew she was not ready to do.

"House is clear," Willet declared from the doorway. "I don't think anything is out of place, but you'll know best."

"That's good news," Grace Ann said.

"Come on in and take a look." Willet waved them closer. "Thank you for your service," he added.

Color rose in Grace Ann's cheeks. What had the police officer seen inside? She hadn't yet given them more than her name, and there was no insignia on her jacket. He waited near the kitchen, as inconspicuously as possible, while she and the police officer walked the house.

With a full view of the spacious front room, Derek decided he liked her home. She'd chosen comfortable furnishings, nothing fussy and cluttered or too sparse and sterile. He noticed the framed flag and a shadow box with an award of some sort on the shelves flanking a big-screen television. He didn't go closer, unwilling to tread on her frayed nerves. On the counter she had a framed picture from her last deployment in Afghanistan. She stood next to his brother, both of them grinning, surrounded by the rest of their team. The date was engraved on the frame. He'd seen a matching piece at Kevin's house.

"Everything is still here," she said when she came back into the main room.

Once again he fought the urge to gather her close. "That's a relief."

"It is." Her smile lacked any real enthusiasm. "It was a long day at work," she told the officers.

The officers promised to look into any connected complaints as Grace Ann walked them out. When they were alone again, Derek caught Grace Ann staring at the broken glass.

"Go on inside," he said. "I'll sweep this up and cover the window for tonight."

"You've gone above and beyond already. It can wait until morning." She glared at the mess. "It's not like I have anywhere to be."

She had yet to sit down with the hot tea and ice pack, and he knew she needed both. Needed to unwind. Though he expected resistance, he had no intention of leaving just yet. "Are you hungry?"

She tugged at that high collar again before meeting his gaze. "A little."

"How is it I don't know if you like to cook?" Camp cooking wasn't the same as enjoying the process of building a meal at home.

"We've never had reason to discuss it." Her lips twitched. "I don't enjoy it much. Unless cookies and brownies count."

His mouth watered. "From a mix or from scratch?" Homemade brownies were his favorite.

"Scratch." Her sharp chin lifted in a way that made him long to nip and taste. "If you're mixing up ingredients, might as well do it right."

"That counts." Baking was one thing he'd never mastered after stepping into a parental role with Kevin. Even with boxed mixes, he'd always managed to mess something up.

He pulled out his phone before she could try to send him away again. "I'll order a pizza and you can make dessert while I clean up the garage."

"How is it I didn't know you're so bossy?" She said it with a sweet smile that made him want to steal a kiss. He resisted. Barely.

"Lawyer." He tapped the wide-bristled broom to the cement floor. "Comes with the territory." He set to work, smiling when he heard the door close quietly behind her as she went inside.

Lawyer, pseudo-parent, oldest child: he supposed he came by his bossiness naturally. In this instance, with a woman with such vivid pain haunting her gaze, he counted it as a helpful trait rather than a hindrance.

Chapter 3

Grace Ann did *not* want company tonight—especially not in the form of Derek. He was temptation personified, the way he nurtured and soothed. She was sore, bordering on miserable and overwhelmed. It would be so easy to let him take care of her.

Easy, but not smart.

She wanted the house to herself because she was afraid to be alone. She needed to prove she could stand on her own, despite the horrible surprises of the day.

Strong. Unflappable. Resolute. Those were the words she kept close to her heart. Words that described generations of her ancestors, whether or not they served in the military. Rileys didn't break and they sure didn't *break down*. How could she maintain any sense of independence if bodyguards intervened or whisked her away? As soon as the Riley Hunter investigators heard about the attack in the stairwell, there would be more protective measures fencing her in. Given a chance, she could handle this on her own. She needed to do so.

Although she desperately wanted to send Derek away, she couldn't do it simply because *she* felt needy and fragile. He was in the middle of a crisis, too. The prior limits of their arrangement had to give a little. Yes, it was weird having him in her personal space—her home—despite what they'd shared on their weekends away, but she'd figure it out.

She had to. She'd been raised with a strict philosophy about hospitality. Together, her parents had led by example and built a reputation for emphasizing the importance of family and community strength to the health of a soldier and the army as a whole. While her father had been blazing a trail as a command officer, her mother had worked with equal fervor developing those support programs.

Grace Ann could be hospitable. She could maintain the no-strings boundaries and keep her feelings in check, even here at home. Letting him help wasn't weakness or fear or clinging, it was friendship. A hearty meal, decadent chocolate and sleep would do them both a world of good. Better than the simple tea and ice pack she'd planned.

Eyeing the time, she mixed up her basic brownie recipe, adding an extra oomph with chocolate chips and a swirl of peanut butter. She smiled. A serious step up from their normal fare on camping weekends.

With the brownies in the oven, she still had a good ten minutes before the earliest possible arrival on the pizza. Plenty of time to scrub away the memory of those brutal hands crushing her throat. She dashed down the hall to her bathroom.

Dropping clean yoga pants and a sweatshirt on the

bench at the foot of her bed, she went into the bath and stripped while the water heated. Her reflection in the mirror gave her a start.

The deep shadows under her eyes only proved it was time to switch to a stronger eye cream. The bruises on her neck were harder to dismiss. Maybe the suspension was a good thing after all. She couldn't treat patients looking like this, and she didn't have the skill with makeup to hide them. This time of year it was too warm to explain a turtleneck layered under her scrubs, though hospitals were notoriously cold.

Turning from the mirror before she could start calculating where other bruises might soon appear, she stepped under the hot spray of water and lathered up, scouring away the remnants of the attack and her frustration over the suspension. The guilt over Kevin lingered. She doubted any amount of time or water would ease that sting.

Aware of the time, she twisted off the tap and reached for her towel. Drying off, she was grateful for the steam-fogged mirror blurring out her reflection. Through the closed bathroom door, she heard a man calling her name and felt the weight of footsteps in the hallway. The voice was deeper and far more agitated than Derek's.

"Grace Ann! Where are you?"

Recognizing the voice, she groaned. What was Hank Lawson doing here? Though he wasn't her brother by blood, her father had practically adopted him over a decade ago. For years, he'd been to every holiday and family gathering unless an assignment interfered.

Currently serving in the Army Criminal Investigation Command, he was the lead investigator on the Riley Hunter case. As such, he had a standing order that any reports involving the safety of the Riley siblings were forwarded to his office for review. She'd hoped to put off this more or less official discussion until tomorrow at the earliest.

"Grace Ann!" Hank's voice boomed through the house. "Who is this guy in your garage?"

Aw, crap. She could imagine Hank gripping Derek by his collar and holding him at arm's length like a mangy cat. Would today never end? Tugging the towel around her to cover everything important, she walked out of the bathroom just as her bedroom door flew open.

Hank filled the doorway, Derek on his heels. Both men were nearly the same height, though Hank was built like a bear and Derek was lean. They both appeared ready to leap into action to remove the other should she give the word. It would be an interesting free-for-all. Derek had the reach, but she knew Hank could fight dirty.

"Far enough." She held up a hand. They skidded to a halt just inside the doorway. "What are you doing here?"

Hank's gaze locked onto her neck and went dark with barely leashed fury. He jerked his thumb over his shoulder. "He do that?"

"If he had, he wouldn't be here. That's Derek Sayer. Kevin's older brother." She spoke with the icy calm she reserved for the worst medical crises and waited for Hank's normally cool head and logic to catch up with the rest of him.

Hank's face relaxed and his lips formed a silent O as the name registered. She'd called Hank right after the news of the crash reached the unit. He knew about Kevin. More importantly, he knew exactly *why* Kevin had been in that helicopter instead of her. Thanks to his full access to the facts, Hank would best understand the guilt weighing on her.

"Derek, this is Hank Lawson."

"More context?" Derek's thunderous gaze collided with hers and then he raised his hands in surrender. "Forget it." He shook his head, backing into the hall. "I'll go wait for the pizza."

Hank slammed the bedroom door closed. "I found him on his phone in your garage. What's he doing here?"

"I invited him." It wasn't much of a fib in the grand scheme. "This is *my* house, since you've clearly forgotten." How dare he overstep and intrude? "Derek drove me home and we found the garage window busted. He's helping. Not that my personal life is any of your business."

Grabbing her clothes, she returned to the bathroom to dress. She blotted her hair with the towel and then folded it over the rack. Dressing with lightning speed, she finger-combed her hair and smoothed moisturizer over her face. It wasn't going to get any better than this without a team of Oscar-winning makeup artists. She was too sore and weary to fuss.

Opening the door, she found Hank pacing. "Why are *you* here?"

His eyes were full of pity when he faced her. "I heard, okay?"

She doubted he was referring to the success of Kevin's surgery. Arms folded over her chest, she cocked an eyebrow, her patience with him nearly gone. Still, she knew better than to volunteer information. "Heard about what?"

"C'mon, Gracie. Your suspension."

If he'd danced a jig she'd have been less startled. She'd assumed he was here to overanalyze the attack in the stairwell.

When the Riley Hunter had gone after Matt, the first,

vague threat of "you will pay" had quickly revealed the son Matt had kept a secret from the family for fourteen years, at the request of his son's mother. Once the madman had all three of them in the crosshairs, every ugly attempt on their lives had been documented and sent anonymously through pictures and live video to torture General Riley.

Having survived the Riley Hunter's violent plan, Matt and Bethany had finally married and were building the family they'd both always wanted. Her mom in particular was thrilled. Despite missing her first grandson's early years, Patricia had been making up for lost time.

"You think the suspension is related to the Riley Hunter?" How could the madman know exactly which buttons to push for Matt and now for her?

"It brings those challenges back to the surface for you," Hank said.

That seemed to be the man's MO. During Matt and Bethany's ordeal, Hank joined the team of investigators working the case, using his connections within the army's Criminal Investigation Division. From her recollection of the latest update, the only motive seemed to be someone determined to deal revenge against the general using his children as pawns.

"Does Dad know about the suspension?"

Hank cringed. "He does."

That was a pretty good indication that the bogus accusation had originated with the Riley Hunter. Her breath backed up in her lungs, fear banding across her chest. What would he try next? Had he sent someone to try to kill her in the hospital?

"I was at the Pentagon on another issue," Hank said. "Dad asked me to check on you."

That was Riley Code for "protect Grace Ann." The

family concern should be a comfort, especially in light of the alarming tactics the madman employed. Would running help? *No.* Where was her fight? She was better than this unfocused dread and uncertainty brewing inside her.

"I rescheduled my meetings as soon as he called," Hank continued. "You know he doesn't believe the accusation. Naturally, he's worried for you, Gracie. With good reason."

It gave her chills to think about how close she'd come to losing her older brother and the new sister-in-law and nephew she was just getting to know. It was bad enough having Matt's secrets revealed, but having him targeted by what amounted to an invisible enemy had been torture. He and his new family had survived, and the Riley Hunter had apparently conceded the contest to Matt. The attacks had stopped, gone dormant. Until now, if she was reading Hank right.

Instinctively, her hand fluttered up to her neck. Hank noticed and she wished she'd chosen a top that covered the tender area.

He stepped closer, studying the marks on her neck. "Who did this?"

"It was random." If Hank had heard about the attack, there was no point rehashing it. If he hadn't, there was no point tossing gasoline on the Riley Hunter fire. "I'm fine." She pasted a smile on her face and spread her arms wide. "Let's go have pizza."

"You can talk to me, Gracie," Hank said.

"I know. I am." She opened the bedroom door and the rich aroma of chocolate wafted in. "Smells like the brownies are nearly done. Come on."

No amount of anger or worry would make Hank dumb enough to let the treats burn.

They found Derek eyeing the oven timer as if he expected the appliance to turn into a man-eating monster when the countdown finished. Ignoring the hard looks the men exchanged, she welcomed the jolt of cold tile on her bare feet as she stepped into her kitchen. Here, at least, was a corner of the world where she was in complete control.

When the brownies were cooling on a rack, she offered each of her guests a beer and poured herself a glass of red wine. She needed something stronger than tea and the idea of an ice pack after the hot shower felt all wrong.

"How is Kevin?" Hank asked Derek as they settled on the stools at the counter that bridged kitchen and front room.

She saw the blatant effort to make amends was skeptically received, though Derek kept it civil. "He looks rough to me, but everyone says he'll make a full recovery."

"Is he in ICU? Is that why you aren't with him at the hospital?"

Hearing the judgment behind the words, she shot Hank the quelling look she'd learned from her mother. She felt Derek's eyes on her throat, as gentle and warm as a silk scarf. She was grateful the sweatshirt hid goose bumps rising on her arms.

"Derek will have plenty of time with Kevin in the days ahead. No one rests well in a bedside chair and he's overdue for some quality sleep." Her explanation put a halt to any speculation or argument. "I've invited him to stay over," she said, daring either of them to contradict her.

"It's stressful when a call like that comes." Hank studied his beer bottle. "Pretty stressful making the call, too."

Her bonus brother had a compassionate streak a mile

wide, though he rarely trusted anyone outside the family enough to show it. "Hank is the fourth son my dad always wanted," Grace Ann said, finally giving Derek the context he'd requested.

It wasn't as if they were in a normal relationship or he had any reason to be jealous. As a friend, though, she was happy to clarify how Hank fit into her life. She and Derek had always been open about seeing other people. For her part, going out had become more risk and far less enjoyable since they'd all been put on alert with the Riley Hunter.

"General Riley practically adopted me out of boot camp," Hank said, a wistful smile brightening his face. "He was a commander at my first post and found out I didn't have any family to go home to over a holiday break."

"He did everything but file a formal petition and change Hank's name," Grace Ann added. "Once Mom fell for him, the rest of our votes didn't count. He's the extra brother I didn't really need," she teased.

"That's me." Hank raised his beer. "Superfluous and proud."

Despite the banter, Derek didn't relax much. Deep lines bracketed his mouth and she suspected questions were fighting to get out. If Hank would leave, she might be willing to give him answers.

The pizza arrived and Hank showed no sign of making a polite or swift exit. Resigned, she pulled out three plates and hoped they could find a conversation topic that didn't have anything to do with her crummy day. The respite wouldn't last, but a distraction would be welcome.

Derek and Hank seemed to reach a truce and were talking cars, something the men in her life seemed to thrive on. Her older brother, Matt, was currently rebuilding a car with his son, Caleb. In true Riley tradition, the sweat equity would make it Caleb's when they finished.

She treasured those grease-stained days when she'd helped her dad with her first car. It warmed her heart to watch Derek's gaze light up as he shared stories of working in the garage or yard with his dad and little brother before tragedy left them orphans.

Though the conversation flowed, she felt Hank's attention on her bruises, her picked-over slice of pizza and the untouched wine in her glass. Soon he'd be demanding the whole story. Buying a few minutes, she ducked into the kitchen and whipped up a quick frosting for the brownies before she carried the treats out on a platter. With luck, the rich sweets would ease the sting of the conversation she knew was coming.

Hank picked up a second brownie and devoured it in two big bites. When he'd swallowed, he pointed at her neck. "What happened?"

"Looks bad, doesn't it?" Grace nibbled at her brownie. "You don't have to worry." She hoped Derek would pick up on her desire to gloss over the incident. "The base security team is on it."

Hank's eyes were cool. "What happened?"

Grace Ann shrugged. "It was a psych patient most likely," she replied as casually as possible. That was a viable explanation until the investigators found hard evidence that the suspension and attack were connected. She was tired of wrestling with what-ifs tonight. "He got confused and things got a little rough in the stairwell. It happens."

"Not to you," Hank stated.

From behind Hank, Derek gave her a quizzical look. She willed him to just let her run with this watered-down version.

"I hope they have him locked in his room for the night," Hank said darkly.

"Base security is top-notch." She managed to keep her hands away from her throat. "Derek was a huge help."

Derek's eyes went wide at the compliment and Hank's narrowed. She wished she could hit Rewind and try that again. Hank bumped Derek's shoulder in masculine approval. "You were there?"

"I saw the, ah, patient push her into the stairwell and followed." Derek took a long drink of his beer, his eyes on her.

She wanted to shower him with kisses for playing along.

"Good man," Hank said.

Derek picked at the label on his beer bottle. "Good timing."

"So when are you heading to Mom and Dad's?" Hank asked her.

She should have known the question was coming, but Hank and everyone else knew she didn't run away when life got sticky. "I'm not going anywhere," she said. "I was planning to call them after my shower. Now I suppose you can fill them in for me."

Thinking about running had been enough of a slip. Her parents had raised her to stand firm. She reached for her wine and changed her mind. Going to the kitchen for a glass of milk, she returned to the sofa. The cold liquid after the smooth chocolate did wonders for her raw throat.

Removed from the shift rotation, she could make Kevin's recovery her top priority. She might not be able to do much right away beyond lending Derek an ear or a guest room as necessary, but those things would help them both. Besides, if the stairwell attack and the busted window were isolated incidents, there was no reason to worry her parents. If the Riley Hunter was behind the suspension or the other trouble, she would handle it right here, on her own. Just as Matt had done when he had been the target.

She would not retreat simply because someone was trying to torment her father through his children.

"Where do they live?" Derek asked, breaking a brownie in two and giving her half.

The man had a way about him. Observant. Kind. How would Hank react if she just leaned into Derek's calming strength? It took some effort to steer her mind back onto the right track.

"They have a new house on the coast of North Carolina," Hank said. "They're hoping to see you, Gracie."

"They will. I plan to go down for Memorial Day weekend. When do you have to get back to DC?" she asked Hank, stuffing the rest of the brownie into her mouth.

He shifted in the chair, not quite meeting her gaze. Suddenly she understood his real intention here. "Oh, *no*. You are *not* babysitting me."

"Adult-sitting?" he ventured.

Her temper lit like a match to paper and she surged to her feet. "No one tried adult-sitting Matt."

Hank stared at her. "Dad sent Alex. Remember?"

Alex Gadsden was Matt's best friend from West Point, currently serving with Special Forces. Her father had called in a favor, putting Alex in DC as extra protection for Matt during the Riley Hunter's attacks. Momentarily deflated, she wasn't ready to give in. "Doesn't matter. I don't need you skulking around playing bodyguard."

Hank stood, forcing her to look up to meet his gaze. "I can work the investigation from the Pentagon office. Since I'm close, Dad asked—"

"Dad knows I'm a capable woman," she interrupted. So what if the suspension and stairwell attack rattled her? She was safe now and those reactions would pass with a little time.

"Dad's concerned, Gracie. Mom's flat-out worried."

She stalked away from him. They could *not* have this argument in front of Derek. This was exactly the angst-filled drama the two of them avoided in their private, friends-with-benefits arrangement. Bad enough she still had to tell him she should've been on that helicopter. How could she explain that some faceless, nameless revenge-seeker was the reason Kevin had taken her place?

She wasn't ready to face her parents, regardless of the potential to surf and soak up the spring sunshine. Her mom, an excellent nurse with plenty of experience with soldiers, would see right through Grace Ann's thin defenses. When she wasn't working or away with Derek, the ugly memories from the tragedy at the village school during her deployment tended to surface, demanding attention. Tears stung her nose and the back of her raw throat. On a silent oath, she struggled to regain her composure. She was an emotional disaster zone and this wasn't the place for the dam to break.

"They'll get over it. I am not running."

She was a Riley, raised to stand proud and serve. To fight for those who couldn't. She would not cave to the antics of a bully, no matter how many thugs he hired to harass her.

Hank's gaze narrowed and she realized too late that she'd moved into a position almost behind Derek, as if he was the shield she preferred over her own family.

"Grace Ann." Hank's voice was edged with ice. "We should discuss this privately."

"I can go," Derek offered. "A hotel is—"

"You're staying," Grace Ann stated. "I invited you." Sort of. She glared at Hank. "Derek gets the guest room." She stepped forward, drilled a finger into her brother's shoulder. "You'll have to take the couch."

"You have three bedrooms," Hank argued.

Grace Ann was already marching down the hall. "My house, my rules. Beds are for invited guests," she hollered back. "Deal with it," she finished before she gave in to a fit of coughing.

She slammed her bedroom door and locked it on principle. Hiding in her room might make her an ostrich, but she couldn't handle another unpleasant or difficult discussion tonight.

Exhausted, physically and emotionally, she needed space. Sore from her head to her toes, she went to her bathroom for some ibuprofen and a glass of water before crawling into bed. If she didn't feel better by morning, she would give in and get an exam.

Sleep didn't come quickly.

In the dark, she could finally admit she'd been braced for more trouble for some time now. Assuming at least part of her wretched day had been orchestrated by the madman set on settling some score with her dad, she needed to come up with a plan to move forward without sacrificing her privacy or independence.

Curling up on her side, she sucked in a breath as the incidents rolled through her mind in an unrelenting cycle: the helicopter crash, the suspension, the stairwell, the broken window. It didn't seem possible that one man could have that kind of reach. And yet Hank, currently working to identify the Riley Hunter, would try and connect the dots.

Derek deserved to know why his brother was in the hospital. Kevin deserved an apology.

Since she didn't believe in procrastination, she could already see that tomorrow wouldn't be much better than today.

Derek watched Hank cautiously. Caring about and caring for a sibling were two different things. He recognized the worry etched on Hank's face and sympathized completely.

Tamping down his curiosity about why Grace Ann would need a babysitter, he cleaned up the dinner dishes and washed the bowl, a little intimidated by her bright red stand mixer. The brownies had been the best he'd had since his mom died. Maybe Grace Ann could do justice to the Sayer family recipe.

He was about to root around her cabinets for plastic or foil to cover the brownies left in the pan when Hank came in, opened a drawer and handled the task.

"She's stubborn," he muttered.

"I've learned most people are," Derek said diplomatically. "I can leave," he offered again. Though he hadn't planned on spending the night, the idea held considerable appeal. He'd expected to feel awkward or pressured. Other than the tangle with Hank, being here felt remarkably right. What did that mean?

Hank let loose a bark of laughter. "If you leave she'll flay me in the morning."

Derek didn't know how to interpret that, so he kept his mouth shut. There was more going on here than just her suspension. There was a reason she'd fudged the details on the incident in the stairwell and he'd honor her privacy until she confided in him about it.

"She thinks the world of your brother," Hank said;

taking two more beers from the fridge, he offered one to Derek.

"Yeah, me, too." Derek popped off the cap and followed Hank back to the front room.

The bigger man flopped down on the couch and drank deeply from the bottle. "What do you make of the busted window in the garage?" he asked.

"Bad luck?" Derek watched the dark, quiet street through the front window. "It rattled her," he added, trying to block the memory of how fragile she'd appeared in the moment. "Reasonable considering how her day ended."

"Did the cops find anything?"

"A partial footprint," Derek replied. "Nothing was stolen or out of place in either the garage or the house. The police think it was kids on a dare."

"You don't sound convinced," Hank observed.

"I'm a corporate lawyer, not a cop," Derek said. "It just seems like a lot of bad luck for one person in a day."

"Some days are like that," Hank muttered.

Derek couldn't argue that. He thought of Kevin and the long road of recovery ahead of him. According to the doctors, his brother had at least two more days in the hospital, then a transfer to a skilled nursing facility for a few weeks. He'd been warned Kevin would need assistance for the first week or two at home. The commander, LTC Bingham, promised Derek all the support the unit could offer Kevin.

Tomorrow, he'd have to coordinate with his office for an extended telecommuting schedule. "I should probably be there when Kevin wakes up in the morning," he mused.

"Probably," Hank agreed. "But since I'm not ready to meet my maker, I'm afraid I can't let you leave without explaining it to Gracie yourself." Hank studied the beer bottle in his hands. Sitting forward, he placed the half-empty bottle on the coffee table. "I didn't mean to make her bad day worse. Patricia will tan my hide when she hears about the way I stormed around earlier. I'm just worried."

"Patricia?" Derek queried. He knew Grace Ann had a big family and wanted to keep the names straight.

"Grace Ann's mom. Mrs. Riley is tough as nails about hospitality and manners. About everything important," he added. "I've been an honorary Riley for about a decade now, but she'll use that mom voice and remind me I should know better. Grace Ann wouldn't have left you in the garage alone, her doors unlocked, if she didn't trust you. I'll get an earful for that, too."

He sounded so miserable about the pending recriminations, Derek considered himself fortunate he only had to worry about disappointing Kevin. Though they lived and worked in separate cities, they got together often enough and stayed in touch through calls and text messages.

Derek was still curious about the real cause of Hank's worry, but it wasn't his place to stick his nose in family issues. "Were the brownies a family recipe?" he asked, hoping to lighten things up.

"Nah. Gracie comes up with that kind of thing off the top of her head all the time. We all tease her about being a stress baker."

"There are worse ways to cope."

"You said it." Smiling a little, Hank stood up and rubbed his hand over his regulation haircut. "Works out best for the people close enough to enjoy the results." He stacked a couple of throw pillows on one end of the couch. "I know she's got an alarm system and you're here, but I'm going to stay over, anyway. It'll ease Dad's mind."

Derek stood up and tucked his hands into his pockets. "Is there anything I should know?"

Hank sighed. "I've trampled enough of her boundaries for one visit. Whatever she wants to share with you really should be up to her."

"All right." Derek moved toward the hallway.

"Hey," Hank said. "One question."

"Sure." Derek paused.

"You saw the patient who attacked her, right?"

Derek nodded. "I did. We gave the description at the base security office."

"Good." Hank's brow furrowed. "Think you'd recognize him if you saw him again?"

"Definitely."

"That is really good news," Hank said. "Sleep well."

"You, too."

After bringing in his overnight bag from the car, Derek prepared for bed in the guest room while the uneasiness of Grace Ann's troubles, known and unknown, circled through his mind. The memory of her being pinned to that rail would stay with him for a long time.

Considering the majority of his next forty-eight hours would be spent in or near Kevin's room, maybe he could use the extra time on the hospital campus to search for her assailant.

Officially he and Grace Ann were only acquaintances. Between them there was the friends-with-benefits thing. Now that the door had been opened for something more personal, more intimate, Derek wanted to march right into that unknown territory.

Chapter 4

The next morning Grace Ann rose early, showered away the aches that had set in overnight and debated what to make for breakfast. It was the least she could do for Derek after the chaos of yesterday. Hank would benefit, too, if he'd stayed, but she wasn't cooking for him.

Today would be better. Despite the hard facts she needed to tell Derek, it had to be an easier day. She assumed he'd want to get to the hospital as early as possible and she planned to ride with him so she could pick up her car. On her way home, she'd check in at the police station for any news about the vandal. Then it would be the hardware store to order a new window.

She tiptoed past Hank and into the kitchen and punched the button to brew a fresh cup of coffee. Maybe if she plied her brother with a stack of pancakes, eggs and sausage he'd install the window for her before he left.

And he *would* leave. Riley Hunter or a string of bad luck, she could handle herself.

Set to silent, her cell phone display lit up with an incoming call. Her father's smiling face filled the screen. She answered, keeping her voice low so she wouldn't wake up Hank. "Hi, Dad."

"Hi, sweetheart. How you holding up?"

"I'm great," she said, ignoring the tenderness in her throat and stiffness in her back. She should get out for a run today and work out the lingering kinks.

"Grace Ann, it's me."

She peered out into the front room where Hank was sprawled uncomfortably across her couch. With so many other things to feel guilty about, she couldn't drum up much for him.

"I know." She kept her voice low as she quietly gathered ingredients for breakfast. "Sure, I'm angry about the suspension." Mad enough to ask him to pull strings. She caught herself before the inappropriate request tumbled past her lips. "I'm livid that my friend is injured." She glanced around to be sure Derek wasn't in earshot. "It should've been me on that helicopter."

"That's my girl." Her dad's pride came through loud and clear. "Be mad. Your mother and I are furious, too. Just don't let temper make you overconfident or blind to your surroundings. All of us need to stay vigilant."

As she whisked together pancake batter, she thought about her broken garage window. It must have been a kid. Maybe Hank would call it wishful thinking, but she couldn't see what the Riley Hunter would gain by such a petty inconvenience.

"Can I ask who told you I was under investigation?" She started the oven to heat the sausage.

"Bingham sent me an email. As a courtesy."

Wow. Relief left her momentarily speechless. The notification didn't seem like the commander's style, yet she'd happily separate the Riley Hunter from the bogus accusation. "Is there anyone you don't know?" she asked.

"Perks of thirty years of service." The warmth in his voice soothed her. "We've met a time or two," he added.

"Clearly you made a good impression," she teased.

"Whatever the reason, I appreciated the heads-up. You would've kept that kind of news under wraps."

Yes. For as long as possible. "Why worry over what is sure to fizzle out soon enough?" She had to believe in a quick resolution so she could get back to work. Helping others was the only thing that gave her any peace.

"What will you do with your time off?"

Since he didn't know about the stairwell attack, she couldn't admit she planned to search the hospital campus for the man who attacked her. "I'll probably do some hiking. Short day trips," she added.

"Not alone?"

His worry came through loud and clear. "Dad, come on. I can't live in a bubble."

"Promise me, Grace Ann. You have to be smart right now. Whoever orchestrated the attacks on Matt is still out there and we still don't have a solid lead."

She moved to the corner of the kitchen, lowered her voice. "He sent you a picture."

When Matt had been targeted, her father had received candid pictures via text message from burner cell phones to prove how close the hunter could get.

The sigh confirmed her suspicions. "He sent two. The first was you hugging someone at the hospital. The second was just a broken window. No people in that one, but there was enough background for me to recognize your house."

"Just when I'd convinced myself it was all a coincidence," she said too brightly. If her dad had mentioned this to Hank, it certainly reframed his arrival and over-reactions yesterday.

"Come stay with us," her dad was saying. "Surf. Hike. Take the boat out. Your mom would love your help shopping for the new baby."

She laughed merrily at that. Matt and Bethany had just announced they were expecting and her mother was ecstatic. "Mom has never needed help shopping." Feeling a smidge closer to normal, she swiveled to start a second cup of coffee and came face-to-face with Derek.

Her laughter faded, replaced by sheer lust. His sandy hair was dark, damp from the shower, and he'd shaved. Her fingertips tingled, eager to touch the smooth line of his jaw. A navy blue T-shirt emphasizing his muscled chest was left untucked over loose athletic pants. Her pulse skipped happily along, troubles forgotten.

He flashed a smile and mouthed the word *morning*. The man gave hot a whole new meaning, she thought as she dragged her attention back to the phone call. "I'll, ah, let you know what I decide. Love you, Dad."

"Love you, too."

She set the phone aside and ordered herself to stop gawking. It wasn't the first time she'd seen him damp from a shower. No, just the first time the scent of his masculine body wash had invaded her kitchen.

"Coffee?" She pulled down a clean mug.

"Please," he whispered, out of respect for Hank.

She waved him in, pointed him to the drawer stocked with coffee pods. Her kitchen wasn't really designed for more than one person at a time and she felt the heat of his body as they slid by each other. "You'll take time to eat before you go in, right?" she asked, pouring batter onto the sizzling skillet. The sleep had erased the worst signs of tension around his eyes and mouth, but he needed to fuel up as well. There were long days ahead for him and Kevin.

He glanced to the wall clock. "You said the surgeons do their rounds pretty early. I don't want to miss him."

"Kevin's surgeon won't come by until eight, at the earliest. If he sends an associate—doubtful in this case—it will be closer to nine, after the morning staff meeting."

The coffee brewer sputtered and Derek inhaled deeply before he took a cautious first sip.

"Then count me in for breakfast."

The reply sounded natural. Perfect. Anticipation shimmered through her. They should have taken this step ages ago. She'd always kept Derek tucked away from the rest of her life, a secret pleasure she didn't have to share. What joys had she been denying herself, and him, with that hard line? Not that he'd made much of an effort to break through it.

Out in the living room, Hank yawned and sat up, stretched his arms overhead. She'd forgotten he was here. "Breakfast is almost ready," she called to him.

"Eggs?" he asked hopefully.

"Pancakes and sausage, too," she replied. "Get moving."

She pulled the first pancakes off the griddle and poured out more batter into perfect circles before starting the eggs.

"You can cook," Derek said, eyeing her over his coffee mug.

"This is just glorified baking," she pointed out, unsettled by that steady gaze.

"It's the most important meal of the day." He shifted the fabric of her lightweight hoodie; she saw his eyes narrowing at the colorful marks on her throat. "How are you feeling?"

His careful touch made any reply impossible. Hearing the squeak of hinges on the bathroom door, she seized on the distraction. "Hank will want coffee."

When the food was ready, he passed platters and tableware to Hank on the other side of the counter.

It gave her an unexpected flutter of satisfaction, watching Derek scarf down food she'd made. Breakfast at a campsite was a team effort. Having breakfast here put all this tenderness in her heart, and she found herself longing for a deeper connection they'd expressly avoided.

This wasn't the time to dwell on it. Not with Hank staring her down. In investigator mode, he made her feel like a bug trapped under a microscope.

When Derek offered to handle the dishes before he left, Hank waved him off. "You've got places to be and I need to chat with Gracie."

Grace's stomach cramped, her appetite gone. She didn't want to chat with Hank. He helped himself to more pancakes while Derek went to change. He returned in a gray button-down shirt, dark jeans and casual shoes, overnight bag in hand. She wanted him to stay, though she knew he couldn't.

"What about your car?" Derek asked.

"I'll take her over," Hank replied for her.

"All right." Derek didn't argue, but he didn't look happy. "Thanks for breakfast."

"It's part of the full-service package." She smiled. "I'll come by Kevin's room in a bit," she promised.

"Great," he said. "I appreciate that."

Her lips felt cheated. They'd always kissed goodbye at the end of their getaways. She stacked up dishes at the table. "When are *you* leaving?" she asked Hank with syrupy sweetness.

He folded his arms and stared her down. "As soon as I convince you to get out of town."

"Save your breath." Irritated with him, she stood up, swaying when the room did a slow spin.

"Gracie?" Hank nudged her back into the chair. "What's wrong?"

"Nothing." The denial lacked confidence. "Just give me a minute."

"Another reason to head south," he muttered. "You're stressed out and Mom would love to spoil you a bit."

She didn't need spoiling, just time and a good distraction. Better to stay right here where she could be useful and spell Derek while Kevin recovered. Derek might be an expert caregiver, but Kevin wasn't fourteen anymore and the road ahead of them was a long one.

A small glass of orange juice appeared in front of her. "Drink up."

Arguing would be petty. She drank it down and felt better. "You could have let Derek take me in," she grumbled.

"He doesn't understand the stakes," Hank said, closing the dishwasher. "He's a civilian."

"You're biased."

Derek's career choices weren't the issue. After speaking with her father, there was no denying the danger to her life was likely imminent. For months now, she'd been walking a fine line between sensible precautions and outright paranoia. She didn't want Derek dragged into the fray. Yesterday's attack had only succeeded because she'd been distracted over the suspension. Now that she was prepared, it wouldn't happen again.

She leaned back against the counter while Hank

wiped down the sink and dried his hands. "There's no reason for me to run and hide. I'm not putting any dependents at risk and I'm not allowed at work. I might as well be bait." She didn't have to voice her additional concern that going into hiding might force the person pulling all the strings to move on her younger siblings. Hank would've thought of that, too.

"Are you crazy?" Hank twisted the towel in his hands. "Those pictures, Gracie. He was close."

"He won't get that close again."

His gaze dropped to her throat. "Derek said he'd recognize the guy from the stairwell. You have to agree the man who did that could've been hired muscle," he said. "If we find him, we might get a lead or a name. I'm sure the hunter is pulling the strings, hiring locals to do his dirty work."

"Why go after us?" she wondered. "Why not just hire those locals to go straight at Dad?"

"Mind games." Hank tapped his temple. "Takes a sick person to punish an enemy by attacking the innocent." He caught her hand, squeezed. "I'm not going to let anything happen to you."

She rolled her eyes. "I've been taking care of myself a long time. While I'm off the rotation at the hospital, can I help you investigate?"

"No."

She ignored the scowl meant to close the discussion. "I'm not an idiot," she protested.

"You are for suggesting that with a straight face," he said.

She wanted to smack him. He might not have been her brother from birth, but he sure was a natural in the role. "I can help," she insisted. She had to do something to stay busy, to keep those ghosts quiet.

"Not with this case." His gaze gentled. "Your clearance isn't valid," he reminded her.

"They grounded me because of the Riley Hunter and Kevin got hurt. That isn't right." She was close to begging. "I need to do something."

"So do something," Hank said. "Go surf. Take out Dad's boat. Relax and recharge."

"Hide," she said, disgusted. "Now who is making idiot suggestions?"

Hank shuffled around her and out of the kitchen. "Get your shoes on and I'll take you to your car."

When they reached her hospital parking space, she understood why Hank had insisted on handling this. Down on hands and knees, he flashed a light under her car, looking for signs of tampering or even a bomb on her candy-apple-red compact SUV. As an Army CID investigator, he would have undergone training that was more up-to-date than hers. Not to mention, he'd thought to look and she hadn't.

Explosives and bombs were for countries far away, weapons of war between powers struggling for dominance, not her car here at home. Just when she thought Hank was done, he popped the hood and continued his search.

"Are you planning to disassemble my car right here?" she demanded, frustrated with both of them.

"If I have to."

"Fine." Antsy, her skin prickling as if she'd been sunburned, she couldn't watch anymore. "I need to get upstairs and check on Kevin." Derek, too. She had to give him the whole truth today. If that was the end of their arrangement, she'd find a way to cope. She always did.

Turning on her heel, she left. Even if she forgot *every*

minute of her training, there were military police stationed all over the base. She could safely get from her parking space to the orthopedic wing without another incident.

Hank caught up with her at the shuttle stop. "Why won't you cooperate?"

"Life is too short to be bullied."

"Precautions do not equal bullying." He gave her a quick hug. "You need to accept that you *are* the primary target." He tapped his phone. "I'll send a picture of the man I assigned to guard your car."

"You did not. Hank, you've become paranoid."

He ignored her. "If he isn't there when you want to leave, call a cab or something. Do not get into your car without assistance."

"That's ludicrous."

"Your father has an enemy whose preferred weapon is inflicting pain on his children. I need to know you'll be careful. Alert." His gaze locked with hers.

"I will." She gave in and hugged him hard as the shuttle approached.

"Check in," he ordered.

"Hourly?"

"If only," he grumbled. "I'm posting a team at the house, too. I'll send the headshots once the rotation is set."

Resigned to the all-out protective detail, she boarded the shuttle. There were worse things than being loved to near-smothering. When Matt had been targeted, she'd been a basket case, full of worry for her brother and his newfound family. She hadn't thought less of him for accepting help from others and he wouldn't have been any happier with the precautions than she was now.

As the shuttle stopped to pick up more passengers, she let it all sink in. The Riley Hunter was taking aim at her, whether she understood the reasoning or not. Dangling herself like bait could bring more trouble closer to Derek and his brother, and that was a bigger risk than she was willing to take.

Being idle or agreeing to hide wouldn't advance the case. She would not stop searching for a solution that exposed the Riley Hunter and kept *all* the people she loved safe.

When Derek reached Kevin's room he was pleased to find his brother sitting up. His first instinct was to let Grace Ann know, but he resisted the urge to send a text. She had enough going on right now, and that was only the things he knew about.

Kevin poked at a bland tray of toast and anemic-looking eggs, admitting his appetite wasn't up to speed yet. Derek didn't mention where he'd spent the night or the details of the amazing breakfast Grace Ann had prepared.

They didn't have to wait too long for the surgeon to come by. He'd explained how well the spinal surgery had gone and assured both of them that the long-term prognosis for healing the broken vertebrae was fantastic. Derek heard the warning that the biggest challenge would be keeping Kevin from doing too much, too soon, once physical therapy began.

"See," Kevin said when they were alone. "You can go on back to work. I've got this."

Derek wasn't going anywhere. "I have plenty of vacation time," Derek said. "Plus I can telecommute for as long as it takes to get you on your feet."

"Better break out the champagne."

The disappointment was brutally obvious. "Well, screw you, too, little brother."

Kevin's laugh turned into a sputtering cough. When he had his breath back, there was a familiar spark in his eyes. "Seriously, man. You don't have to stick around for every pain pill and PT appointment."

"Maybe I want to."

Would Grace Ann extend the invitation for him stay at her place? More than the breakfast or brownies, he wanted time with her. Time to explore this curious longing for something more settled. Watching her cook this morning had reminded him of days when commitment was the norm rather than a terrifying burden.

"What about what I want?" Kevin interrupted his thoughts. "I'm not a kid anymore."

The image of Hank storming into Grace Ann's bedroom flashed through his mind. Was he doing a similar smothering act on his brother? "Did you know Grace Ann bakes?" he asked.

"What did she make?" Kevin struggled to sit up a bit more, his face pinched with the effort as he tried to get a glimpse of the hallway.

So her stress baking was a widely known practice. It bothered him that he'd been sleeping with her and hadn't been aware of the habit. "She made brownies last night," he said.

"What kind? I want one."

Derek swallowed a bitter retort. He couldn't possibly be jealous of his brother for knowing something about Grace Ann. "Peanut butter and chocolate chip."

"With the frosting?" Kevin scowled when Derek nodded. "I knew it."

"Knew what?"

"She's wound up about this whole mess." He dropped his head back to the pillow. "None of this," he motioned to himself, "is her fault."

"What?" Derek asked.

But Kevin was like a dog with a bone. "You could have smuggled one in here," he continued. "Hang on. How did you get a brownie last night?"

"I, ah…" He hadn't thought this through. "There was a problem with her car, so I drove her home," he said.

"Not again." Kevin muttered an oath.

"What are you talking about?" Derek asked, trying to keep his cool.

"Some jerk tagged her car a while back. I gave her a lift that day while the police did their thing."

He didn't like the picture these small pieces of information were building. Was she being stalked? If so, why fib to Hank about the man in the stairwell being a psych patient?

"I can't believe you didn't bring me a brownie," Kevin grumbled. "Use my phone ask her to bring the brownies in."

"Maybe tomorrow," Derek said, slapping a leash on this sudden burst of irritability. It was completely normal for Kevin to have her phone number. They were co-workers. Family, if he bought into that army camaraderie theory. "If she's willing to put me up for another night."

"You stayed with her?"

"She insisted," he said, instantly on the defensive.

"Yeah. She would." Kevin coughed again and Derek handed him a cup of water. "Her brownies are better than Mom's, right?"

Agreeing felt like a betrayal. Disagreeing would be

a lie. "I'm thinking of asking her to give Mom's recipe a try," Derek said.

"That's a brilliant idea."

"I have them once in a while."

A nurse and her aide came in and Derek stepped out to let them work, aiming for the family lounge to grab another cup of coffee.

Last night he'd tossed and turned, more than a little tempted to knock on Grace Ann's bedroom door. The selfishness of seeking comfort from her after the day she'd endured had been enough to keep him in the guest room. Their current agreement aside, she deserved better than him piling on. Of course, her brother snoring in the front room had been an additional deterrent.

Had Hank convinced Grace Ann to leave town? Derek was definitely missing the whole picture, but she'd seemed dead set on staying put. Eager for a distraction, he pulled out his cell phone and scrolled through his email inbox for any news from his assistant.

He glanced up when movement from the corner of his eye drew his attention. Grace Ann walked toward him, a shy smile on her lips. The sight punched right through him, heating his blood. He'd seen her in a dress uniform, her combat uniform, her scrubs and various outdoor gear. She wore the same jeans and soft gray hoodie she'd had on earlier and added high-top sneakers and a sheer scarf with soft pinks and greens that hid the bruising from yesterday's incident and gave her skin a healthy glow.

This was the Grace Ann he knew from their weekends. Almost. It made him want to lay claim to the woman and every brownie she'd ever bake again. Where was all this possessiveness coming from?

"How's Kevin?" she asked, stopping just out of reach in front of him.

Only with her this close, could he see the signs of tension she hid behind the scarf and bright smile. "Pretty well. The surgeon was upbeat and pleased when he stopped in."

"That's great news." She shuffled her feet, her nerves evident as she toyed with the ends of her scarf.

Clearly she wanted more details. "He expects Kevin to make a full recovery and eventually return to active duty."

She did a little hop on her toes, stopping just shy of hugging him. "That's fantastic!"

He wanted that hug, the freedom to hold her close. Except neither of them wanted family or friends to get any starry, happily-ever-after ideas. Meeting Hank last night and hearing a bit of her conversation with her dad this morning only emphasized the wisdom of that decision. Nothing was permanent in this life and steering clear of outside expectations and complications was the only way he knew to get through.

"Why the surprise? This is the same prognosis you gave me yesterday," he reminded her.

"Well, sure. But now it's official."

"Right." Her grin was contagious. "I know you want to see him."

They headed back down the hall and when Grace Ann walked into the room, Kevin positively lit up. Derek wondered—too late—if Kevin had feelings for Grace Ann, but it was soon clear he was interested in food rather than the woman. "Did you bring me something?" Kevin asked.

"Hospital food is the worst," she joked. She reached into her tote and pulled out a small square wrapped in plastic. "Pace yourself and I'll bring another one tomorrow."

Kevin was ecstatic over the treat. She stayed about fifteen minutes, clearly not wanting to wear Kevin out, but Derek wasn't ready to let her go so soon. Making some lame excuse, he followed her out of the room. "Do you have time for coffee?"

"I really need to get home and deal with that window repair," she replied, not quite meeting his gaze.

"I'll take care of the window for you," he offered. Anything to stay close to her. "In trade for advice about the timeline and next steps with Kevin," he added.

She shook her head. "I'm only here as a friend. You should ask his care team."

He didn't need the reminder that they weren't officially more than friends. "You're a friend with expertise." How could he become the person she trusted enough to talk to? Even independent people needed someone to rely on occasionally. "Unless you'd rather I left you alone?"

"Not that," she said in a rush. "You've got a trade." She stuck out her hand to shake on it.

He chuckled. "You make hospitals bearable."

"I'm glad. Feel free to submit a comment card." At the lounge, she selected a coffee flavor and set the machine. "Maybe they'll reinstate me sooner."

He wondered how to bring up Kevin's remark about the training mission as his own coffee brewed. Sitting next to her on a bench that overlooked a grassy courtyard with cheery flowers tucked into the beds, he gave up on being tactful. "Kevin is worried that you feel responsible for his injury. Why is that?"

Her eyes went wide before her gaze dropped to her coffee.

"Talk to me, Grace Ann," he prodded.

Her cup trembled as she raised it to her lips. "You

must have misunderstood him," she said. "Everyone in the unit is upset because he's hurt."

"Well, he is on serious painkillers," Derek allowed. He took in the view, counting to ten twice over until he could trust his voice. "You've always shot straight with me. Why stop now?"

To his shock, a tear hovered on her lashes before she dabbed it away.

"Logic," she murmured. "Logic says it isn't my fault Kevin got hurt." She tapped her fingertips over her heart. "My heart isn't so easily convinced."

She twisted a bit to meet his gaze. "I was on the roster for that training mission. I was ready, willing and able to go. At the last minute, they pulled me and sent Kevin instead." She paused, taking a deep breath. "No, it's technically not my fault there was a system malfunction. Being the senior officer, taking care of those in my command…that's in my DNA. It's impossible not to feel like I should be in that hospital bed."

He understood the ingrained sense of responsibility and high personal expectations, even when those expectations were unreasonable. Still, he sensed there was more to the story. "Why were you pulled?"

"I can't get into that." She laid a hand on his knee when he started to protest. "Not here."

"Can you get into it at your place?"

"Probably." She sipped her coffee. With a small grimace, she set the cup aside and pressed a hand to her stomach. "One cup too many, I guess."

His mind replayed the blows she'd taken yesterday. "You should let a doctor take a closer look," he said. "Make sure you're only dealing with a few bruises."

"I know the signs of serious trouble," she said. "But I do appreciate the concern."

Of course she knew best. It was her body and her profession. Hadn't he called her an expert a few minutes ago? Grace Ann wasn't his dad. His father's visible injuries had been bad enough, but it was the damage he couldn't see that had left him and Kevin orphans.

Derek asked her to dinner at the same time she suggested he get back to his brother. They stared at each other for a long moment. He reached out and adjusted her scarf, better concealing one of the bruises. "I'll walk you to your car first," he said. "I could use the exercise."

"I'm pretty good at seeing through lame excuses," she said as they reached the elevator, a glimmer of amusement in her deep brown eyes. "I don't need an escort."

"So why haven't you kicked me to the curb?" he asked.

"Well, you're cute and I'm shallow." She winked, making him laugh.

When they neared her parking space, she grumbled something under her breath.

"Problem?"

She lifted her chin toward a man in uniform standing near her car. "That's one of Hank's guard dogs. It seems a waste of manpower to post someone here at my car all day long."

Derek stopped, eyeing the military policeman who was dressed differently than the security officer they'd spoken with yesterday. "He's not in the normal base uniform."

"No. Hank surely called in a favor from a nearby unit."

"He means well," Derek said.

She folded her arms over chest. "He elevates over-protectiveness to an art form."

"You know you can trust me, right?" Derek asked before they moved closer.

"That's a silly question, all things considered."

True. "Let me stay at your place again tonight. I'll bring dinner."

She hesitated. They might not have previously shared much beyond a mutual love of the outdoors sex, but he recognized contemplation on her face. "What are you doing, Derek?"

"Talking."

She pursed her lips. "Did Hank put you up to this?"

"No."

"All right." She blessed him with another sincere smile. "Bring ice cream, too," she said. "It'll perk up the reheated brownies."

How had he consistently allowed months to pass without seeing that gorgeous face? "I can do that. Thanks." Relieved to have more time with her tonight, he bent to give her a kiss, turning it into a hug at the last second. He didn't need the guard to report intimate contact and have her big brother crash their dinner.

They'd just reached her car when a sharp bang, followed by a deeper boom, reverberated through the parking garage. A car backfired, he realized. But it was the next sound— a scream chasing the resonating echo— that chilled him to the bone. On the ground next to the rear tire of her SUV, Grace Ann had curled in on herself, hands clapped over her ears.

He dropped to a knee beside her, crooning soothing nonsense, not quite touching her. The MP guarding her car lurched forward.

"Should I call it in?"

"No," Derek replied, waving the man back to his post against the wall. Grace Ann wouldn't want more attention. He eased closer until his knee touched hers, then his hands drew hers away from her ears.

She didn't flinch, but she didn't relax, either.

"I'm right here, Grace," he said. "You're safe, sweetheart." Her limbs shook with a persistent tremor that broke his heart. "You're safe." Her eyes were too wide in her pale face, her eyes glassy and distant. "Grace Ann," he said with more authority. "You're safe now."

She blinked rapidly and then squinted at him. "Derek?"

"Right here." He squeezed her hands.

Her eyes closed tight, shutting him out. "What did I do?"

"Looked to me like you heard a threatening sound and took cover."

"Don't patronize me." She shifted until she was sitting down, her back to the MP guarding her car. Wrapping her arms around her knees, she rocked a little. "I made a scene."

"You did not." Her skeptical glare eased his mind. "Not a big scene. Only the guard dog and I witnessed your moment of weakness."

She rolled her eyes. "Just stop."

"Whatever you say." If irritating her helped Grace Ann feel more like herself, he would do it all day. Standing, he held out a hand to help her up, inordinately pleased when she accepted the gesture and then laced her fingers through his.

They'd rarely held hands on their weekend excursions, unless it was for an assist over an obstacle. Neither of them had come to those weekends for romance. He didn't realize what he'd been missing.

"Give me your keys and I'll drive you home," he said.

She shook her head. "You need to be here."

"I'll use a ride-share app to get back." Her steps were halting and her voice tight as he walked her around to the passenger side.

"I'm okay. Just give me a minute to catch my breath."

"Let me, please. Call it chivalry."

"No, Derek. I can manage. It's not far."

He leaned in so only she could hear him. "Don't make me root through your tote." They could both see her car key on the carabineer clipped to the top zipper.

Stubbornly, she reached for the key, but she needed his steadier hands to get it free.

"Okay, okay," she relented. "You drive."

He opened the passenger door, closing it quietly once she was seated before hustling to the driver's side. There would be time later to sort out the array of feelings pinging through his system. What he was doing for her, he'd do for any friend in a similar crisis.

Buckling his seat belt, he waited patiently for her shaking hands to complete the task for herself. With a nod to the guard, he backed out of the parking space.

Who was he kidding? She unlocked something new inside him. Messy emotions and desires he was running toward rather than away from. Since assuming a parent role for Kevin, he'd sidestepped the typical expectations of relationships.

He suddenly didn't give a damn about preserving his space or independence, not when Grace Ann was hurting. For the first time, he absolutely needed to protect and shelter someone other than his brother.

"I'm sorry," she said as he turned onto her street. "You shouldn't have to coddle me when your brother needs you."

"You keep telling me Kevin is on the mend."

"He is," she insisted. "Still. I know you're close."

"We are." And knowing she'd heard it from Kevin instead of him got under his skin. Being her occasional lover wasn't enough anymore. It was time to restructure their arrangement.

Chapter 5

Hearing the squeak of the garage door rising on the track, he slipped out the back door of the house, leaving a note for Major Riley wedged under the planter on her back step. It didn't matter how long it sat there before she found it. Sooner or later, he'd enjoy the desired effect: abject fear. Thanks to his local contacts, he'd had a key made weeks ago and he could come and go from her home whenever he pleased.

Finished with reconnaissance, he'd planted bugs where he thought it most likely to overhear something helpful. Or titillating. If he gathered enough content, the most innocuous conversation could be edited into something damaging.

He cut through the neighboring backyard and headed to the car he'd left one street over. It amused him that this particular hunt coincided with his annual follow-up with his medical team here at Walter Reed.

From the start he'd known General Riley's second child would present more of a challenge. One he relished since it also gave him a hands-on role. The Rileys weren't fools. The entire family had gone on high alert when he'd put the oldest son in his crosshairs. The kid had surprised him, surviving the traps, so he adjusted to the next, softer target rather than burn through his resources.

Now it was the daughter who would squirm as he systematically dissected her life.

With a daughter himself, targeting the oldest girl made the ultimate goal of revenge sweeter, and he had to tread carefully. Being too eager or bold could result in a shorter game and he wanted to drag this out. The more she suffered, the more the general would suffer and the closer he would be to paying his debt.

He'd combed through the military personnel records, but unlike her brother, she didn't have any obvious secrets to exploit. Again, the creativity required, the twist and doubt he could create, put a smile on his face. He had it on good authority that General Riley had wished for his daughter to find a career outside of the army. Despite her father's desires, his network had provided solid intel that she was well-respected among her peers, and her detractors were few. Even her patients sang her praises, both abroad and here at home.

He would make the most of every detail. All of the praise and respect and love would make for a touching funeral service. Assuming he could successfully manage the pace of events before news of her alleged misconduct overseas leaked to the press.

The investigators were following the crumbs of evidence he'd provided and would continue to do so. Their overconfidence bordered on arrogance. By the time they realized they'd been played, it would be too late for the depressed, renounced and overwhelmed Grace Ann Riley.

Before he was done, she would shatter. More brittle than glass, with no hope of piecing her life or career back together again. He'd toyed with Matt Riley, brought the man to the brink of death and let him live. Let them believe he'd escaped thanks to good friends and cleverness. Let them hope their enemy was cowering, afraid of capture.

The daughter's breakdown and "suicide" would knock them into their new reality with unbearable pain.

He could see it now, General Riley heartbroken, his face tearstained, those once-proud shoulders rounded with grief and loss and guilt. Only then would the general comprehend the pain he had meted out with his calculated decisions and zero concern for the fallout of the people involved.

Riley had once been his hero, a worthy spokesman for the soldiers he sent to carry out orders that would protect and preserve innocent lives. Those days were gone.

Pulling up the app on his phone, he listened to her moving about the house, heard the music swell. The bugs were working perfectly. He finished the coffee going cold in his to-go cup and drove out of her neighborhood, a smile on his face.

Embarrassed beyond words about overreacting in the parking garage, Grace Ann shook the tension from her hands as she paced her front room. At least it had been Derek—cool, competent, steady Derek—to pull her back from that bleak emptiness. He'd known just what to say without coddling or lecturing. If Hank or anyone else from her family had seen that ridiculous display of weakness, they would've nagged her to take leave or talk to someone about letting go or managing her stress. Her early efforts to talk it out with a therapist had only made the nightmares more vivid, so she threw herself into her work.

Once Derek headed back to the hospital after dropping her at her place, she'd called in the order for a replacement window and then cranked up the music to chase away the loneliness prowling the quiet shadows in the house. She'd get through. Being alone had never been a problem until the village school bombing. She couldn't keep relying on patients or family or Derek to keep her balanced.

A kicky song blasted from her speakers. Liking the beat, the happy promise in the lyrics, she put the song on repeat as she scoured her kitchen from top to bottom. Busy was the most effective path she'd found through life's rough patches.

Her hands started shaking again within minutes of completing the task. Grabbing her supplies, she started on the living room. A voice in the back of mind, sounding uncomfortably like her mother, suggested she make an appointment with a chaplain or counselor.

"That didn't work," she said aloud. "It isn't PTSD." It couldn't be. People grieved when things went wrong. Time smoothed things out. She was managing.

Had she seen some ugliness on her deployments? Absolutely. Just like everyone else who'd served in a war zone. Bad stuff happened and some injuries and scars never fully healed. It was the nature of the work. Service and sacrifice would always walk hand in hand.

Further platitudes failed her as she worked until the house sparkled from door to door. Hands on her hips, sweaty and a little breathless, she assured herself this wasn't a big deal.

Everyone had some sort of hang-up. If hers was loud noises she was in good company with many of her peers. At least it didn't interfere with her hospital work.

"It's temporary," she coached herself as the memories floated to the top of her mind.

The first pop...the boom...the reverberation that seemed to come from overhead and underfoot simultaneously. Her breath caught with remembered helplessness as the building came down, dust falling like rain, cries rising and silenced.

"Breathe." She latched onto the chorus of the song. "You're home." She forced her feet to move to the music until the pressure subsided and the memories faded away.

Stowing her cleaning supplies, she went to her bathroom and started the water for a long, luxurious soak in the tub. Perspective was what she needed. The reaction she'd had in the parking garage was rare and it certainly wasn't the end of the world.

Considering everything that had happened, she should've expected a small setback. She had to cut herself some slack before she turned an incident into an issue. When Derek stayed over tonight, she'd make it up to him. Sex would burn away the residual fear and soul-clogging memories and bring on some restorative sleep.

She was alive and well. That alone gave her an obligation to live big and create a full and happy future. It was the best way she knew to honor the lives that had been cut short. By the time she sank into the hot, scented water of her bath she'd convinced herself her earlier fright was part of moving forward.

At the hospital, time seemed to crawl. Derek's attention was fractured as he repeatedly resisted the urge to check in on Grace Ann. It wasn't his place to get clingy and he thought it was best to take her at her word that she'd be fine. When he'd left, he'd seen the team Hank had posted, but it was little comfort when he wanted to be there for her.

The distraction exacerbated his guilt over his brother. He couldn't recall the last time they'd spent a full day together. There was the occasional hockey game and dinner and holidays. Most weeks they did little more than check in with a quick series of texts. He couldn't imagine any reason that would bring Kevin crashing into his house the way Hank had descended on Grace Ann yesterday.

When Kevin woke up, they watched game shows to pass the time. He stayed through dinner, urging Kevin to do more than poke at the food on his tray. Derek channel surfed until he found a baseball game and promised Kevin he'd bring another one of Grace Ann's brownies in the morning.

With the warm scents of the Tex-Mex takeout filling his car, he drove toward Grace Ann's neighborhood, hopeful that she felt better. Her reaction to the car back-fire had left him wrestling with sadness and anger on her behalf. It had been so tempting to grill his brother about her and what might have happened on their last mission.

Derek received plenty of material from the unit's family group on how to support their soldiers at home or overseas. He'd dutifully studied literature on suicide prevention, PTSD and general reintegration, just in case Kevin ever needed him. He never anticipated putting the knowledge to use with someone else.

While the suspension and stairwell attack might have put Grace Ann on edge, today's incident suggested the trouble might go deeper. Whenever he'd seen her at unit functions or on their private weekends she'd been happy, bordering on carefree. He'd never thought of her tendency to pitch in with a ready smile as a mask that hid real pain.

According to the literature, he could make an anonymous call and someone would reach out to her. And he knew that approach would fail spectacularly. She clearly wanted him to think it wasn't a big deal. It would be easier to let them both off the hook but his gut told him that would be a mistake. The army would have him believe they were part of one big family and every member had a responsibility to look out for one another.

He parked in her driveway and grabbed the take-out bag. Her garage door was down, so he went up the front steps and rang the bell, his mind still circling the predicament. She'd promised to tell him why she was pulled from the training exercise. Maybe that would give him an opening to talk about taking care of herself.

He probably would have stood a better chance of reaching her if they'd shared more than a physical relationship. Being detached had worked for both of them. Until it didn't.

She opened the door and his mind blanked. Her cheeks were pink and her hair was styled in a way that emphasized the sparkle in her deep brown eyes. His gaze drifted over her, taking in every sweet detail, down to her bare feet and back up again. Form-fitting leggings showed off her trim legs under the colorful tunic that fluttered at mid-thigh. She hadn't bothered to hide the bruises at her neck, though they seemed to have faded since this morning.

"Hi," he managed.

"Hi." Her lips, shimmering with rosy color, curled into a smile. "What's for dinner?"

He wanted to take a bite out of her as a soft cloud of

tantalizing fragrance swirled out to greet him. Being near her was like walking through the tulip fields in Holland at peak season. Glorious and lovely. Peaceful.

"You look…" *Better. Refreshed.* "Amazing."

"I spoiled myself a little," she said. "It's a start. Tomorrow I'll go for a run first thing. The endorphins will keep up the positive attitude."

Was this one of those compensation things mentioned in the literature? He didn't want to overstep or offend. Neither could he walk on eggshells. "Good for you." He carried the sacks to the kitchen, noticing she'd set the table with two sets of coordinating dishes and tall, slender candles in the center.

"Hot date?" he joked.

Her gaze drifted to his lips, lingered long enough to make him want to forget dinner. "Would that be so bad?" she asked in a voice as soft as he knew the tunic's fabric must be.

She kept showing him facets of her he hadn't seen before. If she was actively trying to seduce him, it was working. And he'd gladly take her up on it, *after* they talked about what had set her off. "As long as food is part of it," he said. "I'm starving."

Her brow puckered and her expression shifted from sensual curiosity to professional assessment. "You didn't eat all day," she accused.

"I grabbed a snack or two out of the vending machine in the lounge." He opened the bags and his stomach growled. "Starving," he repeated. "Couldn't decide, so I got a little bit of everything from the Tex-Mex place."

He set the containers of enchiladas, tacos and carne asada on the table and she brought out serving utensils and drinks. "How's Kevin feeling?" she asked, taking her seat.

"Everyone agrees he's doing well. They expect to release him in another day or two."

"That's great."

Something in her voice caught his attention and he paused, fork halfway between his plate and mouth. "You think it's too early?"

"No, no. If he's ready, it's better for him to clear out." She traced the side of her water glass with a finger. "There have been so many advancements in spine surgery lately. I'm not accustomed to the timetable."

She went quiet, picking at her food bit by bit while he made quick work of his first helping. Wondering where her mind had drifted to, he waited for her to come back around.

When she did, it was with a start and a sheepish half smile. "Sorry for zoning out."

"Welcome back," he said. "Want to talk about it?"

"About Kevin?"

"If that's where your mind went," he said. "You don't like Tex-Mex anymore?" he asked when she sat back, her dinner seemingly forgotten. He could have sworn she'd mentioned loving the spices and flavors during one of the family events.

"It's great. I'm just feeling awkward."

He set down his fork. "Why?"

"We've never done this." She spread her hands. "We should've talked about some of this mess last night, but Hank was in the way."

"I'm listening now." For as long as she needed him.

"You don't need to worry about any of it," she began. "Hank has teams posted everywhere keeping an eye on me. The MP at the garage and you can't miss the car out front. Someone even walks the 'perimeter' apparently," she finished with air quotes.

"That's all good." He used one chip to pile salsa onto another and took a bite.

"What I'm saying is you don't have to hang around here."

"All right." He ate another salsa-loaded chip while she watched him with a wary gaze. "What if I want to hang around, help out, whatever you need?"

"I liked what we had." Exasperated, she pushed back her chair and stood up. "We can't let this get weird," she said, weaving her fingers together.

"Weird how?"

She shot him a dark look over her shoulder. "We don't date."

"Maybe we should start."

Her eyes widened. "That isn't funny. Our arrangement worked so well because we didn't blur the lines or let things get too personal."

"Sharing dinner is too personal?" He leaned back in his chair when she huffed out an impatient breath. "Maybe that was a mistake, Grace Ann."

"You're just saying that because I had a moment earlier and you're a nice guy."

That sounded more like an insult than a compliment. "If you want to talk about it, I'll listen."

"That isn't necessary," she snapped, folding her arms over her chest.

"Would you listen if I wanted to talk about Kevin?"

"Of course."

He smothered a smile at her immediate answer. "What's the difference?"

She opened her mouth and snapped it closed again. "Okay, okay." She paced away from the table. "At least admit this is new territory for us."

"It is." He'd gone too long without really touching

her. Following, he blocked her path and slowly, slowly reached out to trace her cheek, her jaw, eventually bringing his hands to rest on her trim waist. "I like this territory. Don't you?"

"Not the why of it," she replied with the honesty he admired. "But I enjoy my time with you."

"Good." He kissed her lightly, seeking only to comfort. But her lips, warm and yielding under his, ignited the passion always simmering under the surface. He eased back before he got carried away. "I enjoy our time, too."

She studied him from under heavy lids, her eyes full of temptation, and just that quickly he was ready to dive into her. Although sex was their go-to way to communicate and escape, he wanted tonight to be different. He wanted to give her more.

Her eyes cleared, grew serious, and she stepped back, just out of his reach. "I suppose you want to hear the whole story about the accident."

"It's been a rough couple of days." He couldn't imagine ruining this moment with the guilt she'd expressed earlier. "Would you be up for watching a movie?"

She tilted her head, as if confused by his suggestion. She couldn't be any more puzzled than he was. A smile bloomed a moment later, lighting up her face. "How about James Bond?"

"You're a Bond fan?" he asked.

"My parents raised me right."

"I'll say."

When they'd cleared the table and stored the leftovers, she opened a cabinet under her television. He whistled, impressed to see a collector's set of the movies based on Ian Fleming's famous character.

"You choose," she said.

He crouched next to her, giving thought to each story line before choosing one of the films starring Timothy Dalton.

"Perfect," she said. "He's one of my favorite Bonds."

His, too. "I shouldn't be surprised we have so much in common." He knew how and where she liked to go backpacking. He knew how a field of wildflowers would always bring out her camera and an easy smile. He knew her body intimately, exactly where and how to touch to bring her pleasure. But he barely knew *her* and he was determined to rectify that oversight.

Distracted with cuing up the movie, she said, "We haven't spent much time together alone in typical dating settings."

It was the perfect opening to redrawing the lines of their relationship. How could he bring her around to his way of thinking without spooking her? They settled on opposite ends of her couch and as the movie got rolling, she pulled a quilt over her legs, tucking it around her feet. The familiar dialogue of the characters gave his mind plenty of room to wander.

She'd dodged his suggestion about dating. Granted, she had more pressing things on her mind. He should wait. But that didn't feel right, either.

Oh, he'd developed patience by necessity after his parents died. He knew what it was to wait and work and wait some more on the journey to realizing a goal. Though the circumstances sucked, he had to be thankful his eyes had been open. He couldn't go backward with Grace Ann. Maybe it was the pancakes, or the way she looked at him over coffee, but everything he'd been willing to settle for in a partner rang hollow now.

Between her suspension and Kevin's recovery, he saw an unexpected gift. Time they could use to build something new and remarkable. His office was only about an hour's drive away. Her career could take her anywhere at any time, yet she'd bought a house here. He wanted more, beyond helping her through stairwell attacks and cowering from loud noises, but rushing her could flop. He had to be reasonable about his expectations. And hers.

She wriggled, pulling on the edges of the quilt. Faded with age, it wasn't quite big enough to stay around her toes and cover her shoulders at the same time.

"Cold?" he asked as they watched a milkman raise havoc in a safe house.

"Tired, mostly," she replied.

"Come here." He stretched his arm across the back of the couch. The look she gave him was more doubtful than eager. "You've used me as a heater before," he reminded her.

Color flooded her cheeks. "This is hardly the same thing as that night in the Blue Ridge."

That had been the first night they'd let those kisses sweep them away. He'd tried to tell himself it was a one-time deal.

"Well, you know where to find me if you change your mind," he said.

Her lips twitched, but whether at him or Bond, he wasn't sure. At last, without saying a word, she scooted over to sit next to him. Relaxing against his side, Grace Ann dozed off shortly after Bond stole his first kiss and long before overcoming the villain. He enjoyed the peacefulness of it as the credits rolled and regretted that he'd have to disturb her so she could go to bed.

As gently as possible, he scooped her into his arms and carried her to her bedroom. He eased her onto the bed and thought about undressing her. That was more temptation than he could resist tonight. Pulling her comforter over her to keep her warm, he jumped when her hand gripped his wrist.

"Don't go." Her voice was thick and heavy with sleep.

"I'm just across the hall." He kissed her forehead and tried again to leave.

She held on. Tight. "Mmm. You're warm." Her eyes were closed and aside from her grip, she seemed completely relaxed. She had to be caught in that twilight at the edge of dreams. Extracting himself from her grasp, he backed quietly toward the door.

"Derek." Her eyelids fluttered open. "Please stay?" Her slender arm reached for him, fingers waving him closer.

She was awake enough to know what she was asking. He gave in and stretched out on the other side of the bed.

In no time her head was pillowed on his shoulder, one hand resting over his heart and the comforter over them both. It was their first time sharing an actual bed, rather than a bedroll and sleeping bags. He stared up at the ceiling and tried to think platonic, restful thoughts. Instead, memories of her soft lips on his skin, her lithe body moving in perfect time with his, left him aching, body and soul.

It was a desperate act of self-preservation when he retreated to the guest room once she was asleep again. After pouring all he had into raising Kevin, he'd thought he was empty, that there was nothing left to invest in a relationship. Grace Ann reignited that same deep instinct to love and protect and nurture, but this time it didn't feel like a burden. He had no idea that being wrong could feel so good.

Grace Ann woke up alone, caught between the comforter and her sheets, confused for a moment that her tunic was bunched up around her waist. Oh, right. Derek had tucked her into bed and she'd turned all clingy. She dragged a pillow over her face and groaned. She'd begged him to stay with her like some ultra-insecure version of her normal self.

What was one more embarrassing moment piled onto the current heap?

Derek was a camping buddy. He was a *friend* who'd been happy to share great benefits when it suited them both. No matter how kind he'd been, he was here because of his brother's injury. She still hadn't told him everything and she shouldn't—couldn't—take advantage of his decent nature.

It was her responsibility as an adult to deal with the highs and lows in her life with equal competence.

With fresh resolve, she stripped out of the clothes she'd slept in and changed into her running gear, zipping up a hoodie over her sports bra and tank. Tying her shoes, she bounced a little, anticipating the sweet, empowering rush of endorphins. The positive effect would be compounded by a healthy display of independence that would put her back on proper footing with Derek.

Determined, she practiced a smile in the mirror before she went out to the kitchen. An empty mug sat beside the coffee brewer with a note:

Hardware store called. Went to pick up the window. Back soon.—Derek.

She went to the front window and noticed his car was gone. He shouldn't be tackling her repairs; he should be with his brother. This wasn't the sort of hospitality vibe her mother would encourage. This surely qualified her for worst hostess in history.

Her gaze drifted to the dark sedan across the street. Hank's watchful team remained in place, ready to leap into action. Probably a good idea to let them know she was heading out for a run. Looping her earbuds around her neck, she stepped outside, locking the front door before she crossed the street.

A man behind the steering wheel with a youthful smile rolled down his window. "Good morning, Major Riley."

"Good morning," she replied, smiling at the driver as well as the man in the passenger seat. "You guys okay out here?"

"We're fine." They both wore jeans and khaki polo shirts with a unit insignia on the breast pocket. She assumed the windbreakers that would hide their sidearms had been tossed aside in favor of comfort within the car. "Everything okay?"

"Absolutely. I'm headed for a run."

The driver frowned. "One of us should follow you. Give us a second."

She hadn't considered how her run would impact them. Uncertain, she debated going back inside for a long yoga session. Except she'd wanted to enjoy this gorgeous morning. "I'm not leaving the neighborhood," she said. "I can give you my route."

The man in the passenger seat aimed a thumb at the driver. "Tyler will follow you in the car and I'll patrol the block while you're gone."

"That's not very subtle," she said.

"Ma'am, this particular surveillance post isn't about subtle," Tyler said. "Our presence is meant to be a visible deterrent."

"Right." They were here to prevent a vengeful madman from wrecking her life. "Thanks."

Anxiety crept along the back of her neck. Was he watching her right now? If she didn't get moving, the only place she'd be running would be back inside. That was unacceptable. Rileys didn't hide from trouble in any form. "Would it be easier to have someone jog with me?" Being followed by a car would be weird.

"If you're willing to wait, we can have someone here within the hour."

Maybe she should wait for Derek. Did he enjoy running? She really should know that. Casting a glance over her shoulder, she had to follow through or she'd be a mess the rest of the day. Today would *not* be another emotional roller coaster. The first step was acting confidently. "Let's try your way today."

"All right," Tyler said. "Lead on."

She started down the street, the car engine a quiet rumble behind her. Weird. Turning up the volume on her earbuds, she matched her pace to the song on her playlist. None of her neighbors had asked about the surveillance team or the vandalism. If there had been an uptick in petty crimes in the area, they probably appreciated the extra eyes on the street.

Following her favorite route and the music cues on her playlist, Grace Ann upped her pace for a sprinting interval. She intended to push herself until the run consumed her, body and mind, sweating out the stress, embarrassment and this persistent longing for a man who wouldn't stay in the fling column.

Just having Derek within reach was too much temptation. Add in his willingness to let her unload and lean on him when she felt weak, and that cast a new light on their casual dynamic. The course of their relationship should have been simple. That sounded terribly cold and calculating, but the setup had been rooted in practicality and safety for both of them.

Her pace slowed with the change of song. Not once

had she imagined him in her home, but he fit. Well enough that she wanted him to stay. A day or a week, maybe longer. Was changing what had worked worth the risk?

The song for her next sprint came on and she went after it. The cool morning air flooded her lungs; her quads burned. She felt alive, empowered. Strong. *This* was living. She found that sweet spot, where her brain convinced her body she could run forever. This was why she'd come out, to remember who she was. She had the fortitude to wait out the ridiculous, unfounded investigation. She had the courage to outlast the jerk trying to punish her dad. And she could definitely overcome the ghosts of all the small broken bodies she'd known by name.

Reaching the landscaped flower beds that marked her neighborhood's main entrance, she turned back, keeping her promise to the protective detail. She'd expected to see Tyler in the car behind her but the street was empty. Unease chilled her warmed muscles and prickled under the healthy sweat she'd worked up.

Checking her phone, she hadn't missed any messages from the surveillance team. What happened? Concerned, she sprinted flat out, retracing her route. So much for endorphins defeating anxiety. With a passing scan at the first intersection, she rushed across the open space. A loud squeal behind her cut through the playlist pumping in her ears. The sharp odor of hot brakes and burning rubber stung the fresh air. She lunged away from the threat a half step too late.

Her surroundings blurred as something hit her leg and tossed her several feet into the nearest lawn. The breath knocked from her lungs, she floundered. Just as she gained her feet, her knee buckled and she went down again. She caught sight of a car in the road, tires smoking as it backed up. The front bumper scraped along with a fading shriek as the driver left the scene, speeding away.

Dazed, she tried to make sense of what little she'd seen, of what was left. She guessed the driver must have hit the back end of a parked car—the car that was currently angled up on the sidewalk where she'd been a moment ago.

She flopped back onto the soft lawn and worked to catch her breath, let her heart settle. Everything had gone from peaceful to terrifying to peaceful again too quickly. Her blood pounded in her ears, adrenaline sizzled and snapped through her system, while the sunlight bathed her face.

Neither fight nor flight instinct prevailed. She was stunned, flat on her back. In the strange and abrupt quiet, she realized she had lost her earbuds in the spill. She rolled to her hands and knees, fought off the urge to vomit, and spotting the earbuds, she crawled over to pick them up. Her cell phone, in a case on her arm, was a useless paperweight now, the case no match for this tumble.

Who would she call, anyway? There was no danger to be seen. Working her way through a physical self-assessment, she stretched out on the lawn again and stared up at the sky. The chase car would be here soon. Once her heart rate slowed, she'd try sitting up. If the world stayed steady at that point, she might consider standing, though she was in no real hurry. For the first time she was grateful she didn't have anywhere to be.

The danger had come and gone in little more than the blink of an eye. The world was apparently putting her through an adrenaline endurance test. She used the resulting burst of anger to try to sit up. The world

took a slow spin and she dropped her head to her up-
raised knees, waiting it out. Too soon, she realized, and
stretched out one more time.

She'd live. That should give the authorities plenty to
brood over. After all, if it had been an outright murder
attempt, why wouldn't the driver have waited until the
target had jogged into the street?

He regretted he couldn't go back and watch the cha-
otic response in person. The scene and speculation would
be amusing. He would settle for listening to the results
through the bugs he'd planted and taking updates from
those he'd hired to watch her. He couldn't have asked
for better actionable intel than what he'd used to interrupt her morning run.

The Army Criminal Investigation Division would be
scrambling by the end of the day, sifting out the details,
searching for clues as to what about the attacks had been
random and what had been deliberate acts against General Riley's oldest daughter.

Other than the busted front fender, the stunt had gone
nearly perfectly. As sirens swelled around him, heading
toward her neighborhood, he knew he needed to deal
with that noticeable hazard immediately. Plans A and
B were coming along too well to be derailed by an un-
planned interaction with the police.

His pulse skipped a little, anticipating what a rush it
might be if he had to successfully evade a traffic stop.
He took a deep breath, thinking of the timelines and surveillance boards back in his office. Better not to press
his luck. The police would play into his plans—on *his*
terms and schedule.

He'd ordered a thorough scouting report on the area
and done his own reconnaissance, too. Turning off the

main road at the first opportunity, he now found a strip mall that had seen better days. Parking near a scrubby little landscape island to hide the torn-up front end, he climbed out and examined the damage. A scan of the area gave him the confidence to modify his plan and dump the vehicle.

He left the ball cap he'd found in the car when he'd stolen it on the seat. Striding away, he pocketed the gloves he'd worn to hide his fingerprints. He would throw them away or burn them within the hour.

Whistling, he walked along, enjoying the beautiful weather. At this rate, he'd reach his hotel about the time she got home from the emergency room. No chance they'd let her skip a doctor's exam this time. His flight home was booked for the end of the week. Plenty of time to finish his annual follow-ups, create solid alibis to keep him out of the Army CID net, and meet with the team who would finish off Grace Ann Riley, just as soon as he issued the order.

In his pockets, his palms went damp at the idea of handling her himself. He had a key to her house. He could be in and out before anyone could sound the alarm. But the inherent satisfaction of killing her quickly would be fleeting and far too easy on her bastard father.

General Riley's torture had just begun. Sure, his first-born son had survived. That didn't bother him much, not when there were five Riley children to use against the general. Five Riley children to harass and possibly kill before he had his face-to-face confrontation with the man who'd wrecked his career, ruined his family and ultimately destroyed his lifelong dreams.

The general had used him and then turned his back on him, breaking the unspoken promise of comrades in arms by labeling him rogue and making him a scape-goat instead of a hero.

The general must be held accountable for his bad decisions, publicly and personally. And he was the man fate had sent to make General Riley pay.

Chapter 6

Derek turned into the neighborhood as another car went tearing out onto the main road. A block later, he came across a dented vehicle shoved up on a sidewalk and a person sprawled in the front yard. He stopped, ready to offer help, when he saw that person was Grace Ann.

He slammed the car into Park and cut the engine. Terror had him by the throat as he dialed 911. The operator answered as he clambered out of the car. She couldn't be dead. Life couldn't keep stealing people he loved.

Another man, charging up from the direction of her house, was shouting her name. Derek put himself between her and the threat before he recognized it was one of the men Hank assigned to watch her house.

"Sir? Sir, are you still on the line?" the emergency operator asked.

"Yes." Derek swallowed. "I'm here." He found the house number posted over the porch and relayed the information. "There's a woman in distress. We need an ambulance immediately."

"The paramedics are on the way."

"Thank you." He ended the call, giving Grace Ann his full attention. Eyes closed, she was breathing. He latched onto that. "What happened, baby?" He smoothed a hand over her hair, afraid to jostle her. "Can you hear me?" Nothing about the scene made sense. All he could think of was getting her out of here, but he didn't dare move her.

"Derek?" She blinked rapidly and the confusion swimming in her eyes hit him like a sucker punch. "How did you get here?"

"Easy. Don't move. An ambulance is on the way."

The man from the protective detail skidded to a stop, standing over them. Based on the side of the conversation Derek could hear, the man was reporting to Hank. "Is she okay?" he asked, pocketing his phone. "What happened?"

"I don't know." Derek wanted nothing more than to keep her safe behind locked doors for the rest of her days. "I was just coming back from the hardware store. Where were you?" he demanded.

"Tyler was following her in the car when he got a flat."

"Not his fault." She sounded stronger, though she didn't move. "Just a close call."

Too close, he thought. "You're going to the hospital."

"Only to see Kevin," she argued. "After a shower. I think there's grass in my ears."

He examined both ears. "You're clear." Let her think she'd won this round. The paramedics could be the bad guys and insist on taking her in. "Can you tell me what hurts?"

"Everything," she admitted. "I'm one giant dull ache. Nothing's broken."

"Mmm-hmm." He sat down beside her and tried to sort out the scene. "Can you tell me what happened?"

"I got hit by the car that jumped the curb." She lifted a hand in the general direction of the vehicle on the sidewalk.

"You think the car's possessed?" he teased.

She chuckled and gasped, a hand reaching for her side. "Ow. Stop."

"Cracked rib?" he queried.

"More like a battered ego," she replied. "Someone drove into the parked car, the parked car knocked me over here and the first one left."

His temper spiked. He hadn't gotten a good look at the vehicle before it was gone. Maybe it was his turn to overreact, but his first thought was that this was a bigger version of the stairwell attack at the hospital. Isolate her, strike fast and hard, and flee. "When will you tell me what's really going on?"

"I just did." She blinked owlishly.

Hearing sirens approaching, he let that go for now.

Her hand slipped into his and she gave his fingers a squeeze. "I'm fine," she said.

She wasn't as badly injured as he'd feared, though she was far from fine. "It would've been bad finding a stranger here." His heart might never return to a normal rhythm. "Finding you like this? That scares the hell out of me."

"What are you saying?"

This wasn't the time or place to spell it out for her. He cared for her and the feeling grew deeper every time he saw her. "We need to stop meeting like this." He lifted her hand and kissed it softly.

"You may have a point."

A police cruiser pulled up, lights going, followed by an ambulance. Derek moved aside to let the paramedics work. He introduced himself to Hank's team, Tyler and James.

"What did her brother say?" Derek asked James.

"Nothing good," James replied. "He's afraid this was no accident."

Derek shook his head. "To hit her with a parked car?" That required serious skill. "Was it bad luck with your flat tire?"

James shook his head. "Impossible to say for certain, but I don't think so."

Discreetly, Derek looked around. Someone must be watching Grace Ann. There was no other explanation for knowing exactly when and where to strike. He listened as she gave her report to Officers Willet and Radcliff, the same pair who'd responded to the vandalism call. Derek heard her frustration as she explained that she hadn't caught any of the license plate number or a helpful description of the driver, just the general impression of a white compact car.

"The bumper," she said. "The front bumper was dragging as he drove away."

"That'll help. We'll call that in," Officer Willet assured her. "That's a good start."

The paramedics had administered oxygen and helped her to her feet, flanking her as she tried to walk. She was steadier than he expected, the sight soothing his raw nerves.

As they aimed her toward the ambulance, she dug in her heels and refused transport. "You need to go," he said, supporting the paramedics. "Come on. Would you let a friend walk away from this without an exam?"

"Maybe I would." She rubbed her hands over her arms, her fingers catching in the torn fabric of her hoodie.

"No way." He rolled his eyes. "You care too much about your friends," he said. "What if I ride with you and we stop by Kevin's room when you're cleared?"

"What if you take me home to shower and change and then we go see Kevin?" she countered. "An ER visit is a waste of time and resources. I'm fine," she insisted.

He studied her closely; she was only a little shaky and that was probably more about being the center of attention than anything else. He gave in with a muttered oath. "What should I watch for?" he asked the paramedics, relenting under her pleading gaze. Once they were at the hospital, he could have someone from her unit check her out.

"I can—"

He cut her off. "You may be an expert, but I want to hear it from *them*." The paramedics rattled off the signs of shock, warned him about concussions and let her refuse transport with a signature.

He slipped an arm around her waist and guided her to his car. "For the record, I've always wanted to ride in an ambulance. You crushed my dream."

"That's a lie," she said, trying not to laugh. "Kevin told me you hate everything about medicine and hospitals."

"Maybe I'm getting over it." He helped her into the passenger seat. "A certain stubborn, beautiful nurse is giving me a fresh perspective."

He closed the passenger door before she could respond. As he rounded the car to the driver's side, his phone clanged with an incoming call from an unknown number. "Hello?"

"Sayer? Hank. Where's Grace Ann?"

Oddly enough, the cool, official voice put Derek right back on high alert. "She's here sitting in my car."

"Can you put her on the line?"

"Sure, just a second." Derek slid behind the wheel and handed Grace Ann the phone. "Hank. For you," he explained.

"Hey!" she greeted her brother too brightly.

Derek wished he'd had the forethought to put the call on speaker, as he only heard her side of the conversation. Each of her replies was upbeat and brief, and Derek was pulling into her driveway when she handed the phone back to him.

"He wants to talk with you."

Derek stopped her when she tried to get out of the car. "Wait for me."

She wrinkled her nose, though she didn't try to rush off without him. He counted that as progress.

"It's Derek," he said into the phone.

"I know this is a lot to ask, considering your brother's situation," Hank began. "Can you do me a favor and stay with Gracie until I get a handle on this?"

It wouldn't be a hardship on his end at all. "I feel compelled to point out I'm not a certified bodyguard."

On an impatient huff, Grace Ann pushed open her door. "Stop conspiring to babysit me."

Derek scrambled after her.

"She's impossible," Hank grumbled in his ear. "I don't want her left alone. The situation is escalating and I can't get over there myself until day after tomorrow at the earliest. I'm not inclined to trust anyone right now. You're on-site."

Derek locked the front door and waited until he heard her bedroom door slam. "I'll stay," he said. "Does this

have anything to do with why she wasn't on that training exercise?"

"Is that a conflict of interest for you?" Hank asked.

"Yes. No." He scrubbed a hand through his hair. "I'm
staying," he confirmed. "But I'd sure like to know what
the hell is going on."

"Yeah." Hank sounded exhausted. "I'll send you an
email tonight with everything I can share. If she remembers anything about that driver, call me immediately."

A shower and twenty minutes with an ice bag on her
sore hip did Grace Ann a world of good. At least this
time around she had a good reason for leaning on him.
She couldn't drum up much irritation with Hank. If she
had to have a babysitter, she'd rather have someone she
could talk to, someone who put her at ease and distracted
her from wondering who had been driving that car.

Ignoring Derek's protests, she insisted on helping
him replace the garage window. It served to both reassure him and keep her from getting stiff. Plus, the pleasant diversion of watching his muscles ripple under the
T-shirt as he worked couldn't be overlooked.

"How did you learn to do all of this?" she asked when
they finished.

"Construction paid well," he said. "Better than other
jobs, and the hours matched up with Kevin's school
schedule."

She couldn't imagine the pain he'd endured. Naturally, Derek would have factored in school hours as he
attempted to step into the role of provider and parent for
his grieving little brother. She wondered when and how
he'd processed the loss of his parents, or if he'd just buried it under a general loathing for hospitals.

Looking back, his disgust for her profession had been

part of what made him her ideal guy. Sure, the man had sex appeal for days, with a body honed by his love of the outdoors. Being intelligent and interesting only added to the total package. At the start, it was his inaccessibility that worked for her. He had no interest in dropping in or making demands on her time, so she didn't have to think about shifting her life around for a bigger emotional commitment, either.

When they finished with the window, he went to clean up and she headed for the kitchen. They could both use something hearty for lunch. She gathered up bread, cheese and deli meat and dug a quart of homemade vegetable soup from the back of the freezer.

The man deserved more than this for all he was doing, but it was the best thank-you she could offer right now. Dropping the icy block of soup into a pan to heat, she prepped the sandwiches for the griddle. She reached for her phone to turn on some music and remembered it was trashed. Her hip was already achy and she wasn't half done with lunch.

Resentment flared that her morning feel-good plan had been wrecked. Had it been a distracted driver or the Riley Hunter? Not her job to track that person down, Hank's. Better to keep her mind on lunch, a task she could manage. With the busted front end, surely it wouldn't take the police long to find the culprit. When they did, she was pressing all the charges possible. Maybe Derek would have some suggestions on that front.

"That smells amazing."

Derek's voice startled her and she banged her hip on the counter. She hissed through her teeth when a bolt of pain shot straight down her leg to the sole of her foot.

"Sorry!" He gathered her close, massaging the sore spot with gentle pressure and slow circles. "Better?"

"Getting there," she said, breathing through the spike of pain. "Thanks," she added, easing out of his embrace. If he kept touching her, she'd only make a fool of herself.

"Let me take over," he suggested. "You should take another turn with the ice."

"I've got it." At his frown, she explained. "Resting only makes me stiffen up. I promise I'll ask if I need you to take over."

"All right." He moved out of the way and folded his arms, the pose emphasizing the swell of his biceps.

The man kept showing up, doing thoughtful things and throwing her off-balance. She'd gladly accept if he offered her a sexual outlet, but she didn't know what to make of his increasing curiosity about the rest of her life.

When the sandwiches came off the grill, he helped her get everything to the table. "This is fantastic," he said after tasting the soup.

"Family recipe."

He cocked an eyebrow. "I thought you didn't cook?"

"It's soup. You throw stuff in a pot and hope for the best."

His low chuckle was a wonderful distraction. "It hits the spot. Thanks."

His praise left her uncomfortable, when he was the one doing all the heavy lifting. And her troubles had once more interfered with the real reason he was here. "Have you talked with Kevin today?"

"We've exchanged a few texts. Before I picked up the window," he said. "Sounds like he's had a good day." He pulled out his phone and showed her the unhappy face emoji. "He's pouting that I haven't brought one of your brownies as promised."

Frustration turned her stomach into knots. Derek should be with Kevin. Her nose stung with the tears she refused to let fall. Oh, she was tired of feeling sorry for herself. Kevin was facing the long recovery and Derek was stuck here, doing Hank a favor.

"Hey." He reached over and covered her hand. "Talk to me."

Again, she extricated herself from the comforting contact. "You really don't have to stay. I know you told Hank you would. This is me releasing you from that commitment. I shouldn't be your priority."

"What will you do if I go?"

"I'll, um…" She hadn't thought about it. "I'll take myself and the protective detail on a vacation." She'd always wanted to spend some time in Australia. A little extreme, but a valid option. "Getting jumped by a possessed car was a random thing."

The joke clearly missed its mark as Derek narrowed his eyes. "Like the random broken window and random attack in the stairwell?"

"Yes." When he put it that way, it sounded worse. He'd become invested, exactly the kind of relationship factor she actively avoided. She didn't want to worry about her choices affecting someone else. Her father's choices affected the entire family, good and bad, even though the consequences weren't intentional. "It's not like three random events add up to a premeditated plan."

His eyebrows snapped together as he gave his soup his full attention. "Hank said he'd send me an email tonight. I'd rather hear it from you."

"Hear what, exactly?"

"Grace Ann." He stared at her, his expression stern.

Playing ostrich insulted both of them. The recent incidents were almost certainly orchestrated by the Riley Hunter and Derek could well be unknowingly putting his life at risk by sticking close. He'd said it himself; he wasn't a bodyguard.

No, he was a man she could build a life with. She was on the verge of loving him, even knowing he deserved more than she could give. Derek deserved a woman eager to welcome him home every day after work. A woman who would have dinner ready and be available for a spontaneous weekend of rock climbing or an evening walk down a street lined with picket fences. He deserved a woman who'd give him a new family to treasure, a woman who wasn't broken and jaded.

For the first time in months, she considered making another attempt at counseling, so she might eventually heal herself—and also be the right woman for Derek.

"Grace Ann?"

"It's an ugly story." She pulled herself together. "No matter who tells you all the details, you should probably move to Kevin's place. It's where you should've stayed from the start. You were kind to keep me company, but despite the evidence to the contrary, I can take care of myself."

"I disagree." He waved off her immediate protest. "Of course you can take care of yourself. That doesn't mean you should handle everything alone. We were both twisted up after Kevin's surgery. It was nice to spend that time with a friend. With *you*."

She was a pretty messed-up friend right now.

"I'll go stay at Kevin's place," he said. "If you'll come with me."

"That's silly and intrusive. You and your brother need this time."

"We've had plenty of time. I think he'd consider it a favor if you distracted me. He tells me I hover." He shrugged. "I won't leave you alone to deal with whatever is really going here."

She searched for the words to explain she was trying to do the right thing for *him*. "I'm not alone." She waved toward the window and the protective detail outside. "Hank has me covered. I'll go see my parents." Probably smarter than going all the way to Australia. "The surfing will definitely help the hip." Or walking on the shifting sand would make it worse. Only one way to find out. No one could strangle her or hit her with a car or pester her about taking precautions if she was out on the ocean. And if Derek wasn't close by, he couldn't get caught in the cross fire.

She started clearing the table so she could lie down again with an ice pack before they went to the hospital.

"What are you hiding?" He nudged her aside to handle the dishes himself. "Is there any reason you don't want to tell me what's going on?" he asked, blocking her escape from the kitchen.

"Talking about it makes it all sound so creepy and weird." She gripped the edge of the counter. "If Matt survived, I can, too." She didn't like giving the madman behind the harassment that much power or credit. "That's all that really matters."

Her emotions took another nosedive. On the verge of a tantrum, she opened the dishwasher to help him load it. Bending over, her hip locked up and she swallowed a string of curses at the blaze of pain.

Derek drew her back against his lean, warm body and kissed the side of her neck. "Breathe. Just breathe."

It wasn't easy with her heart doing pirouettes and her nerves bouncing between lust and pain.

"In and out," he crooned. "That's it." He held her

closer, taking some of her weight off the battered joint. "Better?"

"Mmm." Words were beyond her now. She'd known he had good hands, though this specific brand of tenderness was new.

"What did your brother survive?"

"It's such a convoluted story." She gingerly boosted herself up on the counter and he returned to the dishes. It made it easier for her, talking to his back as she organized her thoughts. "Did Kevin ever mention the data breach a few months ago, when the personnel records were compromised?"

"Sure. I got an official letter myself," he said. "How does that tie in?"

"Well, some creep used sensitive information to start harassing Matt. Apparently way back when he was at West Point, Matt got another cadet pregnant and didn't tell any of us. The mother of his son received weird messages that amounted to 'you will pay.' The sender didn't want money. Based on the stalker-like pictures and video he sent to our dad, the investigators think he's trying to make Dad suffer for some wrongdoing by hurting us. Matt survived and the attacks stopped, though everyone stayed on alert since the culprit wasn't caught."

"That's seriously twisted."

"An understatement." She accepted the ice pack he handed her. "The creep has reach, I'll give him that. When my car was tagged in the garage with the 'you will pay' note, Hank took that as the opening volley, but the jerk was just playing us. Hank calls him the Riley Hunter, which only aggravates me more."

"Why?"

"He doesn't deserve a title." She couldn't hide her contempt. "And I'm not planning on being anyone's trophy."

"Good." He tossed the towel over his shoulder and leaned back on the opposite counter, watching her. "So I guess it's your turn?"

She hated admitting it. "That is the prevailing theory. Dad got pictures of me hugging you and the broken garage window. I'm not sure if my suspension is part of his plan. I guess it's possible."

"Your dad knew about that, too?"

She nodded. "He sent Hank in here like a one-man cavalry."

Derek's brow furrowed thoughtfully. "What about the car that hit you today?"

She dropped her gaze to her bare feet. "I don't know. Hank reacted damn quick. Then again, his team was here and he's overprotective."

"I'm not sure *over*protective applies in this situation."

"I really think if all of this crap was due to this creep, he'd have sent me another of his infamous messages by now."

"You don't think it's possible he changed tactics when he changed targets?"

"Well, no one tried to strangle Matt," she allowed. "It's possible that my suspension is somehow because of him. If this new approach is because I'm female he's in for a rude awakening. Investigators found out he hired local thugs and rigged things so he could watch Matt's reaction. He used fake email accounts and burner phones."

"He sounds dangerous," Derek said, draping the towel on the hook.

"Which is why I'd like you to let Hank and his guys handle it," she said. "Please."

He was already shaking his head. "No way. I find myself agreeing with Hank. You need round-the-clock protection until someone drops a net on this guy."

"I have it."

"Not inside the house."

This was Derek digging in. She closed her eyes and counted to ten, struggling to find her last scrap of patience. "I do *not* need another brother," she said.

He moved closer, parting her knees gently to make room for his trim hips. His strong hands covered her knees and cruised slowly along the length of her thighs. "Grace Ann, I promise you I've *never* thought of you like a sister."

Sitting on the countertop, her face level with his, it wouldn't take much more than a thought to lay a kiss on him guaranteed to end this conversation. "Derek." She traced his face with her fingertips. His straight eyebrows, the subtle jig at the bridge of his nose. He'd never told her how or when it had been broken. The slant of his mouth, the hard line of his jaw, were softened with a gleam of sandy stubble. He was made up of so many angles and textures. Though she'd explored them all before, it was new having him here.

"Do it," he urged, gently stroking her thighs. "You know you want to kiss me."

She studied the thick waves of his hair, the shape of his ears. What was so different about him in this moment? She laid her lips on his. Softly, slowly, reveling in the fresh sensations, though her heart kicked into high gear. She tasted his lower lip, nibbled lightly, searching for the balance between the familiar and the new.

His hands slipped under her shirt as his tongue stroked over hers. The heat in his lightly calloused palms surrounded her, invaded her. She arched into the sensation as he teased the hard peaks of her breasts, wrapping her legs around his lean hips.

The kiss spun her out onto a cloud where nothing

hurt and no trouble could find her. Craving him was the only risk; the only threat was not following through. She sighed his name, her head falling back as he rained featherlight kisses down the column of her throat and back up again, taking her mouth when she gasped.

She dragged his shirt up and over his head, glorying in the view of his sculpted chest and shoulders. Need pulsed through her, building with every caress of his lips, each rasp of his whiskers against her skin. He was the only thought in her mind. She cupped his erection through his jeans, silently pleading for more. Here and now.

He stilled her hands as she flicked open the button. She groaned, edging toward frantic as she kissed the line of his collarbone where she knew he was ticklish, breathing in that scent that was him alone.

He flinched, chuckled as he carried her to the couch. The man was almost too gentle as he bared her body to his view. Only the hunger in his gaze kept her from begging him to hurry. It was a marvel, being the object of that look, seeing a reflection of the needs and desire crackling though her veins.

At last, he pulled a condom from his wallet and rolled it into place. He buried himself deep into her body and each slow, heavy thrust melted her from the inside out. She couldn't hang on, couldn't hold on a moment longer. The orgasm crashed through her and she clung to that blissful edge until his body shuddered with his release.

He shifted her around until she was sprawled over him, easing those lingering aches with those amazing hands. Fatigue and satisfaction tugged at her and she pulled the quilt over them before dozing off, his heartbeat a comforting echo under her ear.

* * *

Derek relaxed under her pliant limbs, unwilling to disturb her as she slept. They were incredible together, though they still had yet to try this in a real bed. The couch was better than a bedroll, but he suspected her hip would be screaming when she woke up. Probably the rest of her as well, considering she'd been hit by a car.

He wondered how she did it. Most people, himself included, would crumble under the strain of her current situation. The idea of someone coming after her and her siblings was deeply disturbing. Here, in the quiet aftermath, it dawned on him that she must have been pulled off the training exercise as a safety precaution.

So did that make the helicopter accident an accident or had it been the madman's impressive reach? Either way, he had to make her understand no one else put the blame for Kevin's injury at her feet. He didn't have to know anything about the misappropriation accusation against her to know it was all fabricated. Grace Ann wouldn't jeopardize her career. More than that, she wouldn't risk tarnishing her family name.

He'd never met anyone as determined to live up to the legendary standards of their parents.

The stress was getting to her, though. He saw it when her hands were restless, her mind distracted and of course the panic attack when the car backfired.

He slipped out from under her, tucking the quilt around her as she curled on her side. Dressing, he went to the guest room for his cell phone and laptop, automatically checking the street as he went. A new car and team was in place out front. James and Tyler were most likely at the shop getting their tire replaced.

Obviously, he didn't know Hank as well as Grace Ann did, but the man didn't seem prone to drama or overkill.

He didn't care that she hadn't received a fresh "you will pay" note. He would stick around until Hank could get someone else with all the right credentials and training in place. Grace Ann was too important to him. Whatever they might be to each other, he wouldn't take risks with her safety.

He opened his laptop at the table and sat down to catch up on his email. A quick scan of his inbox made it obvious he needed to call the office. He had his cell phone to his ear before he realized noise would likely wake Grace Ann.

He ducked out the back door as his assistant picked up. Loreen was sweet enough to ask about Kevin before filling him in on the current crisis. Summarizing the long list of concerns, they identified the most urgent needs and developed a plan of action.

"You sound good," Loreen said. "Better than I expected."

"Kevin's great." Derek leaned against one column of the pergola shading the patio. "It'll take some time, but his medical team and army unit are on the ball."

"That's really good news."

A hitch in her voice caught his attention. "What? Is Hudson eyeballing my office?"

"No!" She laughed. "Well, yes, he is always after your office. I'm just so glad you're not, um, depressed or something. I know how much you hate hospitals."

"Oh." It wasn't like he didn't have good reasons.

"I've heard Walter Reed has a great campus. You only sound this relaxed after one of your nature weekends."

She didn't know she was referencing his outings with Grace Ann. He had no idea those weekends had made such a noticeable difference to his demeanor. "I was scared as hell for Kevin," he admitted. "You're just hearing loads of relief." He tried to hide his eagerness to get off the phone. "He's expecting me up in his room for dinner," he fibbed. "So I'll get going."

"Great," Loreen said. "We're all thinking of you both," she said. "You *are* coming back?" she queried in a muffled whisper.

"Yes," he chuckled. "I may have to telecommute for a few weeks until Kevin is cleared to be on his own again, but I'm coming back."

"Good. I've got my marching orders. You keep doing whatever has you in such a good mood."

The easiest assignment he'd ever heard. "I'll tell Kevin you said hello."

Ending the call, he stepped into the sunshine, soaking up the sense of peace and contentment. Yes, he was relieved for Kevin and curious about what next step he might explore with Grace Ann. Eager, he headed back inside. Near the decorative stand by the door, he saw a folded card wedged under the potted plant.

"YOU WILL PAY" was scrawled on the card in dark red ink, in all caps.

His pleasant, relaxed mood evaporated in a flash of fear for Grace Ann. This was the message she'd expected. The bastard trying to punish her father had been right *here*. Too close to Grace Ann. Icy fingers danced down Derek's spine.

He took a picture of the note card and sent a text to Hank with a brief message. "I'm taking her out of here."

Let Hank come investigate the scene and collect any evidence. Clearly the Riley Hunter knew where she lived and was making his point. Derek wasn't going to spend one more minute playing along or tempting fate.

Chapter 7

He sat back once the bugs had gone quiet, concerned about the unexpected intimacy he'd overheard. He'd planted the devices to learn her daily plans and routine so he could cause more fear-inducing panic, eroding her confidence and trust in her protection detail. His always being a step ahead would be the last straw for this particular Riley, he was sure of it.

He'd been through her service record and wrung every drop of information from his inside source to get a handle on her mind-set and her personal life. He recognized breakable when he saw it, just as he recognized an ambitious man with something to prove, like his source.

Major Riley had been through hell on her last tour. His source had shared plenty of details about how her demeanor had changed since the unit returned to the States. Her devotion to her patients had become more pronounced and the distance from her friends increased.

The man in her home changed the equation. Either that acquaintance had escalated quickly or his source had missed a critical element in the research. He needed to get a better picture before he left town.

At his laptop, he connected to his cloud service and reviewed his notes. Her last serious relationship had been over two years ago. Since her return to the States, she reportedly hadn't dated at all. If she had an established romantic relationship with the man staying with her, his lead on the ground had failed him. If it was simply an adrenaline response, there were fewer factors to interfere with his ultimate plan to destroy General Riley and everything the man held dear.

After a brief internal debate, he sent the message, demanding a meeting. In planning his attack, he'd eliminated as many face-to-face encounters as possible, assembling his team through referrals and successful test operations. He had a network of select managers in place where the Riley children were stationed around the country, ready to act on his command. Truly, it was a setup that would please even General Riley's passion for organization.

Grace Ann was special to the general, and therefore her takedown had to be special. The general had never outright called her his favorite child, but he didn't have to. The look in his eyes when he shared family stories or shared news of her being honored for one thing or another made it clear she was his pride and joy.

The pride and joy was about to disappoint her father in dramatic fashion. She would be disgraced, humiliated, dishonorably discharged, and if she lived through the hell he was sending her way, she'd be too broken to ever create joy again.

* * *

"Hank," Grace Ann murmured, recognizing the number on Derek's cell phone screen when it hummed on the counter in Kevin's hospital room. Another chill trickled down her spine and she wrapped the panels of her cardigan tightly around her.

Though Derek had woken her gently just over an hour ago, his urgency had been unmistakable. He'd taken her outside and shown her the note from the Riley Hunter. The chills had started immediately. Fear or rage, she couldn't separate one from the other, and she couldn't get warm.

The man tormenting her father had been to her home or sent someone in his place. He'd been at her back door. When? How long had he stayed? Had he peered into her windows? She'd walked her backyard, searching for a trail. Finding everything in order was somehow worse.

When Derek told her they were leaving the house, she hadn't argued, more than willing to go. He'd gathered the few items he'd brought while she packed her essentials. They loaded into his car and she didn't even care where they went or how long she'd be away. In the reflection of the side mirror, she'd watched two men hustle to her house on Hank's orders.

They'd brought Kevin his brownies and chattered about nothing in particular while fear coiled in the pit of her stomach like a rattlesnake ready to strike. She didn't dare let it show or the pictures might get back to her father. The hunter behind these attacks wanted a reaction and she refused to be his pawn. Not even anger cut through the chills. Her house and the hospital were home turf, her domain. She didn't appreciate being chased away from the two places she always considered safe havens.

"You okay?" Kevin asked as Derek stepped outside to take the call.

She rubbed her palms together and pressed them between her knees. "I'm great."

He pointed to his throat. "Feeling better?"

In her rush to get out of the house, she'd forgotten to change into something that concealed the lingering marks. "Better than you, I'm sure," she teased.

"Come on, Grace Ann. Talk around here is a psych patient jumped you."

She couldn't recall sharing that explanation with anyone other than Hank. "Not a big deal," she said. "How'd you hear about it?"

He winked. "Gossip in the workplace is everyone's favorite addiction."

"I thought that was social media," she said.

"Same difference."

"Probably," she agreed. "Speaking of rumors, PT says you're top of the class."

He sat up straighter. "I am a *stud* down in PT," he said with a wiggle of his eyebrows. "It's not as easy as people think to walk away from a helicopter crash."

She appreciated his sense of humor almost as much as she appreciated that he still felt comfortable around her. Of course, he didn't know the whole truth. "They carried you away."

"A vicious rumor." He pretended to get serious. "You could help me out by quashing that one whenever it's spoken."

"Sure thing," she promised. "I can't crush the legend-in-your-own-mind thing you've got going."

"Thanks," he said with such sincerity she laughed.

The normal banter felt good, reassuring, though she still hadn't worked up the courage to apologize to Kevin.

The words kept circling through her mind, like a gerbil on a wheel. Whenever she opened her mouth, the words jammed up, but she had to try. Who knew when she'd have another chance?

She glanced to the door and confirmed Derek was still on the phone. "I'm sorry, Kevin." There, the most important words were out.

"For what? This?" His nostrils flared and his gaze narrowed. "You need to stop blaming yourself for every damned thing."

Oh, she wanted to lay the blame where it belonged, especially in light of the note Derek had found. She just couldn't. Evidence or not, she was 99 percent sure that helicopter went down because someone thought she'd be on it.

"The situation…" She had to stop and hit a mental reset switch or she would have babbled uncontrollably. "It's different." Yes, lousy things happened to good people every day. It had always been harder for her to see a friend hurt than to carry that pain herself. "They put you on that helo in my place because of a last-minute protective order from way up the chain of command. I can't help feeling it should be me in that bed, not you. I'm so, so sorry."

He stared at her a long time. "Are you telling me you wouldn't have needed a stretcher?"

He was gallantly lighting the way out of a dark conversation, and she responded in kind. "Based on my additional training and experience, it's a valid theory."

"But you're a girl," he said with a snort.

The outrageous response had her sputtering and laughing. Leave it to Kevin. "You're too good for any of us," she said when she caught her breath.

"Stud," he said, tapping his chest.

"Yeah, well, the PT department will crack that fragile bravado soon enough."

"Says you." Kevin glanced past her, saw Derek was still occupied. "Seriously. I don't care who pulled you or why. You didn't cause the instrument failure they tell me led to the crash. Tell me you understand it was an accident. It's not your fault."

"Working on it." Logic and common sense said she couldn't be held accountable for the actions of another person—a person determined to wreak havoc on her life. Unfortunately her emotions were rolling around like loose marbles, impossible to wrangle and getting underfoot at the worst times.

"Can I ask you a favor?" Kevin asked suddenly.

"Of course. You know I'll do anything for you."

Kevin motioned her to lean closer. "Keep Derek as far from me as possible." Her confusion must have been obvious as he rushed to add, "He means well, but we can't let him slide back into that caregiver role. I see the strain on his face already."

She suspected the stress lining his face today had more to do with her than Kevin. "I'll do my best."

"If I know him, he'll drop everything and stick here indefinitely." He grabbed her hand. "I love him. That's why I can't let him hang out here too long. He put his entire life on hold for me when we were kids. Make sure he goes home and keeps moving on with *his* life, okay?"

"I will," she promised, hugging his hand between both of hers. Though she'd miss Derek, she had to get him back home where he could be safe, before he shifted those caregiving tendencies to her.

"Good. I think he has someone special at home. I don't want my mess to screw that up for him."

"Someone special?" she asked through the sudden buzzing in her ears.

Kevin nodded. "Pretty sure. He's like Fort Knox with personal details."

She and Derek were only friends with benefits and they'd specifically agreed they were free to date other people. Yet those kisses after lunch had felt different. Special. New. If he was interested in someone else back home, how could he have made love to her like *that*?

"A couple weeks ago," Kevin was saying, "he was completely off the radar and when he did get back to me there was something he wasn't saying. Don't let him blow off someone awesome because I fell out of a helo."

A couple weeks ago. She stuffed the shock and hurt deep to deal with later. Her last trip with Derek had been *six* weeks ago. That meant she wasn't the "someone awesome" Kevin suspected. Considering their agreement, he should have told her. "I'll make it happen."

"What's that?" Derek asked, striding in.

"Kevin wants his favorite burger from Roscoe's when he's moved to the nursing center," she improvised.

"We can definitely do that," Derek agreed. He shot her a look she couldn't quite decipher. "Tonight, if you want."

"Oh, thanks, but I'm all set for dinner tonight," Kevin replied.

"You are?" Derek asked, suspicious.

Grace Ann rolled her eyes. Kevin was too much like her younger brothers. "He's made an attractive friend or two along the way."

"Here?" Derek's eyebrows arched in shock.

"It happens more often than you think," she deadpanned.

"Helps to be the guy who walked away from a helicopter crash." Kevin smirked with blazing overconfidence.

"I suppose we'll have to start calling you Norris," Grace Ann said.

Derek frowned as Kevin gave an enthusiastic cheer. "That's me. Yes!"

"Chuck Norris." Derek groaned when it clicked. "You start that and there will be no living with him again."

They were all laughing when an aide stepped in, a shy smile on her face. Grace Ann immediately noticed that she didn't work on this floor. Picking up the cues, she nudged Derek out, leaving Kevin to flirt.

When they were well away from Kevin's room she asked about the phone call. To her surprise, Derek asked her to take them to a part of the hospital she didn't visit regularly. Concerned, she led him to a canteen that specialized in baked goods and fancy lattes. "What's the problem?" she asked when they were settled at the counter.

"Hank's team found two bugs in your house. One near the kitchen pass-through, the other in the front room."

That was the last thing she expected to hear. Her skin went hot, an improvement on the chills. It was bad enough knowing someone had left the note, broken a window and taken pictures. Knowing someone had been *in* the house and was now listening in on her life was outrageous. Intolerable.

"How long?" It was more growl than question.

"Easy." Under the counter, Derek's thigh bumped hers. "They don't know yet. The note was placed recently or it would have been more weathered."

For a woman who relied on logic and a cool head in the face of dire circumstance, she was about to lose it right here. On the bright side, they weren't far from the psych ward. If she went off the deep end, Derek would have help right away.

"In my house." She murmured the words behind her hand to keep from shouting. The violation simply leveled her, effectively as a punch from a heavyweight champ.. "How? The police didn't see any signs of a break-in when they came out to take the vandalism report."

Derek's brow flexed in thought. "Maybe after that? Hank promised to figure it out. He just needs some time."

She clutched her hands in her lap to hide the shaking. "Hank thinks there are other devices? Here?"

Derek slipped his arm around her shoulders and gave her a quick hug. "Just a precaution."

"I'm not going home." The thought of going back made her skin crawl.

"We knew that already," he assured her.

"I mean ever. I'm never going back." She wouldn't feel safe there again. "I'll sell it as is. Furnishings included."

"Let's not call the Realtor yet," he cautioned.

"He must have heard us," she said, cringing. "In the kitchen. On the couch." She jumped to her feet, too wired to sit still. "Derek." She dropped her head to his shoulder. "What now?"

He tugged her back down to sit beside him and trapped her hands gently on his thigh. "Hank expects me to convince you to go home."

"No," she gasped. Mentally she slashed the budget for Hank's Christmas present in half. "Why?"

"He wants us to set a trap. You've been through so much, Grace Ann. If this is the last straw, if you can't do it, he will understand."

Derek was right, of course. Hank wouldn't hold it against her if she couldn't pull it off. It made sense to try to use the bugs against whoever had planted them. A trap might be their best chance to get a solid lead on the identity of the madman hunting her family.

"I don't suppose he suggested an alternative?" she asked, suspecting the answer before he spoke.

"He said your parents would love to see you."

Her choices were to hold the line or retreat. Deflated, bordering on numb, she made her decision. "I'll go back."

"*We'll* go back," he stated, leaving no room to argue.

Back to where they'd shared a meal before feasting on each other while someone listened. She pinched the bridge of her nose. Another series of good memories tainted by ugliness she'd have to overcome.

"How about this?" He gave her hands a squeeze. "We can replace your phone, grab dinner and then see how you feel about it. If you want to stay at Kevin's apartment tonight, we'll do that. Think of it as a professional consult. Someone should walk me through what I'll need to rearrange to make his life easier when he comes home."

"I, um…" She'd promised Kevin not to let Derek put his life on hold again. His life as a civilian, in another town with someone new and awesome. She pulled her hands free. "I can always get a hotel room or go to my parents' place later tonight." Was he doing a compare-and-contrast thing with her and someone significant? She should just ask. They'd been honest with each other about everything else since the beginning.

It just…hurt. This deep, dull ache radiating through her limbs couldn't be blamed on any physical injury.

"Whatever you decide, I'm not leaving you, Grace Ann."

"You have to," she replied. "You have a job and a life and…" Her throat went dry when she tried to get the words out. "Hank will make sure the protection detail sticks closer." Like a noose around her neck. "I've imposed on you enough."

"Imposed?" he echoed, a whip of impatience in his voice.

"Haven't I?" She tilted her head to sneak a glance at him and found his face stamped with frustration. There were storm clouds in his blue eyes, his jaw set at a hard angle. She fought the urge to kiss and tease him until that slow, sexy smile appeared.

"No." He turned her chin to meet his gaze full-on. "I told Hank I'd see this through. No one can be sure how things will escalate if the Riley Hunter realizes we found the bugs."

"This is a job for the CID." *She* was now a job for an official agency. "You really don't need to—"

"The hell I don't."

The man was gracious to a fault. If he stayed, would there be anything left of their friendship? Worse, if he stayed would he get caught in the cross fire? "You should go back home," she said, determined to do the right thing. "You'll have at least two full weeks of normal before Kevin's released from the skilled nursing center."

"Why are you pushing me away?" he demanded. "What did Kevin say?"

"Nothing." She'd love nothing more than to run off with him and go play in the woods or at the shore. The idea of getting off the radar and exploring more of that incredibly hot tenderness was an astonishing temptation. She wanted to know he was into *her*, not feeling some sense of obligation because he happened to be in the wrong place at the wrong time.

Her fingers fluttered to her throat before she could

stop herself. Derek's gaze latched onto the motion. "Hear me, Grace Ann. I'm *not* leaving you. Or Kevin," he added, belatedly.

She tried again to keep the promise she'd just made to Kevin. "Don't you want to get back to your house, your bed and your routine?"

He scowled at her, as if he couldn't figure out if he recognized her. "Eventually," he admitted.

"Then why waste your vacation time when you don't need to? You're not far away. You can swing by and visit Kevin whenever you want. He'll have plenty of help from professionals and friends until he can manage on his own."

"And you?"

"I have Hank and his team."

"Right." Derek looked past her, out the window, not making eye contact. "First things first. We need to get your phone replaced."

Wow. His bossy lawyer side returned with a vengeance. "And after that Hank and I can figure out what he wants the listener to hear."

"No. After that we'll pick up food and you'll call Hank from Kevin's house."

He made her feel like a teenager who'd been caught out past her curfew. Derek might not be a soldier, but he knew how and when to apply an authoritative voice. "You're not giving me any say?"

He shrugged. "I'm done arguing about the details. Come on."

She'd probably have an easier time sending him on his way once they baited the trap for Hank. Regardless, after that task was done, she'd make sure he got clear before her problems could spill over and hurt the Sayer family again.

* * *

Frustrated was only the tip of the iceberg for Derek. He buried it. If his ultimate goal was to create something more personal and permanent with Grace Ann, he would adjust and adapt to get her on board. Not the first time he'd needed to reframe things. She was swamped by the circumstances. It was her nature to step into the breach rather than put someone else in jeopardy. Pushing him away was most likely her attempt at protecting him.

That didn't make it any easier.

This Riley Hunter had started a game that he didn't intend for Grace Ann to win. Too bad. She wasn't alone in this anymore.

For the hour it took to replace her phone, Derek fumed behind a mask of serenity. Eventually she'd realize there was no chance of him leaving. He replayed every second since she'd fallen asleep on his chest and most of the fantastic minutes beforehand. They were good at occasional sex, but that had been special. And he intended to capitalize and build on that treasured connection.

He debated his strategy while she talked with Hank about how to trap the bastard on the other end of the bugs in her house. She'd started pushing him away once she understood Hank wanted him to stay and help. He supposed the "go home" and "we can only be friends" signals she was dropping between them like orange road-construction barrels were because she cared deeply for him, too. He tried to feel encouraged, but convincing her they could be more than friends with benefits was going to be a tricky process.

"I'm really sorry you're caught up in all of this," she said as he entered her neighborhood.

"Offer still stands," he reminded her. "We can go back

to Kevin's place when we're done." He'd keep using "we" until she got the message.

Hank had told them to talk freely about the incident in Afghanistan. Her job was to plant a false detail, using a name Hank provided. He also asked Derek to make reservations at a specific restaurant in Bethesda for the day after next. He hoped to see how closely the other side was listening and how quickly they could respond.

"I wish you were anywhere but here," she said as he parked in her driveway. "And I'm selfish enough to be relieved that I don't have to go in there by myself."

Her raw honesty loosened the knots in his shoulders. He cut the engine and took her hand, hoping to keep the communication flowing. "Thanks."

Her brow flexed into a frown. "For what?"

"Being you," he said. "You nearly convinced me you were sick of me already."

"Not true." The flicker of a smile didn't reach her eyes. He tilted her chin and leaned over to kiss her. She turned away at the last second and his lips brushed her cheek. "We should get inside." She pushed open the door and climbed out before he could reply.

Her hand trembled as she tapped the code into the panel to raise the garage door. Once the overhead door had rolled down and they were out of sight and before they walked inside where they would be overheard, he drew her into his arms.

"You have my word you won't be alone for any of this, Grace Ann."

She dropped her head to his shoulder, her arms banding tightly around his waist. He hated that some nameless, faceless coward had put this fear into her.

"It might be better for everyone if I was," she said,

leaning back. "Your brother's been hurt by someone after me. If something happens to you…"

He kissed her as her voice trailed off. Her fingers curled into his shirt as she held tight, kissing him back.

This was his only defense against all the words rolling around in his head. He wanted to tell her she was special to him, that he wanted to stand by her through all the joys and trouble life could toss their way. When he gave her those words, he wanted her to believe him.

A minute or an hour later, she broke the kiss. "I don't want to talk about the incident," she admitted. "I'm afraid of it. Of after." She rubbed her palms together. "The nightmares. And I really don't want to make plans that could put you in harm's way."

He touched his forehead to hers. "Then we'll go tell Hank to find another way."

Her fingertips fluttered over his jaw. "You're amazing, Derek."

Was that a goodbye in her voice? He tamped down the knee-jerk reaction to demand clarification. "Same goes." He kissed her again, reveling in the hot silk of her mouth, the taste unique to her. He slid his palms up and down the tense muscles of her back. "Is Hank bad at his job?"

"What?" She blinked up at him. "No."

"Then we'll trust him to use this charade for your benefit. I won't judge anything you're about to say."

"Thanks." She drew him toward the steps. "Once this is done, you should get back to your life."

Why did she keep going there?

The overhead light timed out and she sucked in a breath at the sudden darkness. "Man, I'm jumpy." As soon as they moved, the motion sensor turned the light back on. "Sorry."

"Stop apologizing to me," he said as they went inside. "I'm right where I want to be."

"Really?"

"Yes," he said emphatically. From this point forward, they had to assume someone was listening. "If you'd like to bake something to tempt me to stick around, I won't complain."

They'd decided to use her known strategy of stress baking to help with the performance.

"We just ate."

He cozied up behind her, nibbling her ear. "But what if we get hungry later?" he asked suggestively.

She prodded him with her elbow. "We still have brownies left over."

"Oh, yeah." He moved around her so he could get into the kitchen and steal one. "My mom used to make the most amazing caramel brownies," he said. "Once she died, I tried to replicate them and discovered I'm brownie-challenged."

"I don't believe you."

"You want me to prove it? Point me to your mixer." He winked at her. "Kevin will surely appreciate your effort more than mine when he gets to the nursing center."

She pretended to let him convince her and he pulled up the recipe from the cookbooks he'd painstakingly transcribed to files he shared with Kevin on the cloud. Together they reviewed the recipe, gathered ingredients and set to work.

"Kevin told me you baked at the base in Afghanistan, too." He slipped a hand around her waist as he set Hank's plan in motion.

"It took some negotiating to get time in the kitchen but the facility manager came around."

"What did you make first?" he asked.

"Oatmeal raisin cookies."

She'd brought those a time or two on their weekends. "I bet you had carte blanche after that."

"Pretty much," she admitted with a soft smile. "It was nice to have a taste of home."

They talked more about his mom's brownies, theorizing why the recipe hadn't worked for him. Watching her, he found a sweet comfort in every elegant motion. As ingredients blended, scenting the air with rich cocoa and butter and smooth caramel, memories of his childhood flooded over him.

He should have known watching his mother's recipe come alive again would threaten to rip his heart out. Just when he felt too ragged, as if he might never be whole, Grace Ann brushed against him or shared a quiet smile.

"Altitude is a big part of baking," she said. "I had to make some adjustments with temperatures and baking times while we were in Afghanistan."

"Did you ever give treats to the locals?"

"Like a cookie exchange?" She laughed, the sound brittle but convincing. "That sort of interaction was discouraged. When we saw locals, it was generally for wellness checks. They have high expectations of Western medicine and we did what we could to live up to them."

"You mean vaccines and stuff like that?"

"Pretty much." She slid the brownies into the oven to bake. "You also have to adjust baking time and temperatures for glass pans versus nonstick."

None of those notes had been on the original recipe card. "Do girls just know this stuff intuitively?"

"That's sexist, Mr. Attorney." She stuck out her tongue. "Most of the time those directions are on the boxed mixes."

"Boys don't read directions." He kissed her nose and

then pulled out a counter stool for her as they prepared for the next phase of this farce.

"You're a mess," she teased.

"Bet you can fix me, being an amazing nurse and all."

"I'm suspended, remember?"

She sighed, for the sake of her performance or because she didn't want to do this, he wasn't sure. He massaged her tense hands. She had no idea how much she tele-graphed with her skilled hands. "You said those charges are bogus."

"Maybe 'out of context' is a better way to describe it."

"So tell me," he said.

"It's classified," she murmured. "Or it should be."

"I'm a lawyer."

"Not a lawyer with clearance," she said, her lips curv-ing.

"Just talk to me. You obviously need to get something off your chest."

She sighed again and mimed banging her head on the countertop. "I've told you they suspended me while they investigate a claim that I misused supplies."

"Right." As she talked, he rubbed her shoulders, lend-ing her support and bolstering her enormous courage. It was ridiculous that she had to go through all this for the benefit of a predator.

"There are strict rules about what supplies we can use on civilians and when," she continued. "Our resupply shipments were behind schedule and we were operat-ing on a shoestring whenever casualties came through. It's the same thing every mission deals with. We found a way to keep doing the job. Your brother really is an excellent nurse," she added, twisting to meet his gaze.

Inexplicably choked up, Derek made a small produc-tion over checking the oven timer.

"Anyway, come springtime, the days blurred together. The incident that I believe sparked the investigation came during a particularly bad week."

"Why's that?"

"The insurgents had new weapons to play with." To his surprise, her eyes filled with tears. She blinked rapidly and waved a hand in front of her face. Composed again, she continued. "They also had new targets. There was a new school in the village and the kids, boys and girls, loved it. We'd gone out for a wellness day when it was bombed."

Grace Ann's recitation made it too real. Too evil. "The school was bombed?" Derek had heard about it on the news and been worried sick about Kevin. "Was Kevin there?" he asked for the charade.

She nodded. "Yes," she whispered for the bugs listening in. "That beautiful school was whole, filled with cheerful, healthy kids one minute and a pile of dust and bloody rubble the next."

She stared at the floor, her eyes blank as she relived it. "The bodies..." Her voice faded as tears tracked slowly from her lashes, over her cheeks, to her chin. Her shoulders shook and he wondered if she'd ever talked about this with anyone. Her hands clenched. "Children were scattered everywhere. Most of them dead or close to it. Every single one of them injured. Once I could hear again, the crying was as painful as the scene."

"You must have used whatever you had on hand to help them."

"Of course we did. It's allowed in certain situations, like that one. We treated our own and the locals with the same supplies. We all did everything possible to save those kids. Danny Franklin, one of the MPs on our security team, insisted I treat the little girl in his arms—

she couldn't have been more than eight—before I treated him. Something like that is only a criminal offense on paper."

The fury in her eyes was no act. He wondered if Hank had any idea of the hornet's nest this stunt would kick over. She looked ready to take on the Riley Hunter singlehandedly. And win.

"Do you have any suspicions about who reported you?" he asked.

"It sure as hell wasn't Danny." She rubbed at the tension lining her forehead. "I'm guessing the complaint was filed by someone after my job or a pencil pusher with no compassion."

"Is that two people or one?" He should've asked which facts she planned to embellish for the trap.

"When you're over there, you realize no matter where a person was born, we're all just trying to survive this world." She wiped her damp cheeks with her sleeve. "Unless you're a jerk. The thing is, I didn't do anything wrong or illegal. The suspension is overkill. It was a crisis and I responded accordingly."

"You do have an idea about the person who complained."

She sniffled, paused to blow her nose. "Bingham said the complaint came through anonymously, with enough evidence to make it credible. Until the JAG office shows me the full report I can't know for sure who started this."

"It's just you and me," he prodded. "Spill it."

"I think it's H.B. He was the executive officer on that deployment," she said. "We butted heads from the start on that mission."

The timer went off and she went to the oven to check the brownies. They smelled exactly like his mother's. "I think you did it," he said.

"Hope so. It'd be nice to do something right. We'll know once they cool." She walked down the hallway to her bedroom. Just when he'd decided he should follow, she strolled back into view wearing loose pajama pants patterned with superhero icons and an oversize T-shirt. On a scale of zero to sexy, it should have scored a zero, but he found her off-the-chart attractive, no matter what she wore.

The weariness in her deep brown eyes broke his heart. Apparently they were staying here tonight. He started toward her and she held up a palm, a silent plea for distance. He respected that even as a small voice in his head wondered if she wouldn't be better off with a shoulder to lean on. She'd never looked as vulnerable as she had during these last few days.

If Hank's theory played out, the situation would get worse before it improved. He hated that for her. "Do you want to watch a movie?"

"Not tonight." She turned on her speakers and gentle classical music filled the room. "Is that okay?"

"Sure." Did she think he'd argue over her choice of music after she'd laid herself wide-open for the sole purpose of developing a lead?

Uncertain what else to do, he wrapped her in a hug. She was oddly still for a long moment. At last she hugged him back. "Thanks," she said against his chest, too low for any microphone to hear. "I needed that."

She leaned back and tapped his shoulder. Time for him to follow Hank's script. "Let's go out to dinner tomorrow," he blurted. A rough transition and a day earlier than Hank had requested. Too bad. Neither her brother nor the jerk listening could see the pain etched on her face. He wanted this bastard caught at the earliest opportunity. Grace Ann deserved a chance to heal and move forward.

"We could do Roscoe's and then take a burger over to your brother."

"I was thinking something a little nicer just for the two of us." He reached for his phone and brought up a search for fine dining in Bethesda.

She gave him a thumbs-up and a weak smile, encouraging to keep up the performance.

"Help me decide," he said. "What do you know about this Italian place?" He read off the first listing on his phone.

"They have an excellent reputation," she said. "And a strict dress code."

"I can get my suit cleaned in the morning." It might actually be faster to drive back home for a clean suit, but he refused to leave her alone that long.

She curled into a corner of the couch, stretching her neck from side to side. "It's a date then."

He came over and kneaded the knots in her shoulders. "It will be," he whispered against her skin.

She patted his hand and shifted away from his touch. "I'll just put the kitchen to rights."

Her withdrawal combined with everything else set his teeth on edge. She shouldn't have to relive that kind of tragedy, knowing someone who wanted to hurt her was listening. The bombing of that school had carved deep scars on her heart. She'd warned him there would be nightmares tonight. Did Hank have any idea what he was putting her through?

Their first weekend together after the unit's return, they'd gone rafting in West Virginia. She'd laughed and joked with him, soaked up sunrises and starlight, and not given him the slightest hint of the horrors she'd seen.

He didn't mind being her escape. The trade-offs had been more than worth it. She gave him time and space to have fun, no obligations or strings attached. With Grace Ann he'd never felt the pressure to provide or protect. Now that those things had been forced on them, he realized he wasn't grumpy about it. He definitely wasn't happy with the person behind the chaos, but stepping up, sticking around? All of that felt right.

"Sorry about dumping that whole thing on you," she said, rinsing the soap out of the saucepan she'd used for the caramel sauce.

Grabbing a towel, he started to dry the dishes and utensils. "I can take it."

"So I've heard." She squeezed the excess water from the sponge and dropped it into the holder to dry.

He wanted to put his lips to the shell of her ear and managed to resist the lure. "Talk to me," he said. Neither of them had ever leaned on the other this way. How could he assure her he didn't mind, that he wanted to be her sounding board any time, for the rest of time?

"I've done enough talking for tonight. Your ears may never recover." She went over and cut two brownies out of the pan. "Be honest," she said, handing him one square.

He paused, inhaling the delicious aroma first. Then, biting into the treat, the rich chocolate melted on his tongue, sweetened with the smooth, gooey caramel. He stared at her for the longest time.

"Just like home," he said when he'd finished. "Kevin will *flip out*."

"Oh, good." Her smile bloomed, the first one in hours, transforming her into the confident, glowing woman he recognized. "I can't figure out why you had so much trouble."

Love.

The word planted itself in the front of his brain and wouldn't budge. His mother had often said love made every dish taste better. His dad had teased her about plans to run off with the milkman on the rare occasions when a new recipe turned out poorly. He hadn't thought about that in years, yet he could hear them in his mind as clearly as if they were standing right here in Grace Ann's kitchen.

"Thank you." He brushed a crumb of chocolate from her lip.

With a quick nod, she scooted out of the kitchen and down the hall.

Beautiful, smart and caring. Grace Ann didn't deserve any of this mess. No one did.

Something deep inside Derek shifted and he vowed to see her safely through the crisis until she was laughing and happy again.

Chapter 8

Grace Ann had no idea how to cope with an entire day of nothing to do. Afraid of going outside and being attacked, wary of every word she spoke inside. What could she do? She started with yoga in her bedroom to make up for another restless night. This edgy, unsettled feeling was why she never talked about the village school. Who did it help?

Well, with luck it would help Hank and the investigation.

When she'd dressed for the day and finally mustered the courage to go to the kitchen for breakfast, she found another note from Derek by the coffee maker. He'd taken his suit to the dry cleaner. He'd been thoughtful enough to mark the time so she wouldn't have to wonder when to expect him back.

Her personal safe space had been violated, leaving her raw, nerves frayed. She'd never felt so small. The Riley

Hunter would know she was alone, the closest help out on the street. She hurried over and checked the lock on the back door, then the garage. As fear choked her, she confirmed the front door was locked. She slid to the floor, hands trapped between her updrawn knees. She'd wait right here until Derek rang the bell.

Everything between them would be awkward after last night. As much as she'd like to blame the madman hunting her, this was on her. She'd done the right thing, baiting the trap, but she should have found a solution that also got Derek clear of her issues and trouble.

The man had a life and she had no right to keep interfering. If he'd met a new woman recently, Grace Ann didn't want to get in the way of that, no matter how much she appreciated his steadying influence amid the turmoil swirling around her.

Aggravated with herself and most of the world in general, she sent Hank a text message, asking if he had an update.

The immediate reply was no comfort. No. Sit tight.

She didn't have the energy to dress up for a date. Correction, she didn't have the energy to go on a fake date with Derek, and tonight's outing planned couldn't be defined as anything else.

Hearing a car in the driveway, she tensed. A moment later the doorknob twisted over her head. "Grace Ann? It's me."

Derek. She scrambled to her feet and opened the door. He walked in, his hair windblown and color in his cheeks, and she wanted to keep him all to herself. Forever. Somewhere safe.

What a ridiculous thought. Derek had told her corporate law appealed to him because of the stability and low chance for drama, which made her the last candidate for him in a forever scenario. He'd implied Kevin was all the risk he wanted to manage. And here she was, keeping him hip-deep in the muck.

"Hi," he said, his warm gaze sweeping over her. He leaned in and kissed her before she remembered she shouldn't let him do that anymore.

"Hi."

He held up a tray with two tall to-go cups. "From the shop that shares the strip mall with the dry cleaner," he said.

"Thanks." From now on, she'd associate him with the scents of whipped cream and cinnamon as well as campfires and pine-laced breezes. "Hungry?" At his nod, she turned for the kitchen, hoping her nerves didn't show.

"You doing okay?"

"Peachy." Her left hip sported a riot of colorful bruises, but she was moving better after the yoga. As she cracked eggs into a bowl, she wondered where he'd met the new woman in his life. The office? Maybe the gym where he did his rock climbing training.

"I spoke with the team outside," Derek said as he carefully pried the lid from his to-go cup. "They're confident no one's been around."

She knew he'd given her that report solely for the sake of the bugs. "That's good news."

"How about we head out to Rock Creek after breakfast? We could wander the trails."

And have a conversation that would stay between them.

"Sure," she replied. Hank's team would shadow them, of course, but it would be worth it. It was a beautiful area with tree-lined trails for biking and hiking that opened up on great views. Maybe spending time doing more of what they normally did together would ease this strange pressure in her chest. For the past two years she'd been content to be his weekend pal. Why wasn't that enough anymore?

"Kevin and I talked this morning." He set her coffee to the side of the stove for her.

"How's he feeling?"

"Great. Upbeat and happy. I think you might be right about him having met someone."

Of course she was right. "He knows plenty of people in and around the hospital," she said. She added seasonings, diced peppers and cheese to the beaten eggs and poured them into a hot skillet.

"If it was a normal friend thing," Derek mused, "like he has with you, he'd just talk about her openly, wouldn't he?"

"Probably." Neither she nor Derek had told a soul about their weekend getaways. Her older brother, Matt, had gone more than fourteen years without mentioning the love of his life or their son. "In my experience, the more important a woman is to them, the less information my brothers volunteer."

Derek sighed. "It won't do me any good to ask. It's pretty clear he wants me to stay out of his life."

"Are you looking for an opinion?" she queried. This was her opening to support Kevin's request.

"Absolutely."

The immediate affirmation was unexpected. "I think he wants to make sure you're living *your* life. He knows what you did, how you sacrificed for him when your parents died. He doesn't want to be a burden to you again." She shuffled past him to get the plates out of the cabinet, managing not to tuck herself into his hard body and hang on.

"You'd think that would serve as his reminder that I'd do anything for him."

"Mmm-hmm. Have you forgotten Kevin's all grown up?"

"Well, no." He opened the drawer and pulled out forks for both of them. "Maybe," he added with a lopsided grin.

Butterflies swooped through her belly. She'd wasted so much time holding him at a distance. She'd miss him when he moved on. "He only wants what's best for you, too."

"I was clumsy as a parent," Derek admitted. "Gave him all kinds of crap when he talked about going into nursing. Told him the army wasn't the right solution."

"Hey, be nice to yourself," Grace Ann soothed. "I can't imagine balancing sibling and parent roles."

He sat down across from her at the table. "You remember meeting me. I wasn't exactly family member of the year. Sure, the service covered the cost of his education and he's seen some interesting corners of the world, but all while I'm back here worried about him getting hurt or killed."

Kevin was right that she hadn't caused the helicopter crash, but guilt swamped her again. Ducking her head, she focused on the food on her plate. They really shouldn't be talking about this here. Either one of them could say something that inspired their listener. Unfortunately, she couldn't cut him off without raising more suspicion or losing her chance to hear this piece of his life's puzzle.

"Families play a big role in army life," she said stiffly. "Support is vital."

"I've heard that," he said. The low chuckle that followed sent a delicious shiver over her skin.

Mildly embarrassed, she took a sip of her latte. Of course he'd heard that litany before. "Not trying to bore you. In the nursing corps we see the interaction more directly and more frequently than other units. Believe me, if Kevin didn't understand the pressure on you before, he does now."

Derek tapped his fork to his plate. "He asked you to talk to me, didn't he?"

"Yes." This conversation was killing her already minimal appetite. "At risk of overstepping, you are his hero for the way you stepped up when you were kids. He's afraid you'll put your life on hold all over again, that's all."

He tucked into his eggs, closing his eyes in appreciation. "First, this is amazing."

"Glad you like it."

"And second, how do I support Kevin if I leave?"

She took a bite and swallowed to buy time. "He has resources and a network of friends. No one in our unit will let him flounder. He wants you to visit, sure, but he wants you to go home."

Derek arched an eyebrow. "Why?"

Pinned by that unrelenting gaze, the truth spilled out. "He thinks you met someone. Someone awesome, to use his words. Kevin only wants you to be happy."

"What?" His expression blank, his fork hit the plate with a clatter.

Her heart sank. "You heard me." Exasperation inched closer to irritation. "He made me promise to send you home so you don't miss your chance with her."

Derek's silent shock was better than any excuse he could offer. She poked at the remainder of her breakfast and sipped the latte that didn't taste so sweet anymore.

As if the conversation wasn't bad enough, they both

knew someone was listening in. Giving up on the food, she carried her half-eaten breakfast into the kitchen and scraped the leftovers into a container for later.

For tomorrow, when she was alone again because Derek had come to his senses and returned to the new woman. A woman who wasn't sitting around waiting for a madman to attack.

"You cooked. I'll clean," Derek said, crowding her.

"Super." She gave in and retreated to her bedroom to change into something better for a hike along Rock Creek.

Derek hadn't denied that he'd met someone new. Better to have that out in the open. Her stomach cramped and she had to breathe through her nose to keep from tossing up her breakfast.

As she tied her shoes, her new cell phone hummed. Her mother's face popped up on the screen. Oh, she just couldn't. Not right now. Declining the call, she zipped the device into her pocket. This could very well be her last casual hike with Derek and she wouldn't let anything spoil it. Not even her unruly emotions. They'd agreed from the start that when it was over, they'd part as friends. She couldn't stain every lovely time they'd shared by reneging.

Visiting Rock Creek had been an excellent suggestion. The fresh air and sunshine, the distance from home and hospitals, calmed her inside and out. The water chattering along in the creek, trees swaying across a clear sky, blotted out the ghosts and gruesome images that had given her such a restless night.

"Where's your favorite place to be?" she asked.

They'd climbed out to sit in the warm light splashing across a boulder that jutted out into the creek. Birds sang nearby and puffy white clouds drifted across the wide blue sky as the creek tumbled around them. When he didn't reply, she turned and found him staring at her, his sunglasses pushed up into his hair.

"It changes," he said. "What about you?"

"Asheville, North Carolina, comes to mind." They'd never been there together. "We went as a family the first time, when Dad was stationed at Fort Bragg. I think my sister was only a year old. There was this ice cream parlor that had the best milkshakes. When I was stationed at Bragg I'd drive over whenever I had the chance."

"The ice cream place is still there?"

"It is." She almost suggested they go on his next free weekend and caught herself in time to prevent more embarrassing awkwardness.

"You like being alone more than anyone I've ever met," Derek said.

"If you ever meet my brothers you'll understand," she replied. Of course that wouldn't happen, now that he had someone else.

"We've rarely talked about family. Other than Kevin," he said. "I hope you didn't think I wasn't interested."

But that was exactly where they'd drawn the line. Together. "I thought we didn't want to do that," she reminded him. "We said we'd keep things friendly."

"With benefits," he finished. "I remember." He leaned forward, propping his elbows on his knees, his eyebrows knitting as he watched the creek flow by.

She turned her attention to the happy song of a bird perched on a branch on the other side of the creek, refusing to give voice to the questions burning on her tongue. Let *him* explain the new special someone in his life. After breakfast, there was no denying their arrangement was over. She just had to get through a pretend date and then they could go their separate ways.

His continued silence made her twitchy. She stood up to move on down the trail.

He stood as well and caught her hand. She twisted to get free, but he didn't release her. She looked at everything but his face, knowing she'd cry if he said they were done while holding her.

"Grace Ann, listen. My brother misunderstood. I haven't met anyone new."

"It's not really my business, is it?" She focused on that contented bird as heat scorched her cheeks.

"I would've said this over breakfast, but I couldn't. Not while someone else was listening in. Cowardly, I know, after what you did last night."

Her heart kicked at the compliment and then she braced for the inevitable breakup. This was turning out to be one of the worst weeks of her life. At least in Afghanistan, it wasn't a personal friend who ripped out her heart.

"I went through my phone history trying to figure out what put the idea in Kevin's head," he said. "The last time he couldn't reach me, I was out with you."

"That wasn't recent." Her optimistic heart gave another kick. Maybe they weren't done.

"Six weeks ago." He squeezed her hands. "Want to see my phone?"

"Of course not. I trust you." More than she trusted most people. "I wondered why you hadn't mentioned it." She relaxed, her fingers weaving through his. "So our arrangement still works."

"Does it?"

"What am I missing?" she asked, wary all over again.

He laughed and, drawing her close, gave her a kiss that left her breathless. "Nothing. Everything. However we started, I'd like to make it more."

"More what?"

"Exclusive," he said with far more patience than she deserved.

She frowned, studying him. His blue eyes were serious, but it seemed like his mouth might break into a grin any second. "You and me, exclusive?"

"Yes." He rubbed her shoulder. "Grace Ann, you aren't this dense."

Her heart swelled, all too happy with the notion of more time with Derek. "What if this is a stress response? It happens," she added in a rush when his gaze narrowed.

"Guess we'll find out soon enough if I'm only here for the brownies and excitement."

Her mouth dropped open.

"That's the best you've got?" he asked, slipping an arm around her waist.

"What do you want to hear?" She didn't want to scare him off by stating the obvious ways they were a bad match for the long-term. Being career military pretty much embodied all the unpredictable drama Derek didn't want in his life. Having come to terms with his brother's choice didn't mean he was eager to be listed on another soldier's emergency contact form.

And all of that was jumping too far ahead. He hadn't said he loved her, he hadn't proposed, he'd simply said he wanted to be exclusive.

He brushed her bangs away from her eyes. "I'd like to hear you'll think about it."

Answer or not, she'd be hard-pressed to think about anything else. It was a delicious relief. Pressing up onto her toes, she kissed him. "I'm happy to be your exclusive someone."

"Someone awesome," he corrected, and sent her heart soaring.

* * *

The day had passed in a blur after they'd cleared the air about the "someone awesome" in his life. Grace Ann definitely met that definition and he was glad they weren't wasting any more time.

When she'd stepped out of her bedroom dressed for their date, they'd just stared at each other. The only formal wear he'd seen her in was her army mess dress uniform, and that had only been in pictures. She'd looked amazing, but not exactly sexy and not at all approachable.

Tonight she was both. Her dress reminded him of an orange Dreamsicle, the lightweight layers flowing down over her trim body from a high collar that hid her throat and left her arms bare, her sheer shawl looped over the strap of her purse. The hem of the dress swirled around her knees and all he could think about was skimming his hands underneath the flowing fabric. Dangerous territory, considering they were supposed to be the cheese in Hank's trap for the rats who had planted the bugs in her house.

"Stay put," Derek said, pulling to a stop at the valet stand. "It's our first real date." He hopped out of the driver's seat and came around to her side. He popped open an umbrella against the light rain before he opened her door.

Through text messages he and Grace Ann had learned what Hank expected of them on this working date. Knowing there was an undercover team in the area helped him relax. Derek tried to spot them as they walked to the restaurant.

"If you see them, they're not doing their job right," she murmured.

He smiled, holding her close under the shelter of the

umbrella, though it was illogical to think her frothy, sherbet-colored dress would dissolve under a few raindrops. Inside, they were seated quickly and their water was poured. As they chose wine and an appetizer, he smoothed his tie.

"I'm nervous," he admitted.

"Makes two of us." Her smile took on a wicked edge. "You've seen me at my worst. It feels weird to share my best with you after the fact."

"Have I told you you're beautiful?"

She batted her eyelashes. "I had no idea you were so susceptible to a pretty dress, Mr. Sayer."

"Guilty as charged."

"If we're confessing, you should know I find you irresistible in a suit."

"I'm taking notes." He wagged his eyebrows and made her laugh.

"It's nice to be here. With you," she said as the comfortable laughter faded. "Normal."

"Are we normal?" He hadn't made a habit of studying relationships, but it seemed like theirs was far from typical.

"Oh, probably not. It is nice to pretend for an evening."

They fell into an easy conversation, the topics flowing and spilling into one after another, at last chatting freely like the friends they were. The clothing was different, the atmosphere more posh, but everything between them felt settled. Perfect.

He watched the shadows of stress fall away as she relaxed. Her hands were still, her gaze bright and steady. It made him feel like a superhero, that he could create that kind of safe space for her. He'd treasure this evening for years to come, despite knowing it was all part of an investigation scheme.

"I hope you don't mind that I changed the reservation at the last minute," he said as they waited for a dessert sampler to share.

"As long as you didn't leave Hank in the dark."

It had been Hank's idea, but Derek didn't mention that detail. "We talked." The investigation for the Riley Hunter wasn't his focus; Grace Ann was. It was strange to be attempting a first date in the midst of a potentially life-threating situation.

"Your mind is wandering," she said. "Everything okay?"

"Absolutely." He reached across the table and covered her hand with his.

"Tell that to your eyebrows."

"Pardon me?"

She tapped the space just above her nose. "You get a divot here when you're thinking deep thoughts."

He'd often been accused of being angry when he was thinking hard on something. He rubbed at the spot she'd indicated. "My days and yours are so different," he said, searching for a good way to put his thoughts into words that wouldn't offend her or unravel the progress they'd made.

"We've been so good at avoiding talk about work."

"And I see that as my loss," he replied. "Corporate law is compelling, but rarely dangerous and hardly life-affirming. Not like working in hospitals."

She cocked her head, her gaze narrowed. "You hate hospitals."

"When did I ever say that?"

She circled her finger at him. "I know your kind," she teased. "Skittish and uncomfortable."

"With good reason," he interjected.

"Exactly what I was about to say." She traced the bones of his hand, the feeling of her thumb a cool contrast to the warmth in her eyes.

"My point," he began again, determined to make his thoughts clear, "is that I might have misgivings about the medical field, but I do respect what you do and how you do it."

Her lips opened and closed again as she stared at him. "Where is this coming from?" she asked.

He was saved from answering as the dessert sampler was served. There was a golden cake topped with berries and cream, a dark chocolate dome striped with white chocolate and dusted with cocoa powder, and a cylinder of cheesecake in a puddle of toffee-colored sauce.

Watching her taste each delectable treat made his mouth water for his next taste of her.

"We should figure out how to see each other more," he said with zero finesse.

Her dark eyebrows flexed into a frown that melted as she took another bite of the cheesecake. "We only live an hour apart." She licked her lips. "It's the crazy schedules that pose a problem."

"What if we tried for a long weekend every couple of weeks?" Assuming he could last that long without seeing her. "Your schedule might be crazy," he said. "I'm more flexible." And he would happily flex whatever he needed to be with her. "I can come to you."

Her eyebrows arched. "You want to let people know we're dating?"

"I'd rather not send out formal announcements, but I'd like to tell Kevin and my assistant. That way she'll stop trying to set me up with her friends."

"She does that?"

"She *tries*." He scooped up a berry and a bite of the cake.

"If Kevin knows, the unit will know," she said.

Why was she so cautious? He'd brought it up so they could sort out the next steps with the same candid openness they'd used the first time around. Her lip caught in her teeth, she cracked the dome on the chocolate dessert and revealed a spongy cake and a layer of creamy sauce. The scents of almonds and vanilla filled the air between them.

"Would that be a problem?"

She shook her head and caught him watching as she licked chocolate from her spoon. "In the interest of transparency, you should know that my life's a little messed up at the moment."

He burst out laughing, making heads turn their way. "You have a gift for understatement."

"One of many hidden talents."

He wanted to unveil every last one of them. "For the record, your messed-up life doesn't scare me." It never should have.

"Good to know." She dug into the cheesecake tower and sighed. "As long as you realize it might not be the best time to take this step."

"Let me get this straight," he said with mock severity. "You're saying you don't want to start dating while we're living together."

"Precisely." She grinned, a smudge of whipped cream highlighting the corner of her mouth.

His body coiled to spring, he managed to check himself before he leaned over and licked it away. When they polished off the dessert sampler, he paid the check and they walked through the rain toward the valet stand to claim his car.

Under the umbrella it was easy to pretend they were

alone, though people moved all around them. "Kevin told me you went into nursing to be like your mom," he ventured. It was a safer topic than the others on his mind. Like how quickly he could get his hands under that dress.

"Her career is nearly as impressive as my dad's within army circles." She toyed with the fringe on her shawl. "It's been a lot to live up to, but she'd be the first to tell you I joined the Army Nurse Corps for my own reasons."

"Which were?" Utterly invested in the reply, he caught the shiver that rippled over her skin.

"Helping people. All facets of medicine fascinate me. The army is always making advancements to science and health, and I didn't have the patience to become a doctor."

"I've noticed at formal events you have all kinds of insignia on your uniform."

"You've noticed my uniform?" She looked up at him, eyes wide with disbelief.

Someone bumped into her and then hurried down the street as the valet line advanced. Derek felt her tense up, every muscle battle-ready in the blink of an eye.

"Easy," he said. "He was rude, that's all."

Although she relaxed a fraction, she shifted to get a better look at the man rushing down the street. "He looks like—"

Whatever she might have said was interrupted by a low, deafening boom. The sound, bigger than anything he'd ever heard before, hurt his ears and underscored sudden garish light that turned a rainy night into day. An indescribable pressure followed, pushing him off his feet even as he tried to shelter Grace Ann. Blown down with him, she tucked herself close, the umbrella long gone.

A blast of heat swelled, rolling over them and singeing the air. He opened his eyes, expecting to see the rain turn to steam. He heard car tires and brakes squealing in the street and metal crunching while all around them, people screamed or cried.

Grace Ann gripped his lapels and gave him a shake. "Derek!" Ears ringing, rain in his eyes, he struggled to see her clearly. "Derek, are you hurt?"

"No. Are you?"

"It was a bomb." He saw the words more than heard them. She released his coat, brushing dust from his hair and off his shoulders. Her deft hands cruised over him with an expert, silent assessment. "You're okay," she murmured over and over.

He stilled her hands and tipped up her face to meet her gaze. "*We're* okay."

It was a miracle. On the opposite corner, the landscaping between a restaurant window and the edge of the street was ablaze. People were sprawled everywhere in various states of distress. He counted three cars tangled in the intersection and his stomach lurched in sympathy. How many families would be forever changed tonight?

"Call 911," she said, her voice brisk. "Report an explosion, unknown source." She moved into action, directing people without injuries to clear aside or assist those who were suffering.

Derek stayed with her while he reported the situation to the dispatcher on the other end of the line. Whenever his vision wavered or his knees wanted to give out, he focused on Grace Ann, rather than shocked faces and injured bodies.

Rain had soaked through her dress, the fabric clinging to her skin as she dealt with each victim one by one. The protective detail had closed ranks around them, but she put them to work rather than leave the scene as they requested. Derek was in awe, watching her assess, treat and shout instructions before shifting her attention to the next person in crisis.

This was Grace Ann in her element, doing what she was meant to do.

First responders flooded in. Firefighters and paramedics helped with those trapped in cars. Police directed crowds of onlookers and cordoned off the area. Person by person, Grace Ann kept working her way toward the origin of the explosion as if she were also here in uniform.

Her dress, torn and smeared with grime and debris, was trashed. Both her shawl and his tie had been used for tourniquets; his jacket was somewhere behind him, serving as a blanket for a young man in shock with a broken leg.

Suddenly, Grace Ann cried out in anguish, her calm, detached authority shattered. "It's H.B." She pressed her fingers to the man's throat. "He's alive," she stated. "Barely."

"Isn't he—"

"Your belt," she demanded, hand out. "Damn it. He walked right into it."

Derek hurried to comply. He would have sworn he was the man who'd bumped her just before the blast. "He's from your unit, right?"

"Yes. The commander's assistant. Get someone over here now."

Protection detail or not, he wouldn't leave her alone in this chaos. Looking around, he couldn't tell friend from potential foe. There had been too many close calls for her already, including this one.

This time his knees gave out and he dropped to the ground beside her. His original reservation had been for the window table at this restaurant. He waved and caught the attention of a police officer, who in turn scrambled to find a paramedic. Within minutes the man from her unit was being prepped for transport.

Derek helped Grace Ann to her feet. "Let's get you home."

Her eyes were red-rimmed from the smoke and debris, her face and hands smudged with dirt and soot and far worse. He couldn't think about the "worse." They both needed a shower and several hours to rest and recover.

"This," she muttered. "This is war."

"What did you say?"

"People sometimes ask what it's like." He knew her eyes, glassy now, were seeing streets on the other side of the world. "This is pretty close."

And the terror had struck right here at home. Her sadness was a palpable force blanketing her, pressing him away. He fought it, chafing her arms to warm her up. "I'm taking you home," he said, waiting for the words to click.

"Hospital," she countered. "I should be there for H.B."

Compromising was the heart of his career. "I'll take you to the hospital after we clean up and change clothes at your place." He cut off the expected protest. "Caregivers need care, too."

"Read that in a book?"

"No," he said. "Learned it firsthand."

"That was rude." A tear rolled down her cheek, followed by another. "I'm sorry." The dam broke in a rush and she dropped her head to his chest, letting it all pour out.

"You saved people tonight, sweetheart. You kept families whole," he said.

Her shoulders shook as she fought her demons, past

and present. He gave her the only thing he had left: himself. He turned her away from a nearby news crew and held on while she wept.

Although the device had gone off exactly as planned, he was furious. His inside man had planted the bomb in the wrong place. The explosion had created tremendous chaos, yet Grace Ann Riley had been neither maimed nor killed. Worse still, from every angle he saw on the news, she hadn't suffered a public breakdown.

He wanted more than tears. He wanted her in pieces, emotionally and physically.

Turning off the television, he set the remote aside. The boyfriend was propping her up. Damn it. How had they missed that?

Since returning to his compound, he'd tasked a new team with digging into Derek Sayer. The man seemingly had nothing better to do than get in the way. He had some intel from the bugs, but not enough to understand how to turn the man against her.

He turned up the volume on the television, slightly mollified to hear her voice crack as she told a reporter how devastated she was by the explosion and the near death of another member of her precious unit.

If the injuries didn't kill his inside man by morning, a local hire would finish him off. The weasel had been too jittery the last time they spoke. The man had balked and argued about layering in more details on the case they'd fabricated against Grace Ann.

He didn't tolerate questions or incompetence from the peanut gallery.

At the windows overlooking the canyon beyond his office, he took a moment to appreciate being home. Every move he made was well-hidden and protected.

Should the investigators find him, they'd never get close enough to make an arrest until he was ready for that confrontation.

In a contrary mood, he returned to his desk and worked through the sound files until he found a particular bit of the recording he thought the general would enjoy.

Editing it for maximum impact, he sent the clip as an email attachment.

An evil smile twisting his face, he wondered how difficult it would be to get devices planted in their fancy new beach house. It was a question he'd ask of the man he'd handpicked to infiltrate the small community and move on the general when the time came.

Chapter 9

Sitting next to Derek in the waiting room, Grace Ann slowly adjusted to the cold. Not the shivering sort of cold from the rainy spring night. This was the bone-deep cold of being too late, the icy, unforgiving bite of not having done enough. If H.B. died, his would be one more face haunting her nightmares.

Two men from her unit now bore injuries that traced back to this vicious crusade against her dad. It was more stress and grief than a stateside unit should have to bear. She peered around the surgical waiting room, where nearly everyone from their unit waited for an update on H.B.

She had no recollection of Derek taking them away from the scene. The drive was a complete blank in her mind. She vaguely recalled him undressing her and nudging her into the shower, washing her hair, scrubbing the stains from her hands. He'd applied ointment to their minor scrapes and scratches before he helped her into the clothes she wore now.

He'd handled everything while her mind was stuck in a private hell where she reviewed each treatment and assessment in slow motion, weighing her split-second decisions with the benefit of time and hindsight. What had happened to the protective detail? Who else had been injured because they were too close to her? Had she saved anyone?

"Hang in there," Derek whispered. His arm was warm across her shoulders. "We'll get through."

Because she wanted to let him take her far away, she pushed to her feet and paced to the windows on the other side of the room. On the rain-soaked street below, cars moved like glittering toys under a heavy black-velvet sky. Her memories cast a hazy filter over the peaceful scene below as she replayed the explosion time and again from the moment she'd been bumped to the moment the street corner had seemingly burst apart.

It had been a bomb, she was sure. Not just a flashback, though she understood her experiences overseas exacerbated this post-event disconnect in her mind and heart. The pressure, the sound, the flash of light and the resulting injuries were consistent with a precisely measured detonation.

How had such a thing even happened here, practically in the shadow of Walter Reed, where so many people committed themselves to saving men and women injured in the line of duty?

Where had H.B. been rushing to when he'd bumped her? Being in such a hurry had put him almost on top of the explosion. Maybe if she'd called out and exchanged a friendly word they wouldn't be here, waiting and praying for him to pull through.

"How are you holding up, Major Riley?"

Grace Ann looked away from the street to greet Bingham. Despite the PT uniform and running shoes, the commander's authority was on full display.

"I'm fine, ma'am, thank you." She stood here on her own, breathing unassisted, with only minor scrapes and a few more bruises to add to the current count. The guilt grew with every minute, clawing at her from the inside.

"The doctor who looked you over when you came in told me the same thing. I'm hearing one account after another about your heroism out there," Bingham said.

The suspension flashed to the front of Grace Ann's mind. Her actions shouldn't pose a legal problem, since she'd administered life-saving measures during a crisis. She'd have to go through a battery of tests to make sure she didn't contract any diseases, since gloves hadn't been available. "I only did what I could," she said. "Is it a problem for you if I'm here?"

"Absolutely not. You're part of our team."

The words were a balm over the harsh sting of guilt. "Thank you."

"I'd feel better if you let one of the doctors examine you." She aimed a pointed look at Grace Ann's hands.

Expecting to see an open wound, Grace Ann discovered her hands were locked in a white-knuckled grasp. With an effort, she parted them and tucked them into the pockets of her jacket. "It's a habit when I worry."

"Perfectly natural when good friends are involved."

Grace Ann didn't consider H.B. much of a friend, but as part of the unit, he was family. "I saw him just before all hell broke loose," she said. "He was running straight into danger. We just didn't know it."

Bingham's eyes were brimming with compassion. "Bad things happen every day. All we can do is respond with our best effort. You surely showed your best out there tonight. Go home now and sleep it off."

"Is that an order?"

"If it needs to be," Bingham replied. "I'll make sure you get every update."

"Thank you, ma'am." Turning, she crossed the room. "I'm being sent home," she said to Derek.

"Are you okay with that?"

"Yes." She didn't trust herself to say more without breaking into a tantrum or dissolving into tears.

"Then we'll go." He took her hand as they walked out. "Have you ever wanted to be a personal assistant?" he asked as they waited for the elevator to arrive.

She frowned, trying to put the question into context. "Not really, why?"

"Me neither." He handed her his phone. "Apparently Hank gave my number to everyone in your family." They stepped into the elevator. "They've been grilling me about the incident."

She stared up at the ceiling and counted to ten, then twenty before looking at his phone. "Nosiness is one of the lesser-known side effects of being a Riley," she said, skimming through the surplus of text messages and missed phone calls. It seemed every second or third one had a link to a news outlet reporting the incident. "Good grief, why didn't they just call me?"

"I've checked a couple of those links," he said. "The reporters make it sound like you're the one in surgery."

She choked on a bitter laugh. "No surprise it made national news." She sighed as they walked out of the hospital toward the parking area. "I'll start responding as soon as we're home."

"Start now if you want."

The idea made her stomach twist. It would be easy

to hit Reply and reassure her siblings via text messages. "Hank knows I'm fine, and he should be passing that along."

"They want to hear your voice," Derek said. "I'm guessing," he added when she glared at him. "At your place you run the risk of being overheard."

With everything else on her mind, she'd forgotten her house was bugged. "Thanks for the reminder." She sent a text message to Matt, promising to call tomorrow. Copying the message, she pasted it into replies to each of her younger siblings, her parents, and a few aunts, uncles and cousins.

"That should hold them until morning." At his car, she paused when he opened the passenger door for her. "You've been wonderful. Thank you." She brushed her lips across his.

He angled his mouth and the heady contact burned through the deep, aching cold. "You did all the tough stuff," he murmured, his lips teasing the sensitive shell of her ear.

"Derek?"

"Mmm?"

"Take me anywhere but home." What she wanted to do with Derek, she didn't want anyone overhearing.

"You're sure?"

"If you mention one word about anything other than how much you want me, I will not be responsible for my actions."

His sandy eyebrows arched, then settled back as he considered her. "One condition."

She waited.

"Wherever we go, once you fall asleep, you'll let yourself sleep until you wake up on your own. No alarms. No phones."

"Deal." She hadn't slept more than a few hours straight in months. At home, when she woke up from a nightmare, she'd read a book or magazine until she fell back to sleep. Tonight, she'd have Derek to distract her.

She felt better already.

Derek woke for the second time as the sun slanted through the curtains of the floor-to-ceiling hotel windows. While Grace Ann continued to sleep, he handled a few details from the office through the limited capabilities of his phone. His assistant claimed calls had been coming in all night with interview requests from various news networks.

Though he'd been tempted to make a run to her house for his laptop or an overnight bag, he refused to take a chance that she'd either wake up alone and disoriented or have another nightmare while he was out.

They'd worn each other out, burning off the residual adrenaline from the crisis as well as affirming their survival. He'd never met a woman who shared passion, wild and tender, so openly. She'd been glorious, demanding and oh so generous as they'd loved each other into a beautiful exhaustion.

Having her curl into him and sleep with such trust had been an incredible gift he treasured. A gift that confirmed he was on the right track with his plan to move their casual relationship into something strong and permanent.

As much as he'd hated her having to perform for those listening devices in her home, the conversation had given him valuable insight and fair warning. When the nightmare gripped her and the thrashing startled him awake, he'd taken a few hard kicks and dodged a wide-flung arm. When he'd turned on the light, the tears on her cheeks gutted him. He hadn't seen anything so heartbreaking since Kevin had cried in his sleep as a kid, grieving their parents.

Unable to rouse her, he'd pulled the sheets free of her legs and tucked her close to his side. Soothing her with soft words and gentle, repetitive strokes down her spine, he'd kept watch until her body finally relaxed.

Losing sleep didn't bother him. He was glad to do something truly helpful for this independent and capable woman. He suspected Grace Ann had lost more than her share of sleep to the stresses of her last deployment and the recent events.

The bruising on her hip had turned into a mosaic of purples, blues and greens, and more colorful marks would soon stain her hands along with the scrapes she'd picked up while treating victims. At least the finger-shaped stains on her neck were fading.

Yes, he understood she'd been targeted as some vengeful effort against her dad but last night had really driven home the point that the world wasn't as stable and drama-free as he imagined. Danger and jeopardy were simply a matter of degrees. Having a brother in the military meant he'd kept track of trouble in the areas where he thought Kevin would be assigned. It was so easy to be complacent, to take stateside risks and first responders for granted.

His stomach woke him around nine. This time, he slipped out of bed and showered, then ordered a hearty breakfast for two while he dressed. Grace Ann slept on. The food arrived and he downed a little more than half of everything on the tray, letting her sleep. Noon came and went as she continued to sleep, sprawled across the king-size bed.

With nothing but time, he called his brother to check in.

"About time. Are you okay?" Kevin demanded. "You and Grace Ann are all over the news."

"I'm fine. It was a long night." His gaze cruised over Grace Ann and he wished he'd just climbed back into bed with her.

"Looks like," Kevin agreed, the urgency in his voice subsiding. "They're making it sound like the two of you saved the entire city."

"She did all the tough stuff," he said.

"That's Major Riley." Kevin snorted. "I'm glad you got out of there when you did."

Immediately on edge, Derek turned on the television. "What do you mean?" He muted the sound as he surfed through the channels. Sure enough, last night's tragedy was playing on all the major news networks, along with a ticker giving updates. It seemed no one had claimed responsibility.

"The way she was using your clothing, you would've been naked in another few minutes."

"Right." Leave it to Kevin to get snarky.

The longer Derek watched, the more he wondered who'd caught so many close-ups and details of Grace Ann working triage. No wonder her family had been hounding him for more information. He'd shared the hotel details with Hank last night. Hank, in turn, had verified the surveillance team was still on the house and no further trouble had been noted in the neighborhood.

"How is she coping?" Kevin asked.

"She's sleeping it off," Derek replied. "She told me it looked like war."

"It does." Kevin's voice was as somber as Derek had ever heard it.

He stepped out onto the balcony so his conversation wouldn't wake Grace Ann. "You never talk about what you've seen."

"Not with you," Kevin said.

A pang of regret struck Derek's heart. "I suppose I deserve that."

"Not if you're taking it as an insult," Kevin said. "I know you didn't want me going into the army, but if I hadn't you never would've done anything for yourself."

"Bull."

Kevin scoffed. "Deny it if that gets you through the night. That sibling connection goes two ways. I know how you think."

Derek bristled, not in the mood to argue. "Let's say you're right, *little* brother." He added emphasis for the annoyance factor. "It isn't easy for me to sit at home and wait for a chaplain to show up when you're all gung ho about working in a war zone."

"You haven't opened the door to a chaplain yet."

"You're right. That call about crashing helicopters was so much better."

"Stop," Kevin snapped. "I'm alive."

"A fact that usually makes me happy," Derek replied, his tone dry, as if being alone in the world didn't terrify him. "Get to the point. Why don't you talk about this stuff with me?"

"Because I love you," Kevin replied. "My unit helps me with the worst of it. Besides, you lost enough sleep over me when I was a kid."

Derek had to clear the emotion out of his throat. "Have you heard anything on Major Bartles?"

"They got him stabilized. He's in the burn unit, sedated. I heard he was right on top of the blast."

"Grace Ann found him there," Derek confirmed. "She almost lost it when she recognized him."

"I bet. From the update this morning, I got the impression he wouldn't have lived without her help at the scene. Remind her of that."

"I will," Derek promised.

"Listen," Kevin said. "Do what you can to keep Grace Ann away from the spotlight until this media storm blows over."

Derek nearly laughed. Who could keep Grace Ann from doing whatever she pleased? "Should I find floppy hats and sunglasses to disguise both of us?"

"Not a bad plan, actually."

"Be serious."

"I am," Kevin insisted. "Trust me on this, the last thing she needs on top of the suspension is to be in the spotlight, good or bad."

"All right," Derek assured him. He considered the performance Grace Ann had given for the bugs in her house and the nightmare he'd helped with earlier. "The office was prepared for me to keep working remotely. We'll stop in and see you later."

"No." Kevin groaned. "Aren't you listening? Take her out for a hike or something. Somewhere with no cell service."

"We'll figure it out," Derek hedged. He really should explain that he and Grace Ann were more than acquaintances.

"It's a great idea," Kevin gushed. "You're both into that stuff. She went rafting or something a couple weeks back and came back happier than I'd seen her in ages."

Six weeks ago, Derek mentally corrected his brother. "Really?"

"Yes. Our last deployment wasn't a cakewalk. It was great to finally see her more like her normal self."

Derek glanced over his shoulder toward the bedroom. "I guess if I can't do anything for you right now, I might as well help out your friend."

"She's the best, man. And she really needs a friend who isn't in the military."

The comment caught Derek's attention. "Care to elaborate on that?"

"Her whole family is in one branch or another. It's a lot to live up to. Just keep her out of here. The investigator working her suspension set an appointment to interview me this afternoon."

"What time?"

"Stay out of it, Derek. She needs you more than I do."

"Fine." Derek made a mental note to speak with Hank. "Remember you have rights, even as a witness."

Kevin snorted. "Whoever put this in motion has no idea what they started. Grace Ann is the best of us. I won't let anyone twist up my statement. Besides, I'm fairly sure no one believes they can railroad a Riley."

"Call if you change your mind."

"I won't," Kevin promised.

"If anything—"

"I know how to reach you," Kevin interrupted. "Be careful."

"All right." He ended the call and just soaked up the sunshine pouring over the balcony. Maybe he *should* take Grace Ann out of reach of cell phones before anything else went wrong.

"You weren't kidding about letting me sleep."

Turning at the sound of her voice, he leaned back against the rail, hoping she'd walk out to join him. Her hair mussed from his hands as much as from sleep and her cheeks rosy, she looked positively delectable wrapped in the fluffy hotel robe. "You needed the rest."

"Uh-huh." She seemed almost shy as she stood there in the balcony doorway.

"I ordered breakfast. It's gone cold by now."

"Bacon?" Her eyes lit up when he nodded. "Cold bacon is still bacon."

He laughed. "True."

She abandoned him without so much as a good-morning kiss for the food set out on the table. "There is a microwave."

"I forgot," she said, taking a big bite of bacon.

He removed the covers from the platter and she put seasoned potatoes and more bacon on a plate and heated it up, then added some of the scrambled eggs before giving it a second zap.

"We could order something fresh," he suggested.

"Too hungry to wait." A blush tinted her skin, rising from her collarbones to the tips of her ears.

He poured lukewarm coffee into a mug and heated that in the microwave for her as well. He offered her the pitcher of cream he'd tucked in the mini fridge. So far she hadn't noticed the story playing silently on the television. "Feeling better?"

"A little." She downed another slice of bacon. "More than a little," she amended. "Thank you for keeping watch."

"Anytime." He managed to get the television turned off before she noticed the story. "I just got off the phone with Kevin," he said. "Sounds like he's doing great."

"And H.B.?"

"Kevin says he's stable." That was all Derek wanted

to share right now. Rest was a good start, but food without any added stress would help more. "He suggested I take you away for a nature retreat. He tells me you like outdoor getaways."

She looked up at him, her eyes crinkling at the corners with suppressed laughter. "And you said?"

"I told him I'd think about it." She laughed, the bright sound as welcome as the sunshine. She looked as happy here as she'd been on their last trip. Happier, maybe. "You should sleep long hours more often," he teased.

"Not usually part of the job description." She poked at another bite of her breakfast. "I had a nightmare last night, didn't I?"

"You got through it," he said. "And rested well after."

"Guess so." She sipped her coffee. "Thanks."

"I'm glad I was here for you." Would she try to push him away again, or was she ready to give dating a try?

As if she'd read his mind, she said, "My job is bound to get in the way."

"It doesn't have to." He counted it a positive step forward that she'd brought it up. He poured himself another cup of coffee, currently the best fortification available. "Are you ready to be viewed as a couple?" he asked.

"We were dressed up and together at dinner last night," she replied. "We were together at the hospital. I think the cat's out of the bag."

Definitely. "Kevin said our faces are all over the news this morning. We're being touted as heroes."

She set her coffee aside. "Cell phones and street cams, too."

"Yes." Distress pinched her features. He wished he could snap his fingers and make it all go away. "There are pictures and videos from bystanders and reporters. I think denying we know each other would be a hard sell."

"Of course we know each other." She put the cover over her plate and traced the stitching on the belt of the robe with her fingers. "You've met everyone in the unit by now."

"Meeting them is different than going on a date. And I haven't handed over my tie, jacket and belt on the command of everyone in the unit."

"That's just who you are," she said. "You step up."

Her words surprised him. He didn't think he was really the person she believed he was. Yes, he'd stepped up when his brother needed him. That was different. Personal. He and Kevin were the only family left to each other.

If he'd been alone on that corner last night, he wouldn't have done anything to earn the hero label. "Last night was all you," he said. "I was just a bystander who happened to be wearing the right clothing when you needed it."

She tilted her face up, her lips pursed in a tempting rosebud as she studied him. "I disagree."

"I can't change your mind." Uncomfortable with the topic, he returned to the real issue. "Kevin pretty much ordered me to keep you out of the public eye for a few days."

"That's probably best," she said after a moment. "I'm surprised Bingham hasn't called to remind me not to give a statement or comment."

"We turned off your phone," he said. "But I'm sure she trusts you to remember that on your own." Determined to clear all doubt, he added, "Crisis or not, I have no problem being viewed as your boyfriend or, ah, whatever you'd like to call it."

Her lips twitched. "'Boyfriend' is okay, but you take umbrage at being called a hero?"

"Yes." He sat down in the chair next to hers, wishing he didn't have to give her this news as well. "Kevin also told me an investigator is taking his statement this afternoon about the school explosion."

She stared up at the ceiling and sighed. "You should be there for him."

"He can handle it," Derek replied. "In fact, he told me flat-out not to show up."

She stood up and pressed a hand to her belly, her face pale.

"Grace Ann?" Damn it, she was pushing him away again. "Talk to me."

"I'm fine." Lips clamped together, she shook her head. "I just need a minute. Let me get a shower and talk with Hank. He and I will take it from there."

He didn't care for the finality in her tone. "I beg your pardon?"

"This is an army issue," she snapped. "If Hank says I should go home and lock the doors, I'll do it." She pushed a hand through her hair. "If he tells me to go stay with Mom and Dad or sit for a lie detector or whatever, I'll do that."

She'd promptly shut him out, taking him out of any equation. He agreed Hank would know how best to proceed on the investigation, but he wasn't ready to let Grace Ann walk out of his life.

Derek tamped down his irritation as she hurried to the bathroom. Clearly, she still believed her career, or rather his unfavorable reaction to it, was a wall they couldn't break down. If only he could go back and change his selfish, fear-based grumbling over Kevin's decision to join the army.

He thought of her nightmares and how well she'd slept beside him after he held her. Some part of her knew that she needed him, too. He could build on that, even if she wasn't ready to talk about it. He had no desire to quell her independence. He'd find a way to show her that being together made them both stronger.

He supposed, like any legal case or construction project, it began with patience. And a smart plan.

Chapter 10

In the luxurious hotel bathroom, Grace Ann turned on the shower and skimmed the headlines on her phone. *Oh, man.* Derek hadn't been exaggerating. The two of them led the photo and video footage in nearly every account of the incident. Her stomach did a twist and roll when she saw a picture of her sobbing on his shoulder. She scrolled away quickly, breathing through her nose, refusing to give in to the lingering nerves.

She had to be objective. It was a positive that she hadn't collapsed in a helpless, useless heap on the sidewalk. She'd taken action putting her expertise and training to good use, helping victims and making triage easier for the first responders. That was something to be proud of.

On the flip side, she had definitely caved under the emotional pressure. That scene had tossed her back into the nightmare and forced her to face the ghosts from Afghanistan.

She couldn't decide if crying on Derek's shoulder had been a better or worse coping mechanism than sex in a lavish hotel suite. At least the second option hadn't been captured on camera.

Yes, she still struggled after that bombing at the village school. Who wouldn't? But she *was* getting better. Last night had been a tragedy reminiscent of that dreadful afternoon on the other side of the world and she'd handled herself. Her immediate, professional response last night, now playing across national television, should erase any doubt about her current state of mind.

Dressed again in her clothes from last night, she used her phone to check her email. She had messages from Hank, the JAG office and her mother, in addition to various reporters and media outlets. She swiped the screen to check her voice mails and missed calls. Seeing the latest call from Hank was around eight this morning, she listened to that one first.

"Call me," Hank said. "On second thought, don't." He sounded weary and frazzled. "I'll run down a few things and then Derek and I can make a new plan."

Plan for what? She bristled at the idea that Hank would leave her out of any discussion regarding her safety or the investigation.

Walking back into the main room of the suite, she followed Derek's voice to the balcony. He raised a hand, stopping her before she could step outside.

"All right, we'll meet you there." His thinking face was in full force when he came inside and closed the sliding door behind him. "We have orders to report to your parents' beach house," he said.

"That was Hank?"

He nodded. "He has new information about the man who attacked you in the stairwell as well as the man who set off the explosion last night. He's absolutely sure now that both incidents are connected to the Riley Hunter."

"Hank needs to ditch that moniker," she muttered. "Does that mean the sting worked?"

"Sort of. Hank is pretty sure someone else bugged your house, but it sounds like he has a man in custody willing to give up the ringleader."

She sat down hard on the couch when her knees buckled. Relief made her head swim. She wanted to laugh and cry and do a happy dance all at once. "That's…that's amazing news."

"Hank agrees. He also has new information about a witness to your alleged misconduct in Afghanistan. He forwarded all that to the JAG office."

"Wow. He's been busy." A dozen questions raced through her mind and yet Derek wouldn't have the answers. Finally they were making progress on the madman out to destroy her dad. "Okay. Beach house. I need to stop by my place and—"

Derek was shaking his head. "I'm to take you directly to the beach house. He warned me you'd argue. I am supposed to hold firm and you're supposed to deal with it. Oh, and text him with your packing list."

"What?" No way was she letting Hank root through her closets and drawers. She scrolled through her contacts and tapped the icon to call Hank. He didn't pick up. "He's ignoring my call."

"I got the impression his hands are full," Derek said, ever the diplomat. "When he mentioned the rest of your family would be there, what does that mean?"

Circling the wagons, she thought. Then it hit her. "He means all of us, including my new sister-in-law and nephew."

"Duly noted," he murmured.

"Pardon?"

"I've been ordered to stay with you. At the beach house. Hank will pack my things that are at your house and he's let your mom know."

Good grief. "Hank's out of line." She couldn't imagine a more stressful dynamic for Derek. He'd be miserable surrounded by her loud and boisterous family. "You can say no."

He shook his head. "After last night, it seems I'm no longer an innocent bystander but also a target. Easier for Hank if we're together."

Grace Ann wanted to do what was easier for *him*. Regret swamped her and she closed her eyes, imagining the sweet bliss of jetting off with him to a tiny Pacific island until the Riley Hunter and the rest of the world forgot about them. If only. "You can't, Derek."

"Can't what?"

She searched for the right words as she gazed into his stern face. "I know you can't just drop everything and go with me to the beach. Call him back," she ordered, jumping to her feet.

She couldn't take him to her parents' house. It would take their relationship from zero to over and done in a day. She might not be his forever person, but they deserved more time than this. "Tell him you're dropping me at the house." Frantic when his jaw set, she barreled on. "This is a Riley problem. You've done enough. I won't drag you in over your head."

She wanted to tap out. No way was she up for the challenge of facing her accomplished, confident parents while juggling all these feelings she had for Derek and fears of the unknown. Aside from that, out of her respect for their bond, she would not run him through the gauntlet of meeting the entirety of her family all at once.

"Take a breath," he said. "And please sit down."

She did as he asked and he sat beside her.

"Ready to listen?"

She mimed zipping her mouth closed.

"I think the world of you, Grace Ann," he began. "Whatever is going on, you're my friend first and foremost. I have both the time and the desire to help you."

"You came here for Kevin," she interjected.

His strong, wide hand curved gently over her knee. "Yes. And I'd hoped to see you, too."

"Seeing me shouldn't have meant getting caught up in the drama that is my life."

"No, but now that I'm in it, I'm not running."

She traced the tendons and bones of his hand. "If you come with me, you'll be tossed into the middle of a special brand of chaos. It's more than you bargained for."

"I may only have one brother, but I understand sibling dynamics."

She had to paint a picture that would scare him straight. "This is sibling dynamics on steroids, Derek, with a generous helping of military pride."

He leaned back, glared at her. "Stop using the military angle as a repellent."

She gawked at him. "It's a *factor*," she managed. "Kevin told me you were never excited about his decision, always lukewarm about his accomplishments. You've said as much."

"What I was or wasn't then is between my brother and me."

She'd offended him. *Great.* "My family bleeds army black and gold," she explained. "And navy blue, if you count my SEAL brother."

"A SEAL? I sure wouldn't count him out," Derek deadpanned.

She shoved to her feet, away from him, his touch, the temptation he presented at every turn. "Then why come to the beach house?"

"Aside from the fact that Hank practically ordered me to report there with you in tow?"

"Yes! Aside from that."

"Because I…you…" He stared at her with an intensity that sizzled over her skin. "Because you're important to me," he finished at last. "I want to be with you, wherever you are."

Her heart simply soared, refusing to be grounded by logic. Chalking up the change in their relationship to bizarre and intense circumstances wasn't fair to either of them. Yes, they'd been coping with serious trouble, but no one had forced him to keep going the extra mile, to take such care with her. For her.

She thought about the way he'd touched her last night as they made love. The tenderness he'd shown on her couch. He'd soothed her out of a nightmare that would normally have left her shaking for hours. Her heart and soul seemed to flow toward him with total trust and no regard for common sense.

Her body followed and she hugged him hard. Yes, she was more than halfway in love with him already but it felt like the wrong time for that declaration. "Oh, I hope you don't come to regret it."

A few hours later their impromptu road trip ended as Derek parked his car in line with several others already tucked between a three-car garage and a sprawling, stilted beach house. Assuming one car per sibling, they were the fourth party to arrive. He assumed Hank would be last, and recalling how they met, he had to wonder if he was about to walk into an unyielding wall of Riley men, or if her mother or sister would be more amenable to meeting him.

"You're nervous," Grace Ann observed.

He froze in the act of pulling the key from the ignition. "I am." Why deny it?

"Well, that makes two of us," she admitted. "In case Hank hasn't told you, my mother's been worried about my mental health since I came home from the last deployment. I'm hopeful that our heroics last night will ease her mind. She hasn't used the term *PTSD*, but I know she's thinking it."

"Do you think you're dealing with PTSD?" he asked.

"That's a trick question," she replied. "Isn't denial one of the classic symptoms that actually confirms the diagnosis?"

"You'd know better than I would." He studied her. Her eyes were clear, her lips curved in a self-deprecating smile. He wasn't sure she realized it, but he'd seen her when she was overrun by the worst of her memories. What he saw now was merely surface-level discomfort. "Would you tell a friend in your situation, dealing with the things you've seen, that she had PTSD?"

Her lips parted, then closed. "I might." Instead of enlightened, she appeared defeated.

"Would you hold that against your friend?"

Her brow puckered as she frowned. "Of course not."

"Then why hold yourself to a higher, impossible standard?"

"I'm a Riley." She sighed and glanced toward the house. "Military is part of the DNA around here. You know Dad's a retired general and my mother an accomplished army nurse."

"I've heard," he teased. "What's your point?"

"They both saw a bunch of crap along the way and

they're fine. They cope like champs. Me?" She twisted her hands together in her lap. "Not so fine apparently."

"You're in the midst of it, and being harassed by someone with an ax to grind," he said. "I think processing what you've seen over there takes time. The current circumstances only compound the issue. You're handling things with amazing courage and steadiness."

She gawked at him and he wished he had the guts to risk a kiss right here. "I was eighteen and thought I knew everything when the police showed up on our doorstep," he said instead. "Kevin was a kid, in bed asleep, when our world dropped off its axis."

"Derek."

He plowed on. "Do you know how hard it was for me to get behind the wheel of a car and drive Kevin to the morgue? To the hospital?" He gripped the steering wheel with both hands. "My parents died in the act of driving down a road."

"I'm sorry," she said, laying a hand on his wrist.

He hadn't given a voice to this pain in more than ten years. "It's impossible to describe how terrified I was about killing Kevin or myself. How certain I was that we wouldn't make it home every time we went out. And I wasn't even in the car when it happened. I was nothing but a big ball of stress and grief and fear for months."

"Please, don't do this."

The crack in her voice only confirmed she needed to hear him. "Your parents love you, Grace Ann. I'm sure they had their share of tough stuff, too. They probably just want you to trust them to help. They want you to trust yourself."

"Maybe." Her gaze drifted to the house again.

"I imagine coping with this stuff is the lesser-known part of deployment."

"Being overseas has an impact on everyone," she admitted. "Most soldiers find a way to keep going."

"You've kept going." He shifted in the seat, caught and held her gaze. "Do most soldiers work with wounded warriors stateside?"

"Most in the nursing corps do," she replied.

"Stop being obtuse." It pleased him to see a tiny smile tug at her lips.

"I do hear what you're saying." She closed her eyes and took a slow, deep breath. "Giving all these difficult feelings a label like PTSD bugs me."

"Why?"

"Because I was raised in the heart of the army. I feel like the Riley name on its own indicates an immunity or genetic predisposition to handling things better."

"And would you say *that* to a sibling?" he asked.

"No." Defeated, she dropped her head back against the seat. "You've made your point."

"Then can we go inside before your parents decide I'm a freak?"

Her grin flashed. "Even though that would take some pressure off me?"

"You handle pressure." Tossing away the worry of first impressions, he leaned over and kissed her until her gaze went dreamy and soft. "Whatever the situation, you're the strongest woman I've ever met."

"That, my friend, is about to change." With a wistful smile, she opened her door and shouted a greeting.

He stepped out of the car and saw her family gathered on the landing, each eyeing him with a different expression.

As Grace Ann made the introductions, her mother, Patricia, wrapped him in a warm hug, while General "Call Me Ben" Riley gave him a cool, hard handshake.

Her younger brothers, twins Mark and Luke, followed their father's lead with a cool assessment. Her sister, Jolene, looked like a younger version of their mother and she studied him with a gleam in her eye he wasn't sure how to interpret. Apparently Matt and his family were still en route and Derek expected Hank to be the last one in later tonight.

There was no mistaking Grace Ann had the best of her parents. An inch taller than her mom, she had a similar build. But it was clear Grace Ann's intelligent gaze and deep brown eyes came straight from her dad.

"Come in, come in." Patricia nodded at Ben to open the front door. "Grace Ann can show you to the bunk room when Hank arrives with your things."

"Derek and I are staying in my room," Grace Ann stated.

Mark, or maybe Luke, gave a low whistle while Ben pinned Derek with a disapproving scowl.

"I don't want to bunk with the boys." Jolene's exaggerated complaint failed to sufficiently hide her amusement.

"Too bad," Grace Ann said. "He's here as my guest. We're together and I don't want my little brothers to drive him away. He's endured enough turmoil already, thanks to me."

Mark and Luke visibly bristled at her description or her declaration, but Grace Ann ignored them.

"It is our house," Patricia reminded her. "Our rules."

Grace Ann's bravado held. She raised an eyebrow. Patricia mirrored her daughter's expression.

"I, um, saw there were vacancies at the hotel we passed," Derek offered. Everyone ignored him.

Grace Ann looked to her siblings, particularly Jolene, for backup. "We're all adults, right?"

"A mother can dream," Patricia allowed as they

poured into the big kitchen. "Forgive them, Derek. They know not what pains they are." Her laughter filled the house and broke the tension. "Would you like a drink?"

"Water would be great." Uncomfortable as he was, being even a smidge off his game seemed like a dangerous option. He tried to stay out of the way as Grace Ann's family surrounded her in a swirl of concern, questions and obvious affection.

"Patricia's been watching the news all morning," Ben said while his wife simultaneously juggled three different conversations with her children. "You and Gracie were quite a team out there."

"It was all her," Derek replied. "She was snapping out orders. I just followed them."

"She has a way," Ben said.

"She does," Derek agreed.

"I'd say she gets that from me, but now, having met her mother, you'll know it's a lie." With a smile, Ben wound his way through his family and pulled a bottle of beer from the refrigerator. "Walk with me," he said to Derek.

It was easy to see how naturally Grace Ann came by her authority and leadership ability. Ben showed Derek into a masculine office space off the family room. Though it was tailored to the general's tastes, with dark wood wainscoting and framed awards, it didn't feel as if he'd stepped away from the airy design of the rest of the house. He assumed that was due to the expansive view of the ocean through the wide windows.

"You have a beautiful home," Derek said.

"Patricia had a vision," the general replied, closing the door.

Derek hoped this wasn't about to turn into a "what are your intentions with my daughter" talk. Although after

Grace Ann's declaration about the sleeping arrangements it would be a valid question. If it came to that, he hoped the general would give him points for honesty. Derek knew what he wanted for his future with Grace Ann; he just didn't yet know if Grace Ann might want that, too.

Ben sank into one of the leather club chairs positioned to take full advantage of the view and motioned for Derek to take the other. "Grace Ann is convinced I run a background check on every man she looks at twice." A grin tilted at one corner of his mouth. "If only I was that connected." He set his drink on the table between the chairs. "Through your brother, I know you understand the commitment our soldiers make."

Derek took a sip of his water, waiting for the general to make his point.

"I wanted to thank you for what you've done for my daughter," Ben continued. "Especially in light of your brother's injury."

"Kevin seems to be on the mend and in good spirits."

"I'm glad to hear it." Ben leaned forward. "You've been caught in the middle of a tough situation and for that I'd like to apologize."

That wasn't at all what Derek had expected. "Sir?"

"Ben, please." He relaxed back into the chair again. "Hank said he and Gracie gave you the basics. Apparently there is a vindictive man out there hunting my children to settle a grudge he holds against me. You have no idea how eager I am to figure out who is endangering my family. Can you tell me how Gracie is doing?"

Derek barely kept himself from fidgeting like a kid called into the principal's office. "I'm not sure what you're asking," he began. "She isn't thrilled with the circumstances or the injuries to others, but she's holding up."

Ben tapped the arm of the chair. "Is she? You've been with my daughter for a few days now. I'd hoped maybe she would talk to you. She sure won't talk to any of us."

"Would you like me to get out of the way?" Even making the suggestion cost him. He didn't want to leave Grace Ann, despite her now being surrounded by her far-more-qualified family. What happened if the nightmares came back?

"No, no. Stay. Hank is convinced the bastard has you in his sights now, too." Ben stood, crossing to the window. "Patricia and I saw you with Grace Ann after the bombing. The one thing this country seems to agree on at the moment is that you're both heroes."

"Grace Ann is remarkable," Derek murmured. "I just tagged along."

"You didn't leave her side." Ben let loose a heavy sigh. "Being a father is a lifelong challenge, Derek. You've had a taste of it, raising your little brother."

So the man had done a bit of digging. He wasn't sure muddling through those years qualified as parenting. He'd been tossed into the gig unwillingly, in the midst of heartbreaking grief.

"Being an officer is a similar challenge," Ben continued. "I've made my share of mistakes with both my family and with troops under my command. Sometimes you see those mistakes immediately, sometimes it takes years for perspective and hindsight to kick in." He turned his back on the ocean. "Sometimes your hands are just tied."

"True enough."

"Hank and the investigators have concluded that all of this is connected. From the bogus accusation of Grace Ann's misconduct right up to the bomb last night." Ben reached across his desk for his cell phone. "I'm inclined to agree."

He tapped the phone screen and held it out. Grace Ann's voice filled the room. It was a recording of the "confession" she'd given for the sake of whoever had planted the bugs in her house. Derek's palms went damp. He said a prayer this Riley Hunter creep hadn't sent the recording of them making love, too.

"When the person behind this revenge turned Matt's life upside down, he made sure I had pictures proving how close he could get. Now it seems he's making his point that he knows more than I do. How did he figure out that Grace Ann has never talked so freely to us about any of this?"

"Hank asked her to do it," he began after Ben seemed to expect an answer. "I doubt she would've opened up to me otherwise." In fact, she hadn't.

Ben stared at his phone. "The parts that are false don't worry me." His gaze lifted and the sorrow Derek saw in his eyes was overwhelming. "I haven't let Patricia hear this. She's already concerned that Grace Ann is trying to ignore symptoms of PTSD."

Derek felt completely adrift. He was a brother of a soldier in the nursing corps and his law degree was no help here. He supposed her reaction when the car backfired could be interpreted as a PTSD symptom. Then again, with so much going on, she'd had every right to be edgy.

"She's steady," he replied when the silence got uncomfortable. "Whether or not she has PTSD." What reassurances could he give her father without breaching her trust? "She's aggravated, of course. Sad about the village school and the kids she couldn't save over there. But she's rock-steady. It makes her furious that this Riley Hunter is using her to cause you grief."

"She's her mother's daughter." Ben's weary smile held a wealth of pride. "The way they think is remarkable.

There are few lines they'll cross and then only with good reason." He sighed. "I am sorry your brother was injured. I want you to know we're doing everything possible to identify the culprit who put all of this into motion."

"Maybe the man Hank has in custody can shed some light on the insider feeding intel to the man targeting your family."

Ben's eyebrows snapped together. "Insider?"

Derek shifted in his seat. "I'm sure Hank is going through the unit roster with a fine-tooth comb," he said. "When Grace Ann apologized to me and to Kevin for the training accident, she said she was on the roster for that event, pulled at the last minute," he continued. "Who else but someone within the unit, an insider, would know that?"

Ben swore. "This bastard has reach and influence. He's been far more aggressive with Grace Ann."

"I'm no investigator," Derek said, "but the more I learn, the more it feels personal."

"Oh, it's personal," Ben agreed. "Hank will be here soon and we'll all move forward together."

"Anything I can do to help," Derek said, hoping that didn't include leaving. Through the window, he saw Grace Ann and her siblings heading down to the beach.

"Grace Ann introduced me to your brother at his first pre-deployment family picnic," Ben said, his gaze following Derek's. "I don't recall seeing you there."

"A late arrival," Derek admitted, hoping that error years ago hadn't just destroyed the general's opinion of him. "I wasn't so sure about how to support Kevin back then."

"Are you sure now?"

"I've had more practice," he replied.

Ben nodded. "Family serves and sacrifices, too."

Ben's eyes were suspiciously bright. "My wife did her best to get that through my skull when our family was young. Being retired now, I have a better idea of what families go through. It isn't easy knowing what our soldiers are up against and having no way to affect the outcome."

A chime sounded, saving Derek from finding a response as a monitor behind the general's desk flickered to life. A video from a camera aimed at the driveway showed a minivan parking behind Derek's car.

"That's Matt and his family. As much as we enjoy our empty nest, Patricia loves having all her chicks under one roof." At the sound of footsteps rushing by and boisterous greetings, Ben grinned. "Gracie warned you we're loud?"

"She did."

"Well, it could be worse, son." Ben opened the office door. "Could be Christmas."

Chapter 11

With twilight creeping along the beach, Grace Ann sneaked a glance at Derek as her family relaxed on the deck. Seated at the other end of the picnic table, he was handling the chaos of her family like a pro.

Her nephew Caleb, fifteen now, was talking her ears off with a play-by-play of his latest soccer tournament. The kid was definitely headed for an athletic scholarship if he kept up the hard work. She found it hilarious, considering how much her brother Matt preferred American football, but was now a soccer dad.

"Are you surfing in the morning, Aunt Gracie?"

"Rain or shine," she told him. Her rash guard and board shorts would hide the worst of the bruising on her hip and leg from her family. "You'll probably want to sleep in."

"No way."

Overhearing her son, Bethany snorted. "Why is it the

only time I *don't* have to drag you out of bed is when we're at the beach?"

"Surfing is more fun than geometry."

Caleb ducked when she tossed a marshmallow at him. He flashed the sweet grin the Riley boys always used to get out of any trouble. Grace Ann recognized it easily. Her brothers had applied that same expression to wear down their mother when they misbehaved.

"He comes by it naturally," Grace Ann said to Bethany when Caleb heeded a summons from his uncle Luke down on the beach below.

"Don't I know it." Bethany rested a hand on the first hint of a baby bump under her loose peasant top.

Grace Ann smiled at the telling motion. As much as her dad teased her mom about it, the truth was the entire family was eager to dote on Bethany and the new grandbaby. She couldn't wait to spoil her new niece or nephew from day one. While none of them blamed Bethany, they were all making up for time lost.

"Grace Ann?"

"Sorry." She gave Bethany her full attention. "Zoned out for a sec. What did I miss?"

"I was complimenting Derek. Mark told me he survived the office visit with Ben."

"He did. Though I got the impression your arrival saved him." Grace Ann hadn't had a chance to hear what they'd spent nearly an hour discussing, though she had a good idea. "We're sleeping together," she said without thinking. "Sharing a room, I mean. In case Mark didn't mention that, too."

"If you're looking this way for censure or judgment, you'll be disappointed."

"Thanks for that," Grace Ann said. Bethany had been an instant friend and a welcome addition to the family.

"I'm an adult," she added. "Dad doesn't need to give him the third degree."

"He can't help it," Bethany said, patting her hand. "He's concerned, especially after the hunter targeted you."

"Hopefully Hank will show up soon with some news to put us all at ease." And her luggage. She kept a few basics here, but Derek didn't have anything other than the clothes on his back. Way to make a hard situation worse. She aimed the thought in Hank's direction.

Bethany scooted closer and lowered her voice. "The person pulling the strings is dangerous, Grace Ann."

"I'm aware and taking it seriously." She rubbed her aching hip. It was time to go for another walk. "It's like a puzzle without a border," she mused. "He obviously wants Dad to suffer. I'd like to take him out with my bare hands for that alone."

Bethany murmured an agreement. "If he thinks any of the Riley kids are weak links, he's in for a rude awakening."

Grace Ann sipped the peach tea in her glass. She feared that she was the weak Riley and would fail the next challenge. Oh, she wouldn't intentionally turn on her family or compromise her father, but a PTSD breakdown or being found guilty of misconduct would put a serious stain on the general's otherwise sterling reputation.

"Grace Ann?"

She blinked several times, until her gaze focused on Derek's face. He'd crouched in front of her, his friendly smile setting butterflies loose in her belly. She hadn't even heard him approach.

"Care to take a walk with me?"

"Sure." She popped to her feet, regretting it immediately when her leg protested the quick move. Derek moved close, hiding her bobble and wince from the others.

Once she got moving, her muscles loosened up and the little dig of pain eased back to a dull ache. "I need to remember it doesn't take long for me to stiffen up," she said when they were down on the beach and out of earshot.

"You haven't told anyone but Hank about getting hit by the car?"

She shook her head, then realized he might not have seen the movement in the fading light. "Not much point."

With the ocean rolling in, the breeze in her face and the sand squishing under her bare feet, she felt calmer. "This was a good idea," she said.

"I have them once in a while."

He laced his fingers through hers and she glanced around guiltily. Why did such a casual touch feel so out of place after the far more intimate acts they'd shared?

"Want me to let go?" he asked.

"No." She didn't like needing him, but his touch pushed away the loneliness and worry about what they might have to face when Hank showed up. "Did my dad put you through the wringer?"

"Not exactly. Matt, however…"

She stopped short when his voice trailed off. "Oh, I can take him," she said. "He forgets I fight dirty."

"You do realize you're adults?"

"We're barely two years apart," she said, helpless against the warm burst of affection for her brother. "Conflict is what we do best."

Derek started walking again, continuing down the beach. "To an outsider, the Rileys look pretty united."

She hoped it stayed that way. "Matt's no saint. You don't have to put up with any crap from him."

A low laugh rumbled out of him.

"Why is that funny?"

He laughed harder. "Now I'm offended on *his* behalf. As an older brother myself, I feel a certain solidarity."

With a snort, she shook free and moved closer to the line of moonlit foam gleaming on the sand. The water was cool yet, but it felt good rolling up over her toes and ankles.

"It doesn't make you weak to need someone." He stood just behind her, the heat from his chest radiating warmth against her back.

"I know that." The army was about working as a unit, each person pulling their weight. She knew the value of teamwork. "Fear is eroding everything that makes me feel strong," she admitted.

His arms came around her, his hands loosely stacked at her waist. He was giving her room to make her choice. She could lean into his support or step away with minimal effort.

She leaned back into him. "I keep seeing H.B.'s face," she said.

"Hard not to," Derek replied. "Needing a break from what you do best doesn't make you weak, either."

"Give it up," she said. "Bingham already tried and failed to convince me the suspension had a silver lining."

"You sure about that?" He brushed his lips to her shoulder, followed the curve up her neck. Her nerves tingled in response, all the way to her fingertips and down her spine. "Would we be here otherwise?"

No. Guilt cast a shadow over every sensation and thought. His brother's injury. Her father's reputation. His stable life. All of that was in jeopardy because a madman had taken aim at her.

"Shh. You aren't the cause or reason for any of this trouble, Grace Ann." He nuzzled her shoulder as she stared out over the black expanse of the ocean. "You are strong. Don't let a vengeance-induced crisis blur the truth."

This tenderness was a new layer of him she found addictive. His words floated over her skin, seeped into her system, soothing all the places left raw and aching from recent events. She turned within the circle of his arms and simply stared into the shadows of his face. He didn't move, didn't speak, letting her come to him. Curling her hands behind his neck, she brought his mouth down to hers. In the kiss she told him everything she couldn't say out loud. Not yet.

He made her feel whole and beautiful. He gave her a hope that had gone missing somewhere in the dust of that hollowed-out school. In him she found a love she craved, a love that would last and last. The minute this was over, she'd tell him.

His hands splayed across her back, down over her hips and he boosted her up. On a wordless plea, she wrapped her legs around him, clinging like a burr as the kiss spun out. Feasting on the dizzying sensations, she let everything else fall away. The world contracted to this moment. Her heartbeat originated with his; her breath came from his lungs.

"Don't let go," she said, her lips following the striking line of his jaw. "Don't let go."

"Never." He stood strong, giving her more than she had any right to ask.

She tossed back her head and a flash of heat lightning streaked across the water to the south.

"We should get back," she said as thunder rolled, closer than she expected. "We're likely to get soaked."

She took his hand and started off at a brisk walk until

the first drops splattered against her shirt. Bumping up the pace, they jogged side by side on the softer sand just above the tide line. The rain caught up with them, dousing them as they scrambled over the path through the dunes to the house.

The lights were still on at the corners of the deck, but everyone had wisely moved indoors as the storm rolled in. They came in, laughing and dripping on the rug inside the sliding door, and she felt her entire family staring at them.

Bethany was tucked under Matt's arm on the love seat. Caleb, Mark and Luke were on the floor, the colorful video game frozen on the television. Her sister and mother had turned away from whatever they'd been doing at the kitchen island. Hank stood with her father in the open door of his study. "Hi?" she ventured.

"Welcome back." Patricia waved them in. "You'd best get into dry clothes. Hank and your father have news."

Grace Ann's bright mood plummeted. Maybe she and Derek weren't meant to have more than private moments squeezed in between crises. "We'll be right back down." Before anyone could say anything else, she led Derek up the back stairs to the bedroom they would share.

They changed clothes without a word and Grace Ann gathered up their soaked clothing and dropped it off in the laundry room. She appreciated his stoic silence almost as much as she appreciated his fast kiss loaded with encouragement before they returned to the family room.

Hank immediately waved them into the office, closing the door behind them. "First off," he began, "Kevin's doing great and sends his best."

"You saw him?" Derek asked.

"He asked to see me after his interview." Hank tucked

his hands into the pockets of the windbreaker he hadn't yet removed. "Sounds like that went well. The investigator did ask him about the fictional MP you mentioned for the sake of the bugs in your house."

"Fake news travels fast," Derek muttered. "You protected her against any blowback, right?"

Hank cocked an eyebrow, relenting when Derek didn't back down. "I did. That confirms someone listening to the bugs fed the intel to a legit investigator. The JAG office has been made aware of our effort to identify and trap the Riley Hunter."

"Stop calling him that," Grace Ann grumbled.

Hank ignored her. "Unfortunately, while we're a step closer, there is more bad news."

Grace Ann crossed her arms over her chest, waiting.

"H.B. is dead."

The words didn't register at first. "You're mistaken," she protested. "Bingham would've called. He was stabilized. The burns were bad, but…but he's at Walter Reed. Stable."

"Gracie, I'm sorry." But Hank didn't look sorry. He looked as though there was even more he didn't want to share.

"How?" Her dad stepped over to offer comfort and she held up a hand, stopping him. "When?"

"A few hours ago. We've kept his death quiet while we investigate," Hank explained. "He was stable. This morning, he told his care team he wanted to make a statement about what he saw last night. Because Bingham and I have been in contact since you were suspended, she arranged for me to see him."

Bewildered, she just sat down. "His doctor approved that?" she asked, shocked.

Hank nodded. "But he died before I got there."

Grace Ann didn't know who to look at or where to turn. Part of her mind retreated to the dark beach and the sweet place where nothing could intrude on her time with Derek.

"An autopsy has been ordered. Bingham allowed me to go through his desk and computer files in the office. We got lucky when we found his personal laptop was in the office as well. I've searched that, too."

Based on his grim expression, he'd found something damaging. Although Hank had a mile-wide serious streak, he knew how to cut loose. She was trying to remember the last time she'd seen him relax since taking the lead on the team searching for the Riley Hunter.

"You think H.B. was the inside guy," Derek said.

"What?" She reached for Derek's hand on instinct. Hank's raised eyebrows brought her attention to where she'd sought comfort. She didn't pull away. Derek was involved now, and for better or worse, she wasn't ready to deal with whatever came next without him.

"Derek's right," Hank said. "H.B. was a traitor to your unit and someone used him against you specifically," Hank explained, his voice strained. "He wasn't acting alone."

Ben muttered an oath.

Hank turned toward Derek. "According to files I found on H.B.'s personal laptop, he received instructions on how to create the malfunction that resulted in the helo crash. Reviewing the logs from the training exercise, he wasn't able to get back to the flight line after Grace Ann was benched."

Her stomach pitched. She let go of Derek and dropped her head to her hands. "It should be me in recovery."

"It shouldn't be anyone!" the general bellowed.

Grace Ann jumped. She hadn't heard him raise his voice in anger since Mark and Luke got caught trying to hot-wire a jeep during her senior year of high school. Her dad stalked around his desk and dropped into the chair, his face mottled with fury.

"Someone, presumably the Riley Hunter, turned him against you," Hank said again. "I don't have the full picture yet, but it's clear he was involved. He carried out some orders and passed other orders along to someone else."

"It couldn't have taken much. H.B. and I were like oil and water," Grace Ann said. "We could barely pry him out of the office on that last deployment and he hated how I volunteered for every off-base outreach opportunity."

"He wasn't at the school in the village when it was bombed?" Hank asked.

"Are you kidding?" She shook her head. "He probably wet himself reading the report."

Hank sat on the window seat and extended his legs, crossing them at the ankle. "He filed the report of your misconduct. I found a copy of the letter on his computer, claiming he witnessed you prioritizing civilians over military personnel."

"That doesn't make sense. I mean, sure he hates me, but to fabricate those charges is a little much, even for him," Grace Ann said after a moment. "If he'd been caught his career would've been over, too."

"True." Hank rocked a little, thinking. "The Riley Hunter wouldn't care about the fallout."

She couldn't stop the quick shiver as dread trickled down her spine. Derek propped his hip on the arm of her chair and she leaned closer to him. Every new detail nipped at her confidence, her certainty that the Riley Hunter could be found and caught.

"Did H.B. have a tattoo on the inside of his wrist?" Derek pointed to a spot on his arm. "The person who attacked her in the stairwell had a tattoo right about here."

"No tattoos," Hank and Grace Ann said in unison. "I'll pass that on to the team picking through H.B.'s effects."

"So the attacker in the stairwell was someone the Riley Hunter hired?" Grace Ann asked.

"Probably." With a glance toward Ben, he continued. "H.B. left a letter claiming responsibility for the bombing." He held her gaze. "His letter explains that he planted a device built by someone else that was delivered to him at a predetermined location."

"She's still in danger then," Derek said.

"You both are," Hank said. "H.B. had a file on you and had recently searched through Kevin's personal data. I'd like to tell you nothing will come of it, but I don't know what to expect next."

Hank sighed as Ben continued to fume. "We know the Riley Hunter is the mastermind pulling the strings and we know he uses mercenaries. However he felt about you, these actions seem extreme. I need to find out what our madman had on him. H.B.'s confession bothers me most. Why, when he had no expectation of being hurt, would he leave that kind of damning evidence behind?"

"He expected to die," Derek said into the quiet. "Maybe not at the bomb site, but soon. He'd failed at the helicopter and he had to know the accusation and suspension would eventually backfire. He might have been having second thoughts about what he'd gotten into. Or maybe he was covering his bases, knowing the bomb was his last chance."

"You're saying he was murdered for being a screwup?" The idea was so dreadful, though she could see the logic. She had to hold her muscles tight when they wanted to tremble.

"That lines up with my theory," Hank said. "Everyone expected him to survive his burns. We're going over the surveillance footage, searching for a likely culprit."

"Do you think it was the mastermind himself?" Derek asked.

Hank shrugged. "Sure would be nice if it was."

"Did H.B. break the garage window and bug my house?" The idea of that weasel skulking around her home made her skin crawl.

"I don't think he bugged the house," Hank said. "He had the time to vandalize the window, but he was in a meeting with Bingham the morning you were hit by the car."

Ben sat up straight. "When were you hit by a car?"

Hank, Derek and Grace Ann all cringed. "It was more of a bump, Dad. I'm fine."

"Hank?" the general demanded.

Hank explained what happened with as few details as possible. "The police found the car, but again, no evidence. When you didn't get a text about that, I'd hoped to file it under coincidence."

"And you didn't because?" Grace Ann asked. "The protection detail's flat tire turned out to be deliberate. In light of the bugs in my house, that had to have been done on the hunter's orders."

"Why is he taking such an aggressive line with her?" her father wondered aloud. "If I could protect you from all of this I would, sweetie."

"That may be part of the answer," she said. "You urged me toward a civilian career, but I wouldn't go until I'd proved I could do everything Matt could do, but better.

"H.B. would have been thrilled to have me out of the picture," she continued. "Clears a promotion path for him, at the very least. He had access to everything I've been through and every conversation about it." H.B. had known that she'd been dancing at the fringes of the PTSD issue since they'd come home. As Bingham's assistant, he was privy to her records and all but the most private conversations from their commander.

"But is that enough motivation?" Luke voiced the query at the top of everyone's mind. "I guess people have done worse for less."

She didn't have that answer. Yet. "What would happen to Dad if I'm found guilty of misconduct?" she asked the room at large. "Now, think about what happens to Dad if I'm found guilty of misusing supplies *and* I have a mental breakdown?"

"His reputation takes a hit," Hank said.

"And the *family* reputation takes a bigger hit," she agreed. "When I look at this objectively, I can see that whoever is determined to wreck Dad wants me, personally, to go out in a blazing meltdown. That sort of shameful scene would bring the media down on Dad and the family like vultures on a carcass. Think about it, everything that's happened since the training accident was specifically designed to get under my skin."

And as much as she hated to admit it, those incidents would have succeeded if Derek hadn't been around to steady her.

"It's personal," Derek said.

"Gracie." Ben came around the desk and hauled her into a bear hug. "You're too strong. No one will crack my girl."

She sniffled against the emotions welling up, ready to spill over and embarrass them all. For a moment, she let herself burrow into her bigger-than-life father as she'd done as a little girl. Backing away, she swiped tears from her cheeks.

"I don't matter. Not to the guy calling the shots. *You* do. Your pain is the whole point. He might employ pros to do the dirty work, but this started with something personal between you and him." She backed toward the door. "He turned H.B. against me, against the army regulations he loved so much." To her ultimate embarrassment, Hank's face wavered as she looked at him through her tear-filled eyes. "That takes personal leverage."

She bolted, unable to hang on to her composure for one more second. Her family was a blur of color and sound as she headed for the stairs and the privacy of her room. She needed alone time, terrifying as that prospect was in the grand scheme of things. She didn't want sympathy or support; she wanted to know she could cope under her own power. That's what army officers did.

Sure, she was grateful for all Derek had done, but she realized she'd been leaning too hard. Using him. He deserved better than that. She should probably crash on the couch tonight.

A knock on the door had her curling away from the sound, hiding under the quilt. "I'm asleep."

"I'm sure you'd like to be," her mother replied. She walked in and closed the door. "Gracie, talk to me."

She shook her head. "Hank and Dad can fill you in."

Patricia sighed as only mothers can and the mattress dipped as she sat on the bed. "About the case, sure. Not about you."

"I'm tired, Mom."

"You've been tired before." Patricia smoothed her

hand over Grace Ann's hair. "When was the last time you were on a jump?" she asked.

Grace Ann did the math in her head. "I'm still qualified." She rolled over, too curious now. "Why?"

"Might be time for another one."

As a life-affirming exercise, jumping out of perfectly good airplane was almost as good as sex. "Maybe."

Patricia shifted around on the bed until she leaned back against the headboard, Grace Ann's head resting in her lap. "Do you remember your first jump at Fort Bragg?"

No one forgot their first jump. Pushing past the fear, shutting out the voice in her head clamoring for her to sit down and stay safe, and then the incomparable high of free-falling through the sky. The landing had been rough but once she found her feet she couldn't wait to get back up there and do it all over again.

Grace Ann sniffled. "Never forget your first."

"Ha." Patricia bumped her shoulder. "You've made my point for me. Good or bad, we remember the firsts life dishes out."

Grace Ann groaned. "I'm not in the mood for another Matt-is-the-greatest-child story," she joked, trying to divert the conversation from sensitive territory.

"Well, Matt might be my favorite at the moment…"

Grace snorted. "You say that to all of us."

"And I change the names to protect the innocent," Patricia admitted. "Let's focus on *you*. How did you feel when you graduated from nursing school?"

"Same as you, probably," she answered. "Proud. Scared, but in a good way. Eager to get out there and make a difference."

"That was a wonderful day for us, too," she said. "You

simply are *not* capable of disappointing us, Gracie. We raised you to know you could come to us with anything."

"Mom." She sat up, pleating the edge of the quilt between her fingers. "With Hank involved, you know they'll find the jerk hassling Dad."

Her mother covered her hands, squeezing lightly. There was so much strength in that warm touch. "I won't stop asking," Patricia vowed. "All that tenacity your commanders praise? You got it from me."

Grace Ann sighed. She wasn't escaping this conversation. "What has Dad told you?"

"I want to hear it from you."

"I'm not ready," Grace Ann said in a last-ditch effort for one more reprieve.

"You're past ready," Patricia ordered. She tapped her daughter's forehead. "You've spent too much time in your head since you came home. Oh, you took your leave, but you spent half of it as a volunteer in the pediatric ward."

Grace Ann stared at her. "You knew about that?"

"How can you be surprised? What mothers don't know immediately, they find out eventually." She rolled her eyes. "There have been times these past six months when the surfing doesn't even smooth you out. Talk."

"I'm getting through, Mom."

"Sweetheart, a career in medicine means we see things in ways other people can't. The army intensifies that effect. Burnout happens." Patricia plowed on when Grace Ann didn't speak. "I had your father, almost from day one. I've talked with your sister and brothers. You aren't unloading on any of us."

"Maybe because I'm fine," she insisted.

"If you were acting like yourself I might believe you."

She really was tenacious. "Mom, I really don't need this interrogation."

Patricia simply cuddled her as if she were three rather than thirty-three. "Your father told me about the bombing at the village school shortly after it happened."

And her mother had been waiting all this time for her to open up about it. "I survived." She didn't want to do this, not here, not tonight. Not ever, she thought with a sigh. "Are you trying to push me over the edge, too?"

"No, baby." She crooned in her ear. "I'm trying to keep you on this side of the abyss."

A mean little voice in her head wanted to ask what her mother knew about that dark pit. Except, she knew her mom had seen plenty through her own career and as a mother of five.

A softer voice urged her to snuggle in close and welcome the unconditional comfort being offered. She listened to that voice. "I can't have PTSD, Mom."

"But do you?"

Grace Ann didn't know anymore. "Is that your diagnosis?"

"No," Patricia replied. "I've diagnosed that my girl is hurting. I want to be sure you're open to accepting help from someone."

She closed her eyes and pretended she was talking to Derek again. "The memories don't fade," she admitted. "When I have too much time on my hands my skin crawls."

"You've always liked to keep busy."

"Being forced to think about it is worse than the nightmares."

"Who did you lose, Gracie?"

"None of us were injured," she said. "We were all shocked, furious, but not hurt."

"Not what I meant, Gracie."

"Oh." She couldn't get the words past the emotion clogging her throat. Not even imagining it was Derek here listening helped with this piece of the pain. And wasn't that the crux of it? She couldn't bear to speak the names of the dead. What a coward she was that she couldn't honor them in that most basic way. She just let them float at the edges of her mind, accusing her of not being quick enough to save them.

"They didn't make any arrests before we came back home," Grace Ann said. "I've always felt we should have."

"Is that the resolution you need?"

"It wouldn't hurt." Who knew if it would help? "Don't worry, Mom. I've been doing all right. What's that quote Dad uses about things looking better in the morning?"

"Colin Powell's first rule," Patricia said, smiling a little. "'It ain't as bad as you think. It will look better in the morning.' Is it working?"

"Day by day," she said. "You taught us to live a big life. That's all I'm trying to do, in some little way, living a big life for those kids who didn't make it."

"I'd feel better if I knew you were sharing the burden. A group or a chaplain or…someone." Her gaze drifted to the overnight bags near the door.

Grace Ann knew she referred to Derek. "He's a good listener." And still, she couldn't dump all this baggage at his feet. For him, she was willing to face this, to dredge it up and clear it out.

"I'll let you be," Patricia said, easing off the bed. "But I'll always be here for you."

"You're so strong, Mom. It helps to know you don't hold this weakness against me," Grace Ann whispered.

"Gracie." Patricia's eyes filled. "You know what

makes me strong? Having your father in my corner. Yes, I taught you to live big, Grace Ann. I also taught all of you that you don't have to go through life alone. Get some rest now. Caleb will have you up at the crack of dawn for a surfing lesson."

Chapter 12

The next morning, Derek was roused when Grace Ann slipped out of bed to meet Caleb on the beach again. Her lips had feathered over his and then she'd been gone. Rolling over, he tried to doze off again, but he was done sleeping.

After a quick shower, his mind latched onto the tail end of the conversation he'd overheard outside the bedroom door last night. Patricia's words and devotion had moved him. He tended to recall his parents as perfect, though they certainly hadn't been. Patricia obviously realized her daughter wasn't at a hundred percent, but she'd managed to make that seem acceptable. Grace Ann wasn't quitting or running away and by his count, she had every right to take either option.

Dressed in shorts and a T-shirt, he wandered down to the kitchen and found a fresh pot of coffee. He poured a mug and carried it outside to watch the surfing lesson from the deck. Grace Ann and Caleb were on their boards well out from shore, with Mark and Luke sitting on surfboards nearby. As a wave formed, Mark hopped up and rode it into shore to the cheers of the others.

Derek marveled at the way the family rallied around Grace Ann without smothering her. Though he was sure she recognized what was happening, she didn't push them away or tell them to go back to work. He did what he could to make mental notes, since he planned to become an equally permanent fixture in her life.

He heard the slider and turned, relieved to see Patricia rather than her husband. He wasn't afraid of the general, he just wasn't eager to face him again after Hank's briefing session last night.

"Need a refill?" she asked, patting the coffee carafe she carried.

"Sure." He held out the thick white mug emblazoned with an army logo. "Thanks," he said when the cup was full again.

Patricia set the carafe on the picnic table. "Did she sleep last night?"

"She didn't keep me awake." It seemed the most diplomatic response.

"Good."

She sounded sincere, but it was still awkward. "If you're not comfortable with me staying here, or sharing a room with her, I do understand."

"Nonsense." Patricia waved off his concern. "You're welcome. I taught my children to make friends quickly and to be smart about it. I think they turned out to be pretty good judges of character. So we trust that judgment until we have reason not to."

Sounded like a fair deal, with a hint of a maternal threat added for good measure. "All right. Thank you."

"I noticed right away that you mean something to her."

The words slipped right under his defenses. His heart thudded behind his ribs at how badly he wanted that to be true. Derek sipped his coffee, his gaze on the surfers below. "My brother is our common denominator."

"We've met him a time or two," Patricia said. "He speaks highly of you."

Derek would never get used to hearing that.

"I bet you had your hands full raising a grieving teenager when your parents died."

"It was a rocky time," he admitted, staring into his coffee now.

"And now you're a lawyer?"

"I am," he replied. With fewer years of experience than he'd planned to have under his belt by now. "Inhouse counsel for a firm based in Frederick, Maryland. I enjoy it."

"Ben told me her house was bugged, but he won't share the things that madman has sent to him." Her gaze, fierce and protective, was locked on her daughter as she caught an incoming wave. "Hank's told me a bit of what you've helped her through. I'd like you to tell me why."

"She needed a friend," Derek replied carefully. "Anyone would have pitched in."

"Mmm-hmm. You say that, but she didn't allow anyone else to pitch in," she pointed out. "Thank you, Derek. It takes a backbone and fortitude to hold things together when you have family in the military."

"Kevin is pretty self-sufficient." She lifted an eyebrow and he elaborated. "I try not to dwell on it," he admitted. "I felt better about his career after meeting Grace Ann."

"I bet you did," she said, a grin curling the corner of her mouth.

He felt heat rising into his face. That hadn't come out quite right.

"She's an excellent nurse and a confident soldier," Patricia added.

"It's easy to see where she gets it," he said. "Does she have a plan B?"

"If she needs one, she'll write one for herself." Patricia moved to prune a few spent blossoms from the planter on the deck rail. "Grace Ann has always been the most practical of my children. May I ask how long you and Grace Ann have been seeing each other?"

"It's been a casual friendship for some time now," he said. "We discovered a mutual interest in hiking and camping and we've taken a few trips." How odd that the first person he confessed that to would be her mom.

She hummed in that way mothers did. "And you've been in love with her all that time?"

He set his coffee mug on the railing so he wouldn't drop it. Where had that come from? Well, they were sharing a room and a bed, so conclusions had been drawn. Still, they weren't overtly affectionate in front of her family. He shook his head, the strongest denial he could offer.

"Pardon me," she said. "I've made you uncomfortable. The kids tell me I tend to overstep."

Love wasn't something he'd learned to tie to dating. He enjoyed spending time with women, with Grace Ann in particular. Yes, he wanted to carve out a future with her, but love? How strange to realize he did love her. Not a flimsy, theoretical thought in the back of his mind, but right up front. Until now, love was dangerous, unknown territory. Love led to heartache, either in the short-term or down the line.

With Grace Ann, though, he was ready to brave anything to love her with all of him, as she deserved.

"You're protective," he said. "I respect that and take it as a compliment."

"And you understand it, as a young man who had to fill in for his parents."

"Yes." He couldn't help glancing around for a reprieve. With a family so large, why wasn't anyone interrupting them? "It was just the four of us, until it wasn't." He was a grown man and he'd related the facts of being orphaned often enough through the years.

"Ben and I have seen the best and worst of life. One thing has always rung true for me. Loss pushes everyone around." Patricia nodded to Grace Ann, paddling out to wait for another wave. "She's been rattled since her last deployment," Patricia said. "With good reason, based on what I've heard."

Derek agreed with that as well.

"This nonsense with H.B. and whoever turned him against her isn't helping."

"Not a bit," he said.

"When I saw the news footage of the bombing I had mixed feelings. I was naturally furious at the monster that caused the suffering, but it was clear there was such beauty in the bond between the two of you. Seeing you standing by my daughter was a wonderful illustration of the truest form of goodness in the world."

"I just did what she told me," he said.

"Would you take her away from the danger?" Patricia asked. "Until Hank has the real culprit in custody?"

"If I thought for a minute she'd let me, I would," he admitted. "Even if she wasn't on a mission to prove the Riley Hunter can't break her, you know she'd never let the rest of you handle this without her."

"Sometimes when we're eyeball-deep in trouble, we can't see the right path without help. My Gracie is lucky you're tall," she added with a wink.

He doubted height would be much of an advantage here. Terror and tragedy had interrupted the one real date he'd tried to create for them. He wasn't giving up, but he was naturally wary about the next effort.

"I do love her," he said after a long pause.

Patricia smiled.

Down on the beach, Grace Ann, Caleb and the twins were clustered together. Discussing the water, weather or their boards? Breakfast, he guessed as the surfers turned toward the house.

"Thank you for taking care with her," Patricia said. "It gives me some peace that you've managed to show her it's okay to need someone."

Her words, an echo of his own, lurked in the back of his mind throughout the day and kept popping up at the oddest times. The Rileys were formidable one-on-one, but as a group, he didn't see how anyone would ever wear them down. More, he didn't understand why anyone would want to try.

It was possible he was awestruck. They juggled the various needs, moods and personalities of each person without any visible hitch or strife. Not by luck or denial, but by design. He'd found himself liking the pace and constant flow of conversation more than he anticipated. He'd grown especially fond of the flat-out defiance the family as a whole exhibited. They refused to cower or dwell on the person gunning for them.

Late one afternoon General Riley brought the boat around and they all piled on for a cruise. He and Grace Ann were at the rail near the stern, watching the coast drift out of sight. In her bikini, with a scrap of sheer fabric tied in a loose skirt across her hips, she made him wish they were out here alone.

"Has the guy after your dad ever made a run at them here?" he asked.

She glanced over her shoulder where her dad and mom stood arm in arm at the wheel. "No." Her hands gripped the rail for a moment before she released it. "Hank has security nearby, but the prevailing theory is that he isn't ready to take a direct shot at Dad yet."

"What will you do after this is over?" he asked her.

"Go home, I suppose. I'll find something to paint or mow or plant while I wait for the JAG office to get me reinstated."

"Kevin says he'll be at least another week in the rehab center."

Her lips curved into a smile. "Based on the text messages I'm getting, he's having way too much fun for a guy with a spine injury."

Derek chuckled. "I was wondering if you wanted to come to my place for a few days. I could put in an appearance at the office and you could see just how boring civilian life should be."

"Is this another attempt at dating?" she asked.

"I'd rather not jinx that with an honest answer." Her laughter rolled over him, as warm and happy as the sunlight dancing on the water. "What do you think?"

"I think I'd like that."

He wanted to push her sunglasses up so he could see her gorgeous, expressive eyes. He wanted to be alone with her to tease and hold and relax. "Why don't you talk about your deployments with your parents or brothers?"

"Swap war stories?" She frowned. "Not during family time. It really isn't my style."

"So your style remains ruthlessly independent?"

"Everyone needs a gimmick," she quipped. Turning, she leaned into the rail, her mirrored sunglasses providing an uncomfortable reflection of his serious expression. "Which one of them has been bending your ear to get me to open up?"

"All of them, in one way or another." He took her hand, hoping everyone else was too busy to notice. "They just want you happy," he said.

She lifted their joined hands, pushing her slender fingers between his. "I want to be happy." She nibbled on her lip and his body fired in eager response. "I'm happy right now," she said. "Mostly."

When he had her alone again, he'd make her pay for the teasing. Out of respect for her family, and the possibility of thin walls, they hadn't done more than hold hands, only indulging in a few mesmerizing kisses during their private evening walks on the beach. He'd go crazy if he didn't get her alone again soon.

"Seriously." His voice cracked and her sultry laughter lit a fire in his veins. "There's something else I want to run by you." If he pitched this idea right, it could help everyone. "A reporter has been calling the office, trying to get an interview with me. Preferably with us."

Her eyebrows winged up over her sunglasses. "The bombing was four days ago. Isn't our window of fame over?"

"Apparently it's still wide-open."

"Is this something you want? We don't have any real insight to share. How can interviewing us help anyone?"

Derek leaned on his elbows, putting his face within kissing distance of hers. "Maybe we do the interview to irritate someone."

Her lips pursed and her eyebrows rose. "Go on."

"I've been thinking about it since you said the person

behind all this nonsense wanted to drive you to a break-down." He stroked the back of her hand, his gaze on the receding shoreline. "You didn't break, Grace Ann. I respect why we're here, but wouldn't it be nice payback to do an interview and really triumph?"

She hummed a little, mulling it over. She was too kiss-able and he had to remind himself they were surrounded by her family. Family that was waiting and watching to see how Grace Ann would let him into her life.

The boat rolled and her face paled. She pressed a hand to her belly. "Nerves," she explained. "The idea has merit."

They stood like that for some time before she spoke again. "Do you think I have PTSD?"

"We've had this talk," he reminded her.

"Humor me."

He rose to the challenge. "You've been through a lot," he began. "As a nurse you've seen stuff I don't want to imagine, overseas and stateside." Her face set in muti-nous lines and he hurried on. "I'm not dodging the question. In my opinion, you could use a good, long vacation that doesn't include investigation updates, but you're not unstable. Why are you asking again?"

"Lately nothing feels right," she admitted. "My emotions are too close to the surface." She sniffled. "The memories and nightmares have sharp new edges and leave me queasy in the morning."

"You haven't been restless in your sleep."

She circled a finger in the air. "Woo-hoo. I guess that's something."

"When Hank gets back, let's ask about the interview," he suggested. "Maybe you just need to get proactive, as long as we can do it in a way that doesn't put you or your family in more danger."

She turned to watch her younger siblings at the bow. "I hope Hank has something. We need to put a real name to the man behind this nonsense."

She was out of his sight. Not exactly out of his reach, but he wasn't ready to reveal the full scope of his operation just yet.

The longer the general and the yes-men investigating the situation believed he was limited to the resources of urban hubs and hired hands, the better for the ultimate success of his plans.

He kept tabs on the news out of Maryland, waiting for the announcement of deaths related to the bombing. Major Bartles's name had not been listed as a casualty, although he had confirmation the man was dead.

A wave of resentment swamped him. It had taken months of courting to find the right leverage over Bartles. And the man had chickened out at the last minute, taking the brunt of the explosion meant for Riley's all-too-perfect first daughter.

He knew from his informants that the entire clan had gathered at the house in North Carolina. The house built on the blood and sweat of soldiers the general had sacrificed for his glorious reputation.

The blind rage he'd successfully suppressed long enough to plan out every detail of his revenge bubbled up to the surface. The general would know pain and loss firsthand.

The general *would* be disgraced and he *would* lose the respect and gratitude of the nation.

The Riley children who survived his revenge would forever carry the shame of their father's mistakes. He would see to the exposure and dishonorable discharge of each of them from military service as he had been disgraced and forced out by the general.

Hank returned late the next evening, looking as haggard as Grace Ann had ever seen him. This time he didn't ask to speak with anyone privately, calling a family meeting in the main room. Better this way, she thought, hoping this meant Hank had a name to go with all of the games. Even Caleb had been used by the Riley Hunter, and at fifteen he was old enough to hear hard facts.

"The autopsy proved H.B. was murdered," Hank began without preamble. "The killer used ricin powder in his oxygen line."

"Ricin can take days to kill," Grace Ann said, exchanging a look with her mother.

"I'm aware," Hank said. "The coroner is trying to figure out if he received an initial dose in the days leading up to the bombing. Either way, we've narrowed down a likely culprit who finished him off in the burn unit. One angle shows a tattoo under the sleeve of the lab coat the suspect wore." He dipped his chin toward Derek. "I'll want your take in particular on the images we have."

"Sure thing," Derek agreed.

Grace Ann watched as he studied the photos. "This could be the man from the stairwell. The tattoo is in the right place and the jawline is the same."

"Good start." Hank pulled another folder from his briefcase on the kitchen island. "I brought the pictures just in case any of you might see something familiar." He handed the stack of pictures to Grace Ann.

She studied the picture of the man in scrubs and a lab coat next to H.B.'s hospital bed. "Were his scrubs the same color as everyone else on the floor that day? It's a typical security precaution."

Hank narrowed his gaze as he scanned his notes. "I'm not sure. I'll find out. Regardless, he's not the man pulling the strings."

"He isn't?" Derek asked.

"No." Hank shook his head. "Our man has perfected the art of hiring mercenaries to do the work. He checks résumés, assigns testing tasks. Thanks to the notes on H.B.'s laptop we've unraveled a few of the communications. The hunter issues specific directions and has rigid compliance standards."

"Clearly, he doesn't tolerate errors," Grace Ann said.

"I've spent the past few days picking apart H.B.'s official communications and personal email, looking for motive and contacts."

"You found something," Ben said.

"I sure as hell hope so." Hank turned to Ben. "H.B. was in contact with a former soldier closer to Ben's age. Do you remember a man by the name of John Eaton?"

Her father swore at the same time her mother and Matt gasped. Grace Ann turned toward them along with everyone else. "Eaton was discharged after he went off the rails during a mission in Iraq," Ben explained. "He killed fifteen civilians before his team got him under control. Prior to that, he'd been one of our most reliable snipers."

"About fifteen years ago, wasn't it?" Matt asked. "It still has the potential for a public relations nightmare."

"It was one hell of a mess. We gave the media what we could, though it wasn't nearly the transparency they wanted," Ben said.

"Where is he now?" Grace Ann asked.

"We don't know," Hank admitted. "His medical record shows he was on the Walter Reed campus for his annual exams last week."

"How does he still have benefits?" Mark demanded.

"On my orders," Ben said. "He had family. A wife and daughter. Plus he needed professional help. You said personal? During our years working together, I considered him a trusted friend." He pinched the bridge of his nose while Patricia moved close to offer comfort.

"Why isn't he in jail?" Jolene asked.

"He served his time," Hank told them. "Because his shooting spree happened during an operation to capture a high-value target, the army handled all of the discipline and treatment plans as quietly as possible. He is my top suspect now. From what I can determine Eaton manipulated him, preyed on his basic dislike of you, promising him money and glory if he helped put you in your place."

"All to torment Dad?" Mark shook his head, disgusted.

The horror of that washed over her. Grace Ann waved her hands as if wiping a chalkboard clean. They had to move forward if she wanted to get back to work. "Okay, okay. Something about this has to work in our favor." She turned to Hank. "If he was in Bethesda as recently as last week, we must have his home address, current employer, stuff like that."

"You know, the CID wouldn't mind having an RN on staff," Hank said.

"That's about the only certification she doesn't have," Matt joked.

She made a face at her older brother. "You either."

"The point," Hank cut in before they got into an argument, "is we've sent a team to the home address of record. That's in Illinois. He isn't there. Neighbors say he rents out the house. Wife and daughter moved out years ago. No one remembers them." He passed around pictures of a shabby little house with a sagging porch in a neighborhood that had seen better days.

"What about the emails?" Luke piped up. "Did you get anything helpful about location from the IP address?"

"Not so far. Whatever Eaton's done since he left the army, he's a master at flying under the radar."

"That fits with all the remote feed stuff he did when he attacked us," Matt said, linking his hand with Bethany's.

None of this made sense to Grace Ann. "Email or not, if he's under a doctor's care those communications have to go somewhere."

"Hard copies go to a post office box in the same town as the house he rents. We're still tracking down who collects the mail for him."

"Why is he targeting my kids? I protected *his* kid." Ben's voice boomed through the room. "I'm the one who ended his career. But I made sure his wife and daughter had benefits until she turned eighteen. He should be coming after *me*."

"I believe he will," Hank said. "In time."

Ben shook his head. "Family is off-limits, he'd said it himself."

"Doesn't sound like that stopped him over there," Luke grumbled.

"That's just one reason I didn't believe the first reports coming up the line," Ben said. "I was sure it was a mistake. It wasn't. He eventually confessed to me, though I never understood what made him snap."

"What now, Hank?" Grace Ann asked after a long moment of silence.

"That's about it until we locate Eaton. With luck,

we'll find some evidence he met with H.B. in person last week."

"Surely you can take the rest of the week with us," Patricia said. "You need some time to recharge."

Though her mother spoke to Hank, Grace Ann felt as if the words were aimed at her, a reminder she was supposed to be doing some recharging of her own.

By some tacit agreement, they all moved to cheer up Ben and soon decided a s'mores party on the beach was in order. Graham crackers, chocolate bars and marshmallows were found and the twins had a fire going while others assembled chairs and blankets.

Grace Ann pulled Hank aside while the others settled in. "When can I get back to work?"

"I'm doing my best," he replied. "Eaton has someone posing as the soldier who insisted you treat the little girl first."

"That soldier only exists for the sake of the bugs Eaton put in my house."

"Well, now he's flesh and blood, complete with a service record. It won't hold up, but I'm hoping to tie him or the money he accepted for the job to Eaton or H.B."

She swore. "Hank. I need to work."

"I know, Gracie. Just hang in there. I need a little more time."

She shoved the box of graham crackers at his chest. "What if there was another option? A move that would bring Eaton to us?"

"I'm all ears."

She waved Derek over and as he explained the plan, she started to really believe this next trap would do the trick.

Chapter 13

It had taken another day for Hank to work out the details from choosing the best location for the interview and the transportation and security team for Grace Ann and Derek.

They had consulted the army public relations office and the hospital publicist and eventually agreed to an afternoon taping in Bethesda that would air on the evening news across the country. The station had wanted her to appear in uniform, but she was still officially suspended. Hank negotiated a compromise with a simple, dull gold tailored shirt with a black sweater and slacks. Army colors wrapped up in classic civilian style.

Derek wore a charcoal sport coat and navy slacks with a with a pale blue dress shirt that made his eyes pop and her mouth water. The reporter, blonde and glossy-haired, took to him immediately and simply encouraged Grace Ann to relax.

Before they began, the reporter explained she'd open the segment with a succinct recap of the explosion timeline and a summary of the casualties. Then she started the interview. "It's been a week since the incident and our community is still singing your praises. We appreciate you being here so we can thank you properly."

Derek glanced to Grace Ann, his inscrutable lawyer face in place. She loved him more with every minute. She would never get through this without his steady presence. The whole point was for her composure to push Eaton into making a mistake.

"We were glad to be able to help," she replied.

The reporter walked them through a photo essay of the event, asking for comments along the way. Whenever she felt rattled, Derek's unflappable calm rubbed off on her. Matching his tone, they relived the horror one moment at a time. So far, so good.

Grace Ann's anxiety ratcheted up as she assessed various pictures of the two of them treating victims. She stifled her annoyance and the urge to walk out. That was only the pent-up stress talking. Stalking off the set in a snit would defeat their purpose and make Eaton happy.

Digging deep, she kept the endgame in mind.

The reporter turned to Derek as she paused a bystander's video. She'd timed it perfectly, Grace Ann thought darkly. Derek's brow was pinched and he'd just pulled the belt free to hand it over. She in turn had a bloody palm turned up, while she leaned all her weight onto the man she was trying to save. H.B.

"What made you hand over your belt?" the reporter asked with grave sincerity.

"She asked for it." Derek turned to Grace Ann with a self-deprecating smile. "What you can't see from that angle," he continued though the reporter hadn't asked him to elaborate, "is that Major Riley was in emergency-assessment mode. I did as she asked, obeying or passing on directions as she gave them."

"Miss, I mean, *Major* Riley, what were you thinking as you moved from victim to victim?"

The patronizing tone from one professional woman to another grated on Grace Ann's already-raw nerves. Instead of fuming, she emulated Derek's calm demeanor and dragged up a smile of her own.

This is war. She knew full well the reporter would lap up the truth and the publicist would have a coronary if she dared to give that answer.

"I wasn't. During the crisis I simply followed my training and instincts. Like the other first responders on the scene, my goal was stabilizing the next person in my path."

"And the army runs drills like this?"

"Emergency response is an essential part of our training," she said, keeping her steely officer's smile in place. "The Army Nurse Corps has an excellent record of service in peacetime and in crisis. As a team we work on the cutting edge of medical advancements, as well as manage the day-to-day health of the men and women who serve our nation. We do all we can to prepare to meet that need wherever we find it, be that in the field or a state-of-the-art hospital."

"Major Riley offers a superb example of the greatness we're all capable of," Derek interjected. "This moment stands apart, an unexpected, tragic and unpredictable crisis," he said. "Everyone can make a heroic difference to someone, from highly trained first responders and professionals like Major Riley, all the way to laymen like me. All it takes is stepping up and doing what needs done to assist our neighbors."

"Well said, Mr. Sayer."

Grace Ann had never had cause to hear Derek's professional, legal voice. Oddly enough, it put her at ease at the same time the mellow tones sent an excited tingle along her skin.

When this was over, they were going somewhere private so she could kiss him senseless. The anticipation posed enough of a distraction that she nearly lost track of the interview. Whatever he'd just said, he made no attempt to mute his pride or affection for her, even on camera. It was a heady sensation.

"Major Riley." The reporter tipped her head. "Do you have any advice for the rest of us, should we ever be caught in such a situation?"

"Yes." Thank goodness for training, she thought, breaking out the core message. "Take a first aid course, get certified in CPR," she said. "Remember the value of kindness and compassion," she added, improvising a little. "We can all use more of that, in a crisis or in our daily interactions."

At last they were done and Grace Ann breathed easier once she and Derek were clear of cameras and microphones. Her mother and Hank met them in the hallway between the studio and the greenroom. "Nicely done," her mother said, hugging her close.

"Now we wait," Grace Ann replied, shaking the tension from her hands.

No one was sure how Eaton would react to her serene composure on camera. She'd been eager to push Eaton to do something rash. Now she didn't want to admit how frightened she was that someone she loved might get caught in the cross fire of his next stunt.

"You're not planning on watching this as a family tonight, are you?"

"I think you've had enough," Patricia said. She glanced toward Derek, who was chatting with Hank. "He did an amazing job in there for the two of you, and the rest of us," she whispered. "Are you planning to let that get serious?"

Grace Ann rolled her shoulders. "Is there something more serious than baiting a madman?"

"You know what I mean."

"It's too soon for serious, Mom." She didn't want to share all these feelings she had for Derek. It was too new, too special to let everyone see it.

Patricia hummed. "Not from where I'm standing."

"Well, you're standing in a pool of hopeless romanticism," Grace Ann said. "Let's get to the airport. There's a storm coming in and I'd like to get out on the waves," she said. Between the days of surfing and nights of sleeping well in Derek's arms, she had been feeling better than she had in months.

"Maybe the surfing should wait," Patricia began. "You're a little pale."

"All the more reason to get back to the beach," Grace Ann said. "Nothing will perk me up faster."

"As long as you don't go out alone."

Grace Ann made an *X* over her heart, then kissed Patricia's cheek. "You're the best mom ever."

"The car's here," Hank said, leading the way.

When Derek slid into the back seat with her, she tucked her hand into his. "Feel like coming out to the beach to play lifeguard?"

"Sounds like my kind of fun." He gave her hand a squeeze. "You did great in there. Poised, professional, confident."

"Let's hope the reporter doesn't edit me right out of

the piece. I thought she'd offer to have your babies right there on camera."

His brows shot up and then he broke into laughter and everything felt almost normal again.

Derek felt as if he was dancing on the edge of a razor blade on the flight back to the beach house. Grace Ann had dozed off, her head pillowed on his shoulder, right after takeoff. Hank had thrown himself back into work while Patricia chatted with him, deftly avoiding the real reason they were on the plane.

It was too soon for Eaton to strike back—the interview wouldn't even air for hours yet—but Derek couldn't shake that sense of impending doom. He wanted to put this mess behind them so he could move forward with Grace Ann.

He wanted there to be a *them*. A future. And if anyone was going to have his babies, he wanted it to be her. He could just imagine her face if he suggested it. But a week with the big, rowdy Riley family had him taking another look at dreams he'd set aside in his determination to give Kevin a solid home life after the tragedy. He was ready to grow, to add more branches to the Sayer family tree, as long as Grace Ann was growing with him.

Watching her paddle out over the rollers to catch the next wave, he marveled at her innate resilience. She was a joy to watch, so free out there in the choppy water. Seeing her in a playful mood buoyed his spirits. It seemed she'd finally accepted that leaning on him didn't undermine her independence. For him, he appreciated being needed in a way that didn't mean finding all the answers. Some days he wondered if that trait of stepping in and solving problems had always been part of him, or if it had been honed by necessity when he and his brother were orphaned.

He grinned as she found her balance on an incoming wave and rode in until it broke apart near the shore. His breath stuttered when she went under, smoothed out again as she surfaced a moment later.

He'd gained tremendous perspective on Grace Ann, watching her with her family. Every new layer made him want to stay, to linger until the next surprise appeared. She played poker like a champ, sucked at video games, enjoyed reading medical studies on new procedures, and she could talk for hours with her nephew about metal bands or sports stats.

Given the chance, would he thank Eaton for this nonsense?

It was an impossible and irrelevant question. Without the threats and trouble, it might have taken him longer, but he believed they would have wound up in this direction anyway.

Although Derek had taught himself never to love anyone else the way he'd loved his parents as self-preservation, Grace Ann had been challenging those isolating tactics. The Riley family demonstrated a version of family that made him wish for more. Forced him to realize he was shortchanging himself and the people he cared for by locking away his heart.

Not anymore.

"Looking good, Gracie!" Luke whistled as he walked across the sand to join Derek. "Why don't you ever get out there?" he asked.

Derek shook his head. "I prefer more of a boat between me and whatever's under the waves."

"It's only more water," Luke said, laughing a little.

"I was thirteen when the Pacific tried to keep me," he said.

Luke flicked that aside. "You won the battle, right?"

"Obviously. And yet Caleb isn't out here," Derek said.

"We won't push it while Bethany's pregnant. The kid could totally handle these rollers. Mark and Gracie taught him well."

"Did you enjoy being an army brat?" Derek asked.

Luke leaned back on his hands, his gaze roaming over the water and the bank of clouds closing in on the surfers, driving the waves higher. "Being the son of a command officer carries all kinds of responsibility. At least that's what they told me time and again. You might have noticed Mom is the queen of the castle."

Derek grinned. "I did pick up on that."

"Seriously though," Luke continued. "We had a great life. Different, though you don't know that until you get off base and hang out with civilians. We learned to balance self-sufficiency with teamwork. We saw parts of the world I would never have seen otherwise."

"Did you have a choice about career?"

"Hell, yeah. Our parents were the first to suggest options outside the military for all of us. Of course, they weren't quiet about the benefits, either," he said, smiling. "This situation with Gracie, and with Matt a few months ago, only emphasizes life is short," he continued. Then he swore. "Sorry, that was insensitive."

"It's fine," Derek said. "My parents have been gone a long time now."

Luke let the rollers wash over his feet. "If we haven't scared you off yet, does that mean you're sticking around?"

That was his plan, assuming Grace Ann would get on board. "I enjoy spending time with your older sister," he said. "And the rest of you. It would be nice to do it more often."

"That's good to hear." Luke's mouth slanted into a frown. "Not everyone appreciates our brand of chaos."

"Are you afraid of what Eaton will try next?" Derek asked.

"Eaton should be afraid of *us* if he doesn't back off," Luke grumbled. "He's crossed a line. When we find him, he'll wish he'd never heard of Ben Riley or his kids."

"With luck, the interview will flush him out," Derek said.

"We can hope." Luke lifted his chin toward Grace Ann. "You haven't asked me, but I think you're good for her."

Derek knew better than to let those words go to his head, but it was a tough ask. "We have common interests."

Luke threw back his head and laughed. "Said like a true lawyer. Common interests or not, be careful with her. She'd kick my ass for saying so, but there's a tender heart under that tough shell. It would be a bummer if we had to kill you." On that note, he ran for the tide as his twin brother skimmed his board over the waves and right up to the beach.

When he'd asked Grace Ann about an exclusive relationship, he hadn't fully understood this piece of her life. Family was her cornerstone. He could see how it supported everything she did, and influenced her worldview and perspective.

Testing himself, he contemplated walking away. The immediate ball of icy panic in his gut was all the answer he needed. No further analysis required.

He watched her pop up again as another swell came up, formed into a decent wave. She lost her balance at the tail end of it and splashed into the water, her face alight with laughter. Something around his heart clicked into place and he knew she was the only woman for him. It fascinated him, this all-encompassing knowing.

He vaguely remembered his mom telling the story of falling fast and hard for his father while his dad had worn an expression of dopey contentment. Love had a strange effect on people. He supposed the next question was what Grace Ann would say when he proposed. He looked up as she stopped in front of him, a carefree smile on her face and ocean water dripping into the sand.

"Thinking big thoughts?" she asked, dropping down to sit beside him.

He nodded, turning his gaze to the ocean so she wouldn't see what he wasn't quite ready to say. If he asked her now, she'd blame it on Eaton or pressure from her family. Besides, he hadn't so much as told her how he felt. That should probably come first.

They had time, he reminded himself. He picked up her hand, tracing her long, narrow fingers, the veins and tendons under her smooth skin.

"You okay?" she asked.

"Better than okay," he replied. "Did the surfing help?"

"It did. The hip is all loose again after the flight. Now if I can just keep from going crazy while we wait for Eaton to make his next move."

"I thought maybe we could go out to dinner," he suggested. He had yet to learn if she wanted to watch when the interview aired. He wasn't sure she'd figured it out yet.

"I don't know. That didn't work out so well last time."

"You think takeout would be safe enough? We could bring it back here and eat on the beach."

He thought she'd laugh. To his surprise, she sniffled

and appeared to be fighting off tears. "Ah. You've been thinking big thoughts, too."

"Sure," she confessed with a watery smile. "Hard not to with everything going on. Any word from Kevin?"

He honored the not-so-subtle plea to change the subject. "We talked yesterday. He was upbeat. He tells me he hired a nursing service to help when he's released to go home. Said he doesn't need me at all."

"Are you okay with that?"

He appreciated that she understood. "I didn't think the chick was supposed to push the parent out of the nest," he joked. "Seriously, I'm about eighty percent okay with it," he said. "He is an adult."

"Did you ever hope the injury would end his military career?"

"What? No." He glared at her, offended.

"Take it easy." She bumped him with her damp shoulder. "I know you worry and I assume being the only one worrying is more taxing than sharing the burden with a family."

He hadn't thought about it in quite those terms. "Either way, he's made up his mind. I hear he's good at his work."

"The unit will step up," she assured him. "He's likely to invite you over just to get a break from us."

"It's all good," he said. For several minutes, they watched the water roll into the shore, the storm blowing closer. "From what Hank said, you'll be back in the rotation before long."

"I hope you're right." She wrapped her arms around her knees. "I can't believe Eaton found someone to pose as the soldier I made up that night at the house."

There had to be a way for him to help her. "You should have independent representation."

"Relax." She stretched out her hip. "The JAG office has my back and the right people know the truth. My biggest challenge right now is being patient."

"If you're sure." He mentally sifted through his network of friends for someone who might have some insight or advice that could help her. "At least you have a fallback if the army doesn't come to their senses."

She swiveled to gape at him. "I do?"

"You'd be a superb surf instructor," he pointed out.

"Good point." She grinned. "And there are plenty of ways to be a nurse that don't involve the army."

He didn't believe for a minute that she was ready to leave her military career. "He won't win," Derek stated, sliding an arm around her shoulders.

"What makes you so sure?"

"Could be a hunch," he said.

"Or?"

"Could be your family rubbing off on me."

"You surprise me." She studied his face as thunder rumbled through the dark gray clouds leading the storm. "I like it." She stood up, held out a hand to him. "Let's go have a date."

He dusted off his shorts and she yanked her board out of the sand. Together they hustled up to the house and ducked under the cover as the bottom fell out of the heavy rain clouds.

It was like being caught in the eye of a storm with sheets of rain blowing all around them. Under the house the wind created a chill against his bare legs. In her wet rash guard and swim shorts, she had to be freezing. Thankfully there was a central staircase leading straight to the kitchen.

Instead of heading in, she watched the wind whip up the waves, her arms wrapped around her middle. "You probably don't want to go out in this tonight," she said. "Our date can wait."

Kevin must have told her a heavy rainstorm had contributed to the crash that killed their parents. "It won't bother me," he promised.

"You sure?"

"I am." When she gazed up at him, eyes swimming with concern, he pulled her close. "I am," he murmured again, lowering his lips to hers. He meant to keep it light, but the taste of her laced with ocean salt shot right through him.

"Gracie? Derek?" Patricia's voice carried from the top of the stairs.

Grace Ann smothered a giggle against his shoulder. "Just watching the weather, Mom," she called back.

"As long as you haven't been washed away."

The door closed and Grace Ann's laughter spilled out, like a beam of sunlight breaking through the clouds. "They'll still be checking on me when I'm fifty."

"It's good to know they love you."

"Always," she agreed, darting for the stairs. "And now we'll have to rush if we're going to get out of here before that interview airs."

The speedy shower and quick change of clothes, followed by the short, blurry drive to town, didn't settle Grace Ann. Her nerves were humming after kissing Derek under the house, the mist against her face, her skin prickling with the chilly air and the heat of his embrace. The man had a definite skill and her lips tingled all over again. Though she thoroughly enjoyed sleeping beside him and getting caught up on her rest, she couldn't wait for an encore of the mind-blowing passion they'd shared at the hotel.

He continued to amaze her, in big ways and small, and his ability to adapt and roll right along with her family left a trail of flowery, happy thoughts drifting through her mind. So tempting to let those feelings take root and bloom, but she wasn't sure how Derek felt about a forever kind of thing with a slightly broken nurse.

The spot she'd recommended wasn't a dive, but business casual would've made them vastly overdressed. The bar was doing brisk business thanks to the weather. Derek wore faded jeans and running shoes with a graphic T-shirt that emphasized his chest and biceps. His hair, mussed by the weather, made her want to run her hands through the thick waves. She didn't think she'd ever get this longing for him out of her system.

She wondered what he'd do if she told him she'd fallen irrevocably in love with him. There would be time for that once Hank had Eaton in custody and the Riley Hunter nonsense was over.

At the bar, they ordered two flavors of hot wings and a couple of soft drinks, and waited for a pool table in the back room to open up, since the rain washed out their plans for a beach picnic. They talked about fantasy camping trips and the outdoor experiences they hadn't yet conquered. It seemed both of them had an unending bucket list. He had a thing for rock climbing, which she appreciated if only because the effort had sculpted his arms, shoulders and chest to perfection.

This break would end soon and all of her siblings would return to their normal lives and schedules. Derek needed to get back to work as well, and though the thought made her nervous, she knew Hank would keep an eye on him if necessary. If she was still suspended, she'd have to find something to do. Hanging here with her parents was the logical choice, but it still felt too much like cowering.

For the moment, she was content to admire Derek playing pool. He had a way of moving, of eyeing her as she made her shots, that kept her blood humming.

Taking his turn, he bent low and lined up his shot. "Have you decided to come to my place for a few days after this mess is over?" The stick connected with the cue ball and sent one of his striped balls into the corner pocket near her hip. He straightened, held her gaze. "I'd rather you weren't alone at your place."

"I'm not thrilled with that idea either, but I need to go back sometime." She needed to be an adult and face those demons. Hank told her the bugs were gone and the team continued to keep watch.

She watched Derek sink another ball. He took control of the table and she could only move out of his way as he made shot after shot, finally sinking the eight ball. "And here I thought the big sharks were well off the coast this time of year," she teased.

He laughed and the deep rumble sent another ripple of sweet anticipation down her spine. "Two out of three?" he asked, reaching for the form to rack up another game.

She started to reply when she heard someone swear and ask the bartender to change the channel on the television. Not uncommon, though usually it was a sporting event that prompted the request.

"Rileys are good people," another man said. "That's nothing but fake news."

She caught Derek's narrowed gaze and shook her head. It seemed they weren't going to avoid the interview after all. Moving toward the television in the corner of the poolroom, she read the ticker at the bottom of the screen.

Her first thought was that it had to be a nightmare. The words—the *lies*—were incomprehensible. On the screen, she and Derek sat side by side while images from the explosion were playing in a smaller inset. None of it was enough of a distraction from the ticker. A string of reprimands, none of them true, was being broadcast to the world, making her look like a fraud at best, oblivious and insensitive at worst.

Her career was crumbling under an assault she'd never seen coming.

"We have to get back," she said, reaching for her cell phone.

"On it." Derek had flagged down the waitress and was already settling the check.

She felt every pair of eyes in the place watching her. It wouldn't do any good to defend herself. Someone was likely recording her anyway, for Eaton or to sell to the media, and she wouldn't hand them ammunition to use against her or the army.

"You think Eaton fed her that info?" Derek asked when they were in the car.

"Not directly." She stared out the window, seeking those dark glimpses of the ocean between the buildings and businesses. That darkness called to her and she longed to get lost in it. "The reporter did her legwork, digging into my service record for dirt. Hank purposely didn't hide the suspension when he set it up," she said, thinking out loud.

"I'm sure he didn't expect her to twist it like that."

She was going to have to face her family, to explain those infractions and the kernel of truth that had sprouted and grown into unmanageable rumors.

Whatever Eaton had in mind, a prank she'd pulled in anger downrange had just come back to haunt her.

When they walked in, everyone but Hank was waiting in the family room, gathered around the television. She supposed Hank was already trying to put out the fires. Telling herself it was better to just get it all out, she met her father's flummoxed gaze.

Luke muted the broadcast that had switched over to an analysis of her behavior and the stability of soldiers returning from war zones.

"It's not all true," she began, facing her father.

He waited in silence. It was an effective tactic.

"H.B. was a disgrace to the uniform," she said. "He was a pencil-pushing coward."

"So you threatened his life with a *grenade*?" Her mother glared, quoting one of the claims from the ticker.

Mark's sputtering laugh broke the tension. "The 'homicidal tendencies' deal is a proven deployment exemption, sis. But you toss it out there *before* you go downrange."

She rolled her eyes and got back to the point. "I was ready and willing to get in and get to work on the base or off. H.B., not so much." She met her father's gaze once more. "It was a stupid stunt I pulled a few weeks in. Naturally, he was on the advance party and he'd made a hash of it. Just as we got that sorted out and were hitting our stride as a team, he started nitpicking our scheduling and putting such strict controls on our movements we couldn't carry out any work in the community. Community engagement was core to the *mission*."

"That's no excuse," Ben interjected.

She held up her hands. "You're right. He started a rumor that I only wanted to leave the base to spend more time with our interpreter."

"Did anyone buy that?" Patricia asked.

"Of course not." Grace Ann scrubbed at her face and

then rushed through the next part. "He was scheduled to go out with us, but claimed a sprained ankle."

"You're sure it was a lie?"

She nodded at her father's query, as exasperated now as she'd been then. "On the way back to the base, our team encountered some light arms fire, more annoyance than real danger. H.B. had one excuse after another, week in and week out. I got fed up and put a grenade on his desk."

Mark and Luke couldn't quite stifle their amusement, even when Patricia glared daggers at them.

"You threatened the man's life?" Ben asked.

"He only *thought* I did." She folded her arms, defiant now with the recollection. "It wasn't a live grenade. Any basic trainee could have seen that right away. H.B. panicked and made a fool of himself."

"How did he know it was you?" Luke asked.

She rolled her shoulders. In her wildest dreams, she'd never thought she'd have to explain this poor judgment to her father. "I signed the note."

Patricia sucked in a breath. Her father swore. Her siblings, with the exception of Matt, fell into fits of laughter. Derek, along with Bethany and Caleb, was trying valiantly to stay neutral, with varying degrees of success.

"What did your commander say?" The disappointment in her father's gaze shamed her.

"He laughed," she said. "Privately. I had to publicly apologize to H.B. and deliver a safety training class to the unit."

"Apparently H.B. didn't accept your apology," Patricia noted.

"I thought he did," she said. "We got through the remainder of our time with little more than an aggravated glance here and there. We worked well in the operating room. He never left the base, though he stopped impeding those of us who were determined to do our job right."

Ben and Patricia exchanged a speaking look.

"Were you formally reprimanded?"

The scrolling ticker had implied as much. "No." She flung out a hand toward the television. "And I sure as hell didn't plant a bomb on a street corner last week for him to walk into."

"The ticker reported an anonymous source as well as links to a Wiki page with official reprimands," Matt said.

"Those wouldn't be from *my* personnel jacket," she insisted. "I pushed one prank too far, yes, but that's it."

"Eaton," Ben said. "He must have heard about this from H.B. and fabricated the rest. Hank will handle it."

"I say margaritas for everyone," Luke suggested before anyone else could react. "We've earned it."

She appreciated being shoved out of the spotlight, though the idea of tequila didn't sound smart under the circumstances. She shared a pitcher of virgin daiquiris with Bethany and Caleb and enjoyed the quieter, individual support her family offered throughout the rest of the evening.

The weather cleared and as everyone else headed for bed, Grace Ann slipped out onto the deck. The air was fresh and clean after the rain, the pulse of the ocean the only music at this hour. Derek found her, taking a seat in the chair next to hers without saying a word.

She reached for his hand, savoring that simple, deep connection. "There's only one thing I miss about Afghanistan," she said.

"What's that?" Derek asked.

"The stars."

Scooting closer, he reached over and stroked her

cheek, the curve of her ear. "Do you remember the time we met up in the Smoky Mountains?"

"Of course." Her eyes and heart were heavy with all her mistakes. "It was our second, no, our third trip." Things had felt so easy then. They could slip away from reality and just enjoy each other. Eaton had changed that, turning H.B.'s wounded pride and childish temper against her.

"It was the first time I'd watched a meteor shower."

"No way." He spent too much time outside for that to be true.

"Way," he insisted. "There were shooting stars occasionally when I was a kid, but nothing like that night."

The marvel in his voice made her smile. "How did you break your nose?"

He touched the spot. "Kevin clocked me with a toy train." He smirked. "I got even."

"As you should," she said, understanding.

"Come home with me, Grace Ann." He caressed her chin, his fingers trailing down her neck and over her shoulder and away.

She missed that touch immediately, her body yearning toward him. "This is a bad time," she reminded him. "I'm a liability to everyone, especially now."

"Better if we just go our separate ways then?" he asked. "Or go back to what we'd settled for?"

No. That wasn't what she meant. "Derek, I'm in a heavyweight fight for my career." She propped up on her elbow. "I'm the definition of drama. Assuming I succeed, my work shifts are stressful on a relationship. Not to mention training assignments and overseas deployments."

"I'm aware that *nursing* is a demanding career, in any context. It's what you're built for. Who you are. It's what you love to do, but it's only one facet of what I love about you."

Love? Her heart leaped. Had she heard him right? Stunned, she sat up. She wanted to give him the words back, but she didn't dare. Not until she was sure. She loved being an army nurse. Finding rewarding work in the medical field could prove a challenge after the latest blow to her reputation. No one paid attention to the retractions or follow-ups that cleared a person's name; the dirt, true or not, was much more entertaining.

"You should be with someone stable. Someone who won't trigger you," she said.

He came around to crouch in front of her and she could have sworn there was amusement lurking in his blue eyes. "Do I look triggered?"

He didn't actually. "The light's bad out here," she said.

"You can see me just fine. And you love me, too. You might be caught up in Eaton's web right now, but you're not a victim. I'm not sure you even know how to be."

That was the highest compliment he could have given her. "I've been feeling sorry for myself quite a bit these past two weeks." Longer really.

"If we counted all those individual minutes," he said, "it might add up to an hour or two. I admit, I want to sweep you away from all of this—that's something ingrained in me. Even if I could get away with that, avoidance isn't your style."

He knew her better than she realized. She was too bewildered to know what to do with that. "Derek." *I love you, too.* Why couldn't she get the words out?

"I'm not out to change you," he said. "I'm asking you to keep me around. Let me be the person you come home to. Think about it." He tugged her to her feet. "Come on. You need some sleep."

"I'm not sure what good it'll do," she muttered, letting him guide her up to their room.

She felt off-kilter, a bit more each day, as if her mind and heart and body couldn't quite agree on the best way to go about keeping her alert and upright.

When he tucked her in and stretched out beside her on the bed, she nestled close, holding on to that cherished contentment she'd only ever found with him.

Eaton turned up the volume as the interview aired, looking for a chink in her damned Riley armor. She hadn't broken. Hadn't been driven to despair with the various attacks. Now she was on the news, basking in the praise of a grateful city.

He swore. He'd been so sure of his plan, trusting his research into her personal life as well as the ugly moments of her career that he could exploit.

Then the ticker started and he laughed.

The information he'd fabricated with Bartles for the misconduct case was working. And better than he could have hoped now that it was out there for public consumption. Oh, this was rich. Karma was in his corner after all. This gave him still more ways to torment General Riley, tarnishing that sterling reputation everyone went on and on about.

Eaton considered, again, the likely results of each of his options. Even with the reporter inadvertently playing his cards for him, he suspected the investigation he'd started would soon fall apart. His people in DC and Maryland and North Carolina were keeping him informed about everyone's movements.

Thanks to the weak link that had been Bartles, the CID had his real name as well as the house where he'd once lived with his family. They might never find him here, but he wouldn't leave anything to chance.

He turned to his board, where the five Riley children filled out a timeline that culminated with a cartoon sketch of the general on his knees, thoroughly defeated, begging for mercy.

Eaton visualized it every day: the moment when General Riley realized he'd lost the only battle that mattered. If he didn't have his children, what was left? All those motivating addresses and pep talks, the briefings and awards, were nothing more than hot air when the man threw his best soldiers under the bus as it suited him.

So what if he'd killed fifteen civilians in some craggy hovel on the other side of the world? The soldiers he'd been protecting at the time had made it out, made it home to their families. General Riley had made an example of his efforts, robbing him of a chance to raise his daughter, to grow old with his wife. Now he'd make an example of the general's children. Make the man understand the suffering he'd inflicted.

He picked up the phone. The first call set in motion a plan guaranteed to bring the oldest Riley daughter to her knees. Finally. The second call ensured that his ultimate plan would continue to roll like an avalanche, even if, by some miracle, the authorities found him.

Chapter 14

The next morning at breakfast, Patricia announced she was taking her girls shopping and the guys would be on their own. Derek hoped the outing perked up Grace Ann. Her phone had been humming all morning with updates from Hank, though she didn't share details. He only knew some of the messages left her cringing, while others put a battle light in her eyes.

Regardless of the circumstances they were trying to ignore, he felt he needed to speak with Ben about his plan to propose to Grace Ann. Yes, they were all adults, but traditions mattered, too, and Derek had too few of those in his life. He'd just about worked up the courage to ask for a quick meeting in the general's office when Ben announced the men should take out the boat for a fishing trip and see if they could catch enough for dinner.

Maybe there would be time out there for a private word.

Or maybe he'd just have this conversation with all of the Riley men at once.

* * *

In the maternity department of one of the outdoor mall's bigger stores, Grace Ann slid hangers from side to side on the rack. They'd decided to start the day shopping for work clothes for Bethany that didn't scream "I'm pregnant!"

When her sister and sister-in-law moved out of earshot, she caught her mom's eye. "Maybe I should just resign." There, she'd finally given voice to what felt like the worst-case scenario. If anyone would talk her though every side of the decision, it would be her mother.

"You certainly could do that," Patricia said. "Is that what you want?"

"How do I know?" She'd woken up queasy and irritable again, unable to decide on anything. Not even a quick surf lesson with Caleb had settled her system. "I had what I wanted, Mom." Respect among her peers, a positive and challenging environment. She pulled out a square-neck top and held it up for an opinion. Patricia shook her head.

"With Eaton pulling the rug out from under me…"

"He's a sick man. You can't let that factor in."

"But it does, Mom. This isn't like Matt's situation. He was innocent."

"Your brother is hardly innocent," Patricia muttered.

Clearly her mother hadn't quite forgiven Matt for keeping his son a secret from the family for nearly fifteen years. "He was honoring Bethany's request. You know that. Matt sure didn't let Eaton make a spectacle of him or the family. That was all *me*."

"We're all people, as flawed as we are special. Some more temperamental than others," she added with a wink. "Hank and the JAG office will salvage your career, you know that."

Did she? "My reputation is in tatters after the broadcast last night." She forced out the real problem. "Derek's reputation might take a beating, too, and he's only here because he was trying to help me."

"Derek seems to handle whatever life tosses at him. I like that."

"Just because he can doesn't mean he should have to." She stopped, hearing the echo of his supportive words to her from a few days ago. "He must wish he'd never met me."

"Hmm."

"What's that mean?" she demanded.

"It means he seems to be exactly where he wants to be. Next to *you*."

There was an itch between her shoulder blades. She should have told him she loved him back. "I can't imagine why. We're too different. I'm the embodiment of everything he doesn't want to be part of."

"That's nonsense," Patricia said with too much cheer. "And I think you know that."

"I love him." Just admitting it made her feel better, from the inside out.

"You should tell him, not me."

Once again, her mother was right. He'd said he'd loved her and she'd been a big chicken. That wasn't like her at all. "How did you raise us to live so fearlessly?" she wondered aloud. "We knew Dad worked in bad places, risky places, but you kept us straight."

"Sometimes." Patricia pulled out another blouse, held it up. "Bethany, what about this?"

Her sister-in-law glanced over. "Oh, that's pretty." Then she frowned at the soft green colors. "Will I look like a frog?"

"Not a chance." Patricia beamed. "Go try it on." Turning back to Grace Ann, she said, "Have you forgotten that living big is about where you put your focus? You have to be logical, reasonable, and then you have to decide how to be happy in the midst of it."

Grace Ann was chewing on that bit of wisdom when an emergency signal sounded. The store lights flashed off, though there was plenty of sunlight coming in through the plate glass windows. The three of them stared at each other for a split second as an order to evacuate the mall came over the speakers.

"Jolene, go get Bethany," Patricia said.

The emergency signal clanged again, and a rapid burst of gunfire echoed from somewhere nearby.

"That's in the courtyard." This end of the mall was anchored with the food court, including a large carousel, a playground, and seating indoors and out.

Instinctively, Grace Ann started toward the sound, but her mother caught her elbow.

"No, Gracie. Not today."

Jolene and Bethany rushed back into view, faces pale. Her mom was right. Getting Bethany out safely was the top priority. They moved along with the other shoppers, rushing toward the nearest exit as more gunfire preceded a crash of breaking glass.

Sirens howled as emergency vehicles approached.

They were almost to the parking lot when a mother's cry of dismay was cut short by a gunshot. A child screamed in terror and Grace Ann froze. She knew that sound. In an instant, she wasn't in the States anymore. She and her ghosts were right back in a dusty village on the other side of the world where she'd failed a little girl who'd made a similar plea on a bright spring day.

Without a word to her family, she turned, weaving through the sea of people to get closer to the crisis.

Derek and the Riley men were at the dock, loading the bait coolers into the boat when Matt called out for Ben. He held up his phone. "There's a hostage situation at the mall."

"Where the girls are?" Ben asked. "Damn it. Ten to one, Eaton's involved."

"Bethany." Matt cleared his throat, his face set in grim lines as his son stepped up beside him. "I've gotta go."

"We're all going," Derek said, thinking of Grace Ann. Whether or not Eaton was behind it, he couldn't let her face the crisis alone.

"I'm driving." Mark grabbed the keys from his dad. "Let's move."

They all piled back into Ben's SUV. From the front seat, Ben tuned the radio to a news station. Derek and Caleb scrolled through footage on their phones, Luke and Matt reading over their shoulders.

Ben pushed a hand through his hair. "Eaton is determined to break my baby girl," he murmured. "To prove that a soldier pushed past the limit isn't responsible for the fallout."

"You don't believe that," Mark said.

"Even if I did, there are consequences for the actions we take. At one time Eaton knew that himself." He went quiet as the reporter interviewed a witness who described a man dressed in an old military uniform entering the food court and taking several hostages.

Derek searched social media and found the thread already growing. He enlarged a grainy picture on his phone to see five women and two men tied to a picnic table near a playground. A man wearing a suicide vest held them at gunpoint. He showed the picture to Ben.

Ben pounded on the car door. "It's the village school all over again."

"What are you talking about?" Matt asked before Derek could.

"That school bombing in Afghanistan originated with a man strapped to a bomb. He took a classroom hostage and only a few survived."

"Gracie told you?" Derek queried.

"No. Her commander and I discussed it." He swore. "Eaton successfully worked oversight on a similar mission a year before he went off the deep end. It's all connected in his twisted mind."

Personal, Derek thought as his phone rang. "It's Grace Ann." He answered in speaker mode so they could all hear her.

"Derek?" In that one word, he knew everything. She was on the scene and ready to act.

"You're on speaker," he said.

"Seven hostages, five female, two male. Two perps, male, in ski masks with rifles and plenty of bullets. One perp is wearing a vest."

They all looked at one another. "Two perps?" Derek asked.

"One holding the hostages, and the vest looks like the real deal. Second man is on the roof of the building west of the playground. He has a clear shot of anyone trying to help the hostages."

"Where are you?"

"Food court, up to my elbows in mostly superficial gunshot wounds."

"Has anyone recognized you?" Matt queried.

"Not yet," she whispered.

Gunfire at the scene came through the phone speakers. When it was quiet again, Derek realized the call had ended. He swore.

"Call Mom," Mark said to Ben, goosing the engine. "First we find them, then we give Grace Ann backup."

"I'll tell the police about the guy on the roof," Luke said.

Derek just stared at his phone. There was no one to call, nothing to do in the back of Ben's SUV but wait it out.

Grace Ann had done what she could to warn her family. Now she had to do something proactive here. She and several other people were hunkered down behind the concrete wall separating the doors that opened to the playground and courtyard, but it wasn't enough. There was too much open space.

Anyone who tried to get to the hostages was fired on from the guy on the roof. Anyone making a move toward the parking lot took fire from the guy with the vest.

The sounds of panic and weeping at the scene were too close to what had happened at the village school to be a coincidence. Had to be Eaton. The recognition of his tactic, this blatant attempt to unnerve her, had galvanized her instead.

Grace Ann considered going out, hands raised, and dismissed the idea. This team wasn't here to negotiate; they were here to break her down and capture it for Eaton's viewing pleasure and her father's dismay.

Several feet away, the wife of one hostage wept inconsolably. Understandable. Grace Ann's more immediate concern was that the security guard who'd tried to intervene would lose his leg if she couldn't get him to a hospital.

She pressed her cell phone into the guard's hands. "Call the police, tell them everything we know." She shifted toward the next victim, a teenage girl with a chunk of glass jutting from her calf. "Tell them there are two mercenaries and any request they make is a diversion."

"You were on the news last night," the guard said.

"I was." The glass, embedded deep, was keeping the girl's bleeding to a minimum. "This looks worse than it is," she lied to the girl.

"Well, it hurts worse than it looks then," the girl replied. "Can't you get it out?"

"You're better off leaving it right where it is." What she wouldn't give for some tape to be sure the girl didn't mess with it. "What's your name?"

"Tori."

"All right, Tori, promise me you'll leave that alone." She nodded. "Super. Too bad the leggings won't make it." To her relief, Tori smiled. "Hey, can you do me a favor?"

"As long as it doesn't involve walking."

"Not a bit," Grace Ann said. "When the paramedics get in here, make sure the guard gets out for treatment first."

"Yes, ma'am."

She peered around the corner to check on the hostages. The bastard with the bomb on his chest had wedged them between the carousel and an overturned picnic table. The device she assumed was the bomb's trigger was clipped to his belt and he held his gun with both hands, sweeping the weapon side to side to prevent anyone from making a rescue attempt.

The security guard waved at her. "Police are five minutes out," he whispered when she crept back to his side. "They know about the sniper on the roof."

"Nice job." She picked up the guard's gun, a revolver. There had to be a way to make a difference here, before that vest blew by accident or on purpose. "Do you have a knife?" she asked the guard. If she could create a diversion, she might be able to sneak around the landscaping and get the hostages free.

"I do," the teenager said. She reached into her bag and pulled out a hefty switchblade, sliding it across the floor to Grace Ann.

Grace Ann shot her a look, but who was she to judge? She tucked the knife into her pocket and looked around for anything she could use as a distraction and heard the thumping rotor of a helicopter overhead. It was the opening she needed.

Leaning around the concrete pillar, she saw both men were eyeing the police helicopter. Crouching low, she fired twice, hitting the knees of the man wearing the vest. He pitched forward, away from the table, and she ducked out of the way as he screamed in pain, gunfire spraying in a wide arc as he went down.

Thankfully, the bomb didn't detonate and the hostage taker had fallen unconscious from the pain. She rushed to the playground, kicking the gun out of his reach on her way to check on the hostages.

To her immense relief, all seven people were unharmed.

She shouted the good news back to the security guard as she cut them free and ushered them away from the hostage taker on the other side of the table. Paramedics and police descended on the scene and when she glanced up at the roof, she saw the man in the sniper's position being cuffed by a tactical team.

Despite her protests and efforts to get back to her family, she was loaded into an ambulance and rushed to the hospital along with others who'd been injured. Dazed and light-headed as the adrenaline rush faded, her first and only thoughts were of Derek.

She'd never hold back an "I love you" again.

Although Eaton had been set on forcing her into breakdown, his stunt had actually created a break-*through*. If she was going to live the big and full life she wanted—with Derek—it was past time to seek out a PTSD evaluation and the right support.

Derek thought he would go crazy with the lack of news. They'd almost reached the mall when they got word the crisis was over and victims were being transported to the nearest hospital. He'd called Grace Ann repeatedly, but she didn't pick up. A thousand dreadful scenarios rolled through his mind. Where was she?

When they reached the ER handling the crisis, Ben blustered until the staff told him she was indeed in the back, under a doctor's care. Patricia, Bethany and Jolene joined them, unharmed, after Bethany had an ultrasound to verify the baby was fine. No matter how Patricia cajoled, they wouldn't let her back to see her daughter.

It was over an hour before Hank joined the family in the waiting room. He confirmed what they already suspected. The sniper on the roof confessed that Eaton ordered the men to launch the attack at the mall. He was eager to trade insight on the intricate communication relays for leniency. Grace Ann had not only saved lives, she'd denied Eaton a meltdown and any victory points by taking action before the news crews were set up.

"Did he give up Eaton's location?" Ben asked, his arm around Patricia.

"He's not that high on the food chain," Hank replied. "For now, let's celebrate this win over the Riley Hunter. Hey, Derek, is this the guy you saw in the stairwell?"

Hank showed him a picture of the hostage taker who'd worn what had apparently been a fake bomb vest. Derek recognized the face, and pointed to the tattoo on his wrist. "That's him."

"Sweet," Hank said with a lethal tone. "Once he's out of surgery, he'll talk, too."

The doors to the treatment area parted and a nurse stepped into the waiting room. "Derek Sayer?" He raised his hand and she waved him forward. "Follow me, please."

"Is she okay?" he asked as he matched her brisk pace down the hall.

"Grace Ann has been asking for you." The nurse held back a curtain dividing the ER bays. "Go on in."

He hesitated, relief making his movements sluggish. She was dirty, her clothing torn and stained, but she seemed to be all in one piece. And alert. "They won't let me leave without a workup." She reached out to him and her wobbling smile cut through the last of his fear.

"About time someone got you to hold still." He came closer and smoothed her hair back from her face, kissed her forehead, her nose, her lips. "Were you hurt?"

"I got grazed by a bullet or something." She raised her upper arm where someone had cleaned her up and applied a bandage. "Didn't even need stitches."

"Grace Ann, you amaze me."

"I'm sorry, Derek." She wouldn't look at him. "I know I should have stuck with mom and the girls. I know I worried everyone but…"

"Shh, now. You did the right thing. The *you* thing." And seven hostages would return to their families alive and well, thanks to her.

"I need to say something first." She sniffled.

"First?"

She looked him in the eyes. "I love you, Derek. So much." She held his hands tightly. "I love you. I'm selfish to say it now, knowing you really should throw me over for someone who doesn't have drama and daredevil tendencies."

He was laughing. After hours of hell, she made him laugh. "Say it again."

"I love you."

He kissed her. Finally he had the words. Or maybe it was sooner than he'd expected. He didn't care about the timing. His heart simply floated, pumping out pure joy that washed away the hours of angst and worry. He realized those three words, from her, would always hold that power.

"You're not a daredevil, you're a Riley. I love you, too." He'd planned a more romantic moment, but it seemed foolish now. Unwise since they had yet to get through a date without a problem. That wrinkle would be gone when Eaton was in custody, but why wait for happiness?

"Grace Ann, will you be my wife?"

Her eyes rounded in her smudged face. "You're serious."

"I am." He cradled her hands in his, giving her all the strength she needed. "Dating hasn't worked so well for us. I figured we should just skip the formalities."

"But I'm a career nurse for the army. If they'll have me back."

"They will," he promised her, giving her a quick kiss

along with all his confidence. "When they do, I'll be honored to be your emergency contact." No words had ever felt so true or right. "Marry me, Grace Ann. Go wherever you need to, as long as you let me be your home base."

"Oh, you are. You already are," she whispered as a tear rolled down her cheek. "I love you so much."

He erased it with a gentle sweep of his thumb. He couldn't wait to get her home, help her wash away the fear and terror. "Is that a yes?"

"Absolutely." She cradled his jaw and kissed him. "It's a big, huge yes."

She'd said yes! His ears rang with her answer, his heart thudding in his chest. At the sound of a gasp and sniffle, he turned to see her mother at the break in the curtains, eyes and cheeks damp. "Happy tears?" he asked.

Patricia nodded vigorously, and then stepped aside, allowing an exasperated medical team to enter. Leave it to Patricia Riley to adjust the priorities to accommodate family and romance, even in an emergency room. How had she even gotten back here? He suspected the whole family would be calling for champagne within the hour.

"Major Riley," the doctor began, "everything on your scan looks normal and the bloodwork is clear. I'd like you to rest for the next several days. You've been through an ordeal and your body needs some extra time. I have two prescriptions here for you. One is for pain."

Derek saw her brow furrow as she read both small squares of paper.

"We've taken the liberty of scheduling your first prenatal exam with the practice associated with your primary care team in Bethesda. You're about eight weeks along. If you'd like, I can arrange for you to hear the baby's heartbeat before you leave."

"Baby?" Derek directed the question at Grace Ann, but she appeared as dumbstruck as he felt.

"I'm pregnant?"

The crack in her voice snapped him out of the shock. "Yes," he answered for them. "Yes, we'd love to hear the baby's heartbeat before we go home."

"You didn't know?" he asked in a whisper as a nurse moved the equipment into position.

She shook her head. "No idea."

"Well, you have been distracted."

Moments later, her hand locked in his, he heard their baby's rapid-fire heartbeat for the first time. Grace Ann giggled, her eyes sparkling.

"What?" he asked.

Catching her lip between her teeth, she tried to quell the laughter. It was a hopeless cause.

"Just say it," he urged.

"Seems you found a way to rebuild that Sayer family tree double-time," she said between snorts of more laughter.

"I've always appreciated efficiency." He drew her into his arms and held on while his heart adjusted and settled. They were definitely rebuilding and reframing. Together they'd just created two joyful, life-altering happy memories right here in an emergency room.

"We're going to be parents," she murmured, laying his hand on her flat belly.

"Good thing I have invaluable experience with broody teenage boys."

"Well, that settles it. I'm not letting you get away."

He grinned. "You were locked in when you said you loved me," he said. "The rest is just paperwork," he joked. "Do you want to tell your family tonight?"

"Not yet." She touched her forehead to his. "We have

plenty to celebrate tonight. Let's keep this for us, just for a few days. We've earned it." She kissed him, long and sweet. "Take me home?"

"It would be an honor, my love."

* * * * *

Don't miss Matt and Bethany's story,
A Soldier's Honor,
available now from Harlequin Romantic Suspense!

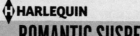

SPECIAL EXCERPT FROM

H HARLEQUIN

ROMANTIC SUSPENSE

*After a suspicious death on her team, environmentalist
Emma Copley knows someone needs to investigate.
When the authorities won't, she decides to do it herself,
despite Beau Kingston's warnings. He may have a
financial incentive to stop her investigation, but he
certainly doesn't want her hurt. Can they trust each
other long enough to find the real culprit?*

Read on for a sneak preview of
Deadly Texas Summer,
the latest thrilling romance from Colleen Thompson.

She looked up at him, her expression stricken. "You don't
believe me either, do you? You don't think I can prove
that Russell was on to something real."

"I'm reserving judgment," he said, keeping his words
as steady as he could, "until I see more evidence. And
you might want to consider holding back on any more
accusations until you've recovered from this shock—and
you have that proof in hand."

"Oh, I'll find the proof. I have a good idea where, too.
All I have to do is get back to the turbines as soon as
possible and find the—"

"No way," he said sharply. "You're not going out
there. You saw the email, right? About Green Horizons'
safety review?"

She gave me a disgusted look. "Of course they want to
keep everyone away. If they're somehow involved in all

this, they'll drag out their review forever. And leave any evidence cleaned and sanitized for their own protection."

"Or they're trying to keep from being on the hook for any further accidents. Either way, I said no, Emma. I don't want you or your students taking any unnecessary chances."

"I'd never involve them. Never. After Russell, there's no way I would chance that." She shook her head, tears filling her eyes. "I was—I was the one to call Russell's parents. I insisted on it. It nearly killed me, breaking that news to them."

"Then you'll understand how I feel," Beau said, "when I tell you I'm not making that call to your folks, your boss or anyone else when you go getting yourself hurt again. Or worse."

She made a scoffing sound. "You've helped me out a couple times, sure. That doesn't make me your responsibility."

"That's where you're wrong, Dr. Copley. I take everyone who lives on, works on or sets foot on my spread as my responsibility," he said, sincerity ringing in his every word, "which is why, from this point forward, I'm barring you from Kingston property."

Don't miss
Deadly Texas Summer
by Colleen Thompson

Available March 2020 wherever
Harlequin Romantic Suspense
books and ebooks are sold.

Harlequin.com